THE WISE AND THE WICKED

THE WISE
AND THE
WICKED

REBECCA PODOS

BALZER + BRAY
An Imprint of HarperCollins*Publishers*

Balzer + Bray is an imprint of HarperCollins Publishers.

The Wise and the Wicked
Copyright © 2019 by Rebecca Podos

Library of Congress Cataloging-in-Publication Data

Names: Podos, Rebecca, author.
Title: The wise and the wicked / Rebecca Podos.
Description: First edition. | New York, NY : Balzer + Bray, an imprint of
    HarperCollinsPublishers, [2019] | Summary: "Ruby comes from a family
    with a rare power: to see the moment in time when they are to die"—
    Provided by publisher.
Identifiers: LCCN 2018055696 | ISBN 978-0-06-269902-2 (hardback)
Subjects: | CYAC: Extrasensory perception—Fiction. | Sisters—Fiction. |
    Family life—Fiction. | Fate and fatalism—Fiction. | Vendetta—Fiction.
Classification: LCC PZ7.1.P63 Wis 2019 | DDC [Fic]—dc23 LC record
    available at https://lccn.loc.gov/2018055696

Typography by Sarah Nichole Kaufman
19 20 21 22 23 PC/LSCH 10 9 8 7 6 5 4 3 2 1
❖
First Edition

TO LANA POPOVIC AND
JORDAN BROWN, FOR EVERYTHING

Who has not asked himself at some time or other:
am I a monster or is this what it means to be a person?
—Clarice Lispector

For small creatures such as we the vastness
is bearable only through love.
—Carl Sagan

●●●

I n an old house built of bloodred bricks, with a tea shop in the converted front rooms, there lived three sisters and their mother.

Solnyshko, the eldest, was willow-tree tall and sweet. Zvyozdochka, the middle child, was beautiful and sharp as a cut diamond. The youngest, Zerkal'tse, was small but hard, like an unshelled nut. Each was different as could be from her sisters, except that all three had their mother's eyes, the deep green of leaves in the part of the forest where sunlight doesn't reach. Of course they did; you can always recognize heroines in stories by their eyes, a sign of powerful gifts within. And this was a family with very powerful gifts.

Or they had been, once upon a time.

Once upon a time, their ancestors had lived inside an immense forest of towering pines beside the republic of Russian Karelia, south of the White Sea.

Once upon a time, the forest was cold and foreboding, and braved only by those seeking miracles. Those who'd heard whispers that the woman in the woods could foretell a person's fate, could grant wisdom and health, and—if the seeker was worthy—could ward off death itself. She and her daughters were revered and respected by those who believed. They were legends.

But the world around them changed, as it does. The cities to the west were touched by war. Political factions wrestled for the land, fighting and dying and destroying, in the way men do. Farms lay fallow; bridges and buildings were demolished. Factories and processing plants sprouted up. Typhus and cholera and diseases of deprivation burned through settlements, killing thousands.

So it was that the people became fearful for their lives. Stirred by rumors—by stories—and hungry for the power to save themselves, a band of city-dwelling men went into the forest. They trampled brush that had gone unstirred for centuries, hacked through delicate black thorns, and sloshed through clean river water with their foul boots to steal the secrets of the woman in the woods for themselves.

Long had the woman believed they would come. She had heard the tales of the settlements from miracle seekers, caught the stench of desperation and decay and greed on the westerly wind. She knew of the darkness in these men that stained what was good, like blood in water. And so she was prepared. She sent her daughters away on a ship bound for America to protect them. But they left their greatest secrets behind, and by the time they'd crossed the ocean, they had become shadows of themselves, believing it better to be small and safe than strong and hunted.

This was the legacy of Solnyshko, Zvyodochka, and Zerkal'tse. Deep green eyes, greatly weakened gifts, and the stories their mother—the granddaughter of the woman in the woods—told them in their beds in the old brick house. Each night, she passed along what diminished wisdom their ancestors had brought with them to their new home, this foremost: that the world has never been very kind to powerful women.

• ONE •

Ruby was in the tub with a teacup of Stolichnaya, when her sisters rattled the door.

"Occupied!" she called, hunting for a spot to stash the cup before they barged in. There wasn't any. Their only bathroom was tiny, stuffed with a pedestal sink, toilet, and a cracked claw-foot tub that took up three-quarters of the black-tiled floor. The whole house was like that: small, splintered, overcrowded. There was nowhere to hide, and no space to keep secrets, at least not between the sisters. With a resigned sigh, Ruby plunged her cup beneath a veil of bubbles and let it sink, hitting the bottom with a small, sad *thunk*. She squirted another dollop of Dahlia's Flower Empower bath bubbles into the water, snatched whichever book topped Ginger's pile on the toilet tank, and settled back just as the door burst open.

When the steam cleared, Ginger leaned against the frame, long fingers twisting the doorknob back and forth in its socket. "A little Tolstoy before bed?" she asked, lemon-mouthed.

Ruby glanced down at the spine of the book. *"Anna Karnina* is awesome."

Her sister snorted. *"Kar-e-nin-a."*

"I said that."

"Uh-huh. Just get out of the tub. I need the mirror."

"But I'm at the best part," she protested as Dahlia slipped into the bathroom beside Ginger.

"What part is that?"

". . . Where everyone is like, 'Oh my god, Anna Kar-e-nin-a, she's so crazy.' You know?"

"Ah, yes, that classic scene," Ginger deadpanned.

Ignoring them, Dahlia smiled sunnily. "Time to get out, Ruby! Polina's coming over."

"Okay, yeah," Ruby relented. She reached for her towel, but stubbornly waited to take it until they'd turned to leave.

"Whatever, it's all fogged up in here anyway," Ginger muttered on her way out.

Once they'd gone, Ruby fished the teacup out of the bath. The Stoli had been hard-won; her sisters kept the vodka in the back of the highest kitchen cabinet, not an easy climb for her five-foot body. She didn't know why they bothered. A little vodka wasn't going to kill her.

That isn't how Ruby dies.

She scrubbed a towel over her head until her jaw-length brown hair puffed up around her ears like ruffled feathers. She wrapped the towel around herself and headed toward her bedroom at the end of the narrow hall, but paused in Dahlia's doorway.

As always, her oldest sister's bedroom looked like an occult shop rammed by a tornado. Colorful beaded necklaces glittered in piles on the rug. Tarot cards and finger-thick crystals spilled across her desk beside a day-or-two-old bowl of cereal.

Ruby liked this room. She liked that she could plunge her hand into any pile and pluck out something she'd never seen there before: a silver ring with an opal the size of a grape, or a black candle that smelled like pepper, or an entire loaf of bread in its plastic package.

Her middle sister settled at the vanity and cleared a spot with her elbow, scowling but silent. Dahlia had three years on Ginger and eleven on Ruby, and was undeniably in charge, even if it was Ginger who made sure their bills were paid, their groceries shopped, and their small, scrubby lawn weeded in spring.

Ruby was banned from Ginger's room, and that was fine. From the hallway, it looked like a dentist's office—softly colored, clean, and cold.

"What's up, Ruby?" Dahlia chirped as she stepped into a silky, voluminous skirt patterned with blackbirds and ivy vines, the one she wore for clients. Ginger had a skirt just like it.

"Is Polina bringing somebody?" she asked, eyeing her sister's outfit.

"Someone's meeting us here."

"Who?"

Dahlia hesitated, sorting out how much to tell her, Ruby knew. She wasn't allowed to see clients with her sisters, judged too young for the "sensitive nature" of the family practice. She did not yet have her own skirt. Ginger dotted on cherry lipstick in Dahlia's mirror, pressing together and then popping her lips. "She's from out of town. Nobody you know." Recapping her lipstick, she swept a highlighter stick above her cheekbones, flecked with the same perfect constellation of freckles as Dahlia's. They'd inherited them from their mother, just like the straw-gold hair they dyed regularly. They did this at home, so every six weeks when they emerged from the little bathroom, it was splashed and stained, as if they'd been in there murdering fairies with jewel-colored blood—right now, Dahlia's was a bright sky blue, Ginger's a bold sapphire. They'd tried to convince Ruby to join them, but her overgrown pixie cut was too dark for dye to show; it only made her look pale and ambiguously Goth. Although her mother's nickname for her had been zerkal'tse—little mirror—she'd never looked much like her, or like Ginger (zvyozdochka, the little star) or Dahlia (solnyshko, the little sun.)

Except for their eyes—Chernyavsky eyes.

Ginger cut those familiar eyes toward Ruby. "Were you gonna dress for company, or . . ."

Remembering her nakedness, Ruby shoved off from the wall and trudged on down the hallway.

If Dahlia's bedroom looked like it belonged to the Mad Hatter, and Ginger's to an accountant, then Ruby's looked a bit like it belonged to nobody, but was frequented by drifters who sometimes left possessions behind when they moved on. The bookshelf was bare except for strange little trinkets—a tube of lip gloss she'd never worn, with a unicorn's head on the cap; a fist-sized garden stone with a rooster painted on it; a striped yellow billiard ball. On her nightstand, on top of a library copy of Carl Sagan's *Pale Blue Dot,* sat an unopened jar of Vegemite she'd taken from the World Market three months ago. Some would've kept their acquisitions stashed in the back of a closet or deep in an underwear drawer, but Ruby preferred to hide things in plain sight. There was one photo taped to the wall above the bed—Ruby and her cousins Oksana, Mikki, Lili, and Cece on the front steps of Polina's house, arms slung around each other—but that was one of few identifying artifacts.

She dressed quickly in sweats and a T-shirt, then met her sisters in the kitchen. Dahlia was boiling water, silver bracelets with tiny bells tinkling against her graceful wrists as she scooped loose tea into the strainer. Squeezing passed her in the tight space, Ginger extracted cups from the cabinets and placed them on saucers on the counter. Three in all, none of them meant for Ruby.

In the next room, the front door opened and shut without a knock to warn them, and before the sisters could move to greet her, Great-Aunt Polina stood in the kitchen in her steel-gray coat, unwrapping a black headscarf from her steel-gray hair in its tightly braided bun. Her broom skirt, unlike Dahlia's or Ginger's—embroidered with silver moons and stars— was plain black, brushing the tops of her dull black oxfords. "Girls," she said in her Russian accent, the curled *R* and guttural *L* and the single syllable stretched into two. Nearly eighty years in America had not stamped it out.

She lowered herself into one of the mismatched chairs around their kitchen table that still had its cushion. Dahlia set a steaming cup of tea in front of her at once, while Ginger whisked her coat and scarf off to the living room closet. Ruby stood without a specific duty, waiting to be summoned.

"Come sit, kroshka," Polina said as expected, pointing to the chair beside hers.

She did so as her great-aunt riffled through the compartments of her oversized brown handbag, pulling out a little bag of homemade pastila baked in the old way, with honey and egg whites and sour apples from Polina's backyard. Even the traditional Russian bakery in Portland didn't make them like that anymore. Polina plunked it down on the table, waiting until Ruby slipped a square into her mouth to ask the usual questions.

"How are you going in school?"

"Okay. We were on Christmas break, but it ends tomorrow, so—"

"Science is A, yes? What about English?"

Ruby grimaced. "Maybe a B . . . minus."

"You're too smart for B minus."

"I'm trying."

Polina patted her cheek once, her hand wrinkled and liver-spotted, but strong for ninety-five, and perfectly steady. That was her great-aunt all over. "You must work harder, because life is also hard. But you can do it. You are tough, kroshka. If only that cousin of yours is so tough. I see her yesterday, and she is dressed like a payats! Like a little clown! I tell her she is a woman now, a true Chernyavsky woman. She must act like it."

Polina could only be talking about Cece, who dressed in clothes as bright as she was.

"What do you mean, she's a true Chernyavsky?" Dahlia spoke up, settling on Polina's other side with her own cup of tea. "Do you mean . . ."

Polina nodded gravely. "Anfisa's daughter sees her Time."

Ruby's heart stuttered. "What? When?" There was a proud light in Polina's still-clear green eyes, despite her harsh words.

"Yesterday, I say this already. Her party is being planned now."

Ginger, standing behind Polina with the third cup in hand, raised a pale eyebrow at Ruby. "She didn't tell you?"

Ruby shook her head, fist tightening around the bag of pastila. While there were a few Chernyavsky cousins close to Ruby's age, most of them attended private schools in nearby towns. Cece and Ruby went to Saltville High and were in the same class. Anfisa, who went by Annie and was their mother's younger sister, had married a respectable gastroenterologist named Neil Baker. They lived on the west side of Saltville. Aunt Annie didn't work, but was on the PTO as a full-time volunteer, decorating their gym for the annual Halloween dances and making cupcakes for every bake sale.

They were nothing like Ruby's small branch of the family—if the Bakers' home was a tulip, hers was an old cactus—but it didn't matter. Cece had always been her best friend.

And yet a whole day had passed, and she hadn't mentioned her Time.

"I can't believe she's old enough." Dahlia smiled down into her tea. "I remember when she was born."

"Whatever, she's sixteen. That's three years older than Ruby was," Ginger reminded her. "And I was only twelve. I handled it fine."

"Okay, enough chat, girls." Polina tapped Ruby's cheek again, a bit more sharply to catch her attention. "It is almost time for us to work, so now you must go away," she commanded.

Though Ruby loved Polina—of course she did, Polina was blood—she knew her great-aunt wasn't easy to like. Cece was a little terrified of her; most of the cousins were.

Not Ruby. True, Polina looked at her from time to time as if searching for something Ruby was pretty sure wasn't there, and it made her skin itch. But she preferred that to the way Aunt Annie watched her, as though Ruby was barely herself; as though she was just the glass pane in a picture frame that held a photo of her mother behind it. Aunt Annie's face would twist with pity and betrayal at once. Polina's never did. She hadn't mentioned Ruby's mother, hadn't even said her name aloud since the night she left them all.

Whatever her great-aunt did or did not see in Ruby, at least she *saw* her.

Rising obediently, Ruby pressed a light kiss to Polina's leathery cheek as tradition dictated, then slipped away to her room.

Collapsing onto her bed, she stared up at Cece in the photo on the wall over the headboard. Pretty, chubby, colorful Cece. Cece, who'd never kissed a boy with tongue. Cece, who'd once collected caterpillars in a paper milk carton so they'd have someplace safe and warm to become butterflies, and peed her pants with grief when the girls peeled back the lips a week later to find a pile of dried husks.

Cece, finally seeing her Time.

Ruby had been waiting for this day for three long years,

and now it was here. She wanted to meet up with Cece, now. She thought about texting her cousin their Super-Actual-Emergency Code, but as she imagined sitting across from Cece in their booth at the Rooster, ready to compare futures at last, Ruby's throat closed tight as a fist. She suspected she'd need the rest of the bottle of Stoli to loosen it.

She was still trying to work up the courage to send the text when she heard the car. The sputtering engine grew louder, and she crept to the window, kneeling with her elbows propped on the sill to peer out as the car turned into their driveway.

Once upon a time, Ruby and her sisters would've been sought by despairing folk who trekked through the cold, endless woods to reach them. Now a woman climbed out of a gray car spattered with rust, stuffing a tissue under her nose. She looked up at the yard, and Ruby knew what she saw: a tiny house, the orange paint blistered, curling away in spots like half-peeled fruit. Battered wind chimes over a front stoop hardly any wider than Ruby.

If they'd still lived in the big brick house where Ruby had been born, if their mother were still around . . . but she didn't like to think about her old life, and neither did Dahlia or Ginger. They pretended their family had always existed in this diminished state. That was the story they all told themselves. On most nights, anyway.

By day, they were the kind of people who seemed to belong in the house on Stone Road. Ruby went to school while her sisters worked the part-time jobs they could get without college degrees, scrambling to save for Ruby's own (ultimately pointless) college fund. Ginger was an office assistant at a feed store, while Dahlia currently worked at 'Wiches and Wings, a butterfly conservatory and sandwich shop in one.

And then some nights, rare but constant for the last few years, they were different people altogether. Polina would come with a client, or one would follow. Always women, always in dark plain clothing, in stained pants and with no jewelry or lipstick. Often, their cars had out-of-state plates. They looked desperate, as though they would have walked through the woods all night to get here, if necessary. Ruby wasn't sure how clients actually found Polina, or where Polina found *them*. Nor was she completely sure what went on after she was sent to her room, but she knew enough.

Her sisters, with Polina's guidance, did what their ancestors had always done. They helped people. They welcomed them into this unextraordinary little house, listened to them, counseled them with the gift that remained to the Chernyavskys: the empathetic, righteous rage of women who knew what it meant to have everything taken away from them.

So it wasn't like the stories their mother had told them, which she'd been told by Polina when she was a girl. They weren't fortune-tellers or miracle workers any longer, if they ever were. Polina insisted it was so, but she was the family matriarch, the oldest daughter of the woman in the woods and the keeper of the family myths, so she *had* to say that. Yes, they were special. Strange. They had their Times, and she had never read anything that could explain them. But it wasn't exactly the kind of magic that existed in fairy tales.

Whatever the truth, it didn't make much difference to Ruby now.

And anyway, it was a legacy she was proud to be a part of . . . even if she wasn't really a part of it. Someday, her sisters had promised, she'd join them in the family practice. When she was older. More mature. When she was ready.

She wasn't holding her breath.

Out in the driveway, the client stopped to gather herself before hunching forward against the wind and making her way up the walk. She disappeared from Ruby's sightline, and then the front door opened. The wind chimes jangled out of tune as Polina's voice, unlovely but beloved, welcomed her inside.

· TWO ·

Though it was freezing cold and snowing on Monday morning, Ruby parked the dented gray Malibu she'd inherited from Ginger—who herself had inherited it from Dahlia—in the very back of the Saltville High student lot. She was claiming the spot closest to the loop of pavement where the buses dropped off. If she wanted any time with Cece before school, she'd have to catch her cousin as soon as she disembarked. In the same grade but six months younger than Ruby, Cece had just turned sixteen in October. And though she'd likely have a beautiful Prius topped with a bow waiting in her driveway the day she finished driver's ed, Cece had yet to sign up for the class. Unlike Ruby, she was happier in the passenger seat.

Ruby left the engine running and her phone plugged in so she could keep listening to *Solving for X-traordinary* over the speakers. It was her favorite podcast, a drama about the ongoing adventures of Kerrigan Black, college student, who'd been catapulted back through time after an unfortunate Bunsen burner explosion in her chemistry lab. By engineering explosions to blow herself up in each era, she hopped around throughout the centuries, using her present-day knowledge and the scientific method to solve mysteries and right wrongs, pausing occasionally to kiss sexy land barons and peasants alike. It was cheesy, and as Cece often reminded her, Ruby had little patience for fiction.

But this, she loved.

Maybe because she loved science, and had since she was a kid, and would've studied it in college if it were possible. She'd taken her first book by Carl Sagan out of the Saltville Public Library when she was just shy of eleven, and then another after that, reading them all again and again over the years with the goal of understanding each word; by now she had page-long passages memorized. In seventh grade, she'd researched a science camp in Boston and campaigned for months for Dahlia to send her, revisiting the website until the description—"campers use the scientific method to uncover the mysteries of the world around them"—was engraved in her hippocampus (which she knew about from her extracurricular research on the human brain.) And she'd been fascinated by their unit on genetics last year, particularly the section on genetic abnormalities, and done her final report on Barbara McClintock.

Her science classes were the only ones she regularly did the homework for, much less showed up for. Dahlia would look at the Cs on each report card, earned with the barest of efforts, and proclaim Ruby to be "differently talented."

Ginger said she was just lazy.

Either way, she was obsessed with *Solving for X-traordinary*, began every bimonthly episode the moment it was posted. Ruby cranked up the volume to better hear it above the heat roaring out of the vents:

> *The last thing I see as the flame alights, licking down the hollow bamboo tube toward the huo yao—the mixture of saltpeter, sulfur, and charcoal I'd heated and dried to black powder in the kitchens these past few nights—is the sturdy face of Xuan Bang through the smoke. I see his lips move, though he stands too far away for me to hear and answer. Instead, I press my fingers to my own lips just as a thunder-like rumble rents the air, and I'm lifted off my feet.*
>
> *When I land, I know at once I'm not in eleventh-century China anymore, nor am I safely back in the chemistry lab at Princeton. I'm standing in a flat*

expanse of pale orange desert, a herd of sturdy cows
grazing on spiny tufts of gray grass all around me. In
the near distance, a tiny village just darker than the
sand.

I'll miss Bang and the sensual fit of his military
tunic, but I have work to do. Once again, I must learn
everything I can about this time and place if I'm ever
to return to mine.

The episode ended just as she saw her cousin. Or rather, just as she saw a sturdy pair of legs in bright pink tights shuffling through the slush, and knew immediately that it was Cece in the middle of her pack of friends. Ruby leaned across the seat and cranked open the passenger side window, letting winter in.

"Cece!" she screamed. "Ceceeeee!"

Her cousin's friends stopped all at once, a school of fish scared by the cry of the common loon.

Cece peered between them until she spotted Ruby, then waved them off and trudged toward the Malibu. She bent down to stare expectantly through the driver side window, her hair sequined with snowflakes. As usual, she wore her piles of ice-blond waves in a perfect sloppy bun, so that with her pale skin and the massive globe of her pale hair, her head was shaped like a luminous snowman.

"Hey, Bebe."

"Hi. What, um, how was your weekend?"

Cece's nearly invisible eyelashes flickered twice against her pink cheeks, and the breath puffed from between her parted lips. "Fine," she said. "Boring. You know."

Cece had never lied to Ruby, so she hadn't been sure what her cousin's lie face looked like. She guessed she was seeing it for the first time.

The warning bell toned over the loudspeakers in the entranceway.

Straightening quickly, Cece swiped melted snow from the tip of her nose. "I gotta get my books out of my locker. See you in the caf, okay?" She hurried for the propped-open school doors.

A likely story, Ruby thought, watching her go.

Cece wasn't in any classes with Ruby, mostly because her cousin took all AP courses, while Ruby was lumped in with the rest of the "differently talented." So Ruby had to sit through US history, hide out in the bathroom during wood shop, and make it through a gym period where they didn't even change into their uniforms, only sat on the dull floorboards while Mr. Pfeffer explained the anatomy of a tennis racket and the artistry of the backhand grip. All the while, Ruby thought about nothing but the next chance to talk to her cousin.

Finally lunch arrived, and she snaked through the food line

in the cafeteria as quickly as possible, pausing only to palm a Nutty Bar from the rack and stuff it up her sleeve.

Like everything in Saltville with the exception of the Chernyavskys and the pollution level of the tea-brown river that cut through downtown, their school cafeteria was impeccably average. There was a small stage for announcements, and below that, rows of tables crowding the white cinderblock walls. The third on the left was Cece's, and so of course it was Ruby's table, too.

Ruby's first real, true memory of her cousin—beyond blurry birthday parties and backyard swings—was a county fair in Bluebar. Uncle Neil took them one year, and a fortuneteller read their palms inside her tent. She wore glittery eye makeup and had big white arms that oozed out of her costume like batter from a waffle iron. She told the cousins they'd been a single soul in their past lives, only recently split into two bodies in this life. They'd been born by the sea two centuries ago, and they'd painted the face of an Egyptian princess for a living. They'd once been a man with three wives in Utah (here, Cece's dad had groaned from the door flap of the tent).

At that, Cece turned to Ruby and smiled, a lollipop tucked in the pouch of her cheek, smudged with sunburn. Five-year-old Cece had looked like a baby Disney princess; Ruby, meanwhile, was pale and dark-haired, less Snow White than Samara from *The Ring*. Ginger once put it bluntly: "You looked like a creep when you were a kid. I'd get up to pee at night, and

I'd check behind the shower curtain for *you*." It was the shape of her mouth, Ruby thought, a permanent frown carved by nature; Cece's pink lips were curved upward, always.

But Ruby remembered smiling right back at Cece across that stuffy dim tent and thinking, of course they were the same. It seemed they had been born knowing each other.

Cece, a rare and shining double rainbow of a human being, was the best luck that being a Chernyavsky had brought Ruby.

She slid onto the bench across from her cousin, who was in the process of twisting half of Talia Mahalel's waist-length black hair into a pigtail braid. Talia was helping by hoisting Cece's slice of pizza up for her, and Ruby studied her cousin as she bit down. Did she look different? Older? Sadder? Did they look more alike now than they had before Christmas? On the outside, Cece was the same. A baggy band T-shirt (today's was Neutral Milk Hotel) over a long-sleeved waffle shirt, a not-too-mini yellow miniskirt and her neon pink tights. It was her customary ensemble, except that the colors of her tights rotated, and the band tee was occasionally switched out for a shirt advertising some indie movie theater in New York they'd definitely never been to.

Ruby squinted across the table, searching for deeper marks that Cece's Time might have left on her.

That was when boy's-name-that-started-with-a-D dropped his tray down beside Ruby, from a great enough height that it clattered against the table and then partway onto her tray.

His pizza slice flopped over the side, dripping grease on her unwrapped Nutty Bar. As he slipped onto the bench, his elbow knocked the Nutty Bar to the floor. He didn't seem to notice as he flashed a white, impersonal smile, then turned and said, "Hey, Cee."

Swiveling her head, Cece dropped Talia's hair and yanked the pizza out from between her teeth, her pink cheeks glowing mauve.

Ruby took note.

Boy's-name-that-started-with-a-D was Talia's brother—the other half of the Mahalel twins, who'd moved to Saltville last summer from "The South." "The South" could be any place below Bangor, but Ruby guessed they'd come farther than that. Their naturally olive skin was still beach-tanned despite the winter months, and sometimes, a long vowel would stretch taffy-like from their full lips. Talia was a regular at Cece's table of popular AP kids (plus Ruby) while her brother was the smallest and darkest of the unironically flannel-wearing bros who normally sat a few tables back. Despite being a transplant, he'd slotted right in with the townies. They were boys who got stoned around bonfires and snowmobiled through the woods in winter; summers, they got stoned around bonfires and went mudding in their pickups, and maybe worked on their uncle's fishing boats. If any of them had ambitions beyond that—if they dreamed of being professional basketball players, or doctors, or tech-startup starter-uppers, or whatever boys dreamed about—they certainly weren't letting on.

"Can I still get your trig notes?" he asked Cece, rhythmically zipping and unzipping his Creatures Such As We hoodie. CSAW were a big-deal indie band that played electric guitars and ukuleles in the same songs. Ruby despised them.

Talia rolled her eyes. "I already said you could have mine."

"*Your* handwriting looks like you dipped a chicken in ink, set it on fire, and let it run across your notebook. *Cece* types."

His sister threw a greasy balled-up napkin at him, which he batted aside smoothly as he jerked his head to knock his black bangs out of his eyes. Under the harsh strip lighting of the cafeteria, his hair looked as soft as his brown skin. "This class . . . Cee, I'm doomed."

"At least it won't be *bubble letters* hard," she said, some inside joke that cracked him up, showed his pointed canines.

Ruby glanced between them to keep from rolling her eyes. Not that she was jealous. Not of him, or Talia, or any of them. Just because Cece was Ruby's only friend at school didn't mean that Ruby had to be hers. Ruby knew that wasn't how it worked. And Cece was always trying to rope her into group hangs, no matter how many times Ruby refused.

Still, she took pleasure in interrupting them to ask, "Cece, can I sleep over tonight? Levi's coming for dinner. I think he's gonna stay."

"Yeah, obviously." Her cousin smiled.

Of course she'd say yes to Ruby. Cece was good to her

because Cece was *good*, the way that summer rain and ripe fruit and kittens in wicker baskets were good. It was just that she was different around these people than she was with *their* people. It would be pointless to try and get anything out of her now, so Ruby would bide her time.

Cece only said true things, important things—Chernyavsky things—when they were alone.

• THREE •

Levi Dorgan, Ginger's boyfriend, did indeed come for dinner that night, and he brought their mail with him. Levi was the sorter at the Saltville Post Office. Ginger claimed she was dating him because it was helpful for a mostly fake psychic to know everyone's secrets, and Levi usually did. Not only because of his job, but because he was also everybody's friend's cousin's dealer, who grew his own plants in the root cellar of the house he'd inherited from his parents.

He dropped onto the couch beside Ruby and propped his boots on their chipped coffee table, nearly taking out Dahlia's salt lamp, softly glowing pink. While Ginger was fetching him a beer, gushing that he was *the best* even though he could've just let their mail carrier bring their mail five hours earlier, he tossed Dahlia a small twist-tied baggie of weed. She disappeared with it into her bedroom before Ginger could see.

Levi was handsome, his biceps straining the sleeves of the T-shirts he wore all winter, his teeth impossibly straight, and his hair perfectly fluffed and sprayed, graceful in its architecture, like a beautifully constructed cake. But his usefulness as a busybody aside, Ruby wasn't sure why Ginger genuinely seemed to like him, or any of the substandard boys she'd been bringing home since high school.

Still, she wasn't worried. The romance wouldn't last, and soon enough it would be only the three of them around the dinner table again.

Ginger was a Chernyavsky, after all.

Though Ruby had been edging up the TV volume to block them both out, she suddenly wasn't interested in the Real Housewives or their impressive lip augmentations. Their purses and personal chefs blurred into watercolor as she watched from the corner of her eye as Ginger climbed into Levi's lap and kissed him gratefully. No longer caring which Housewife was mad at which for forgetting to chill the pinot grigio, Ruby levered herself off the couch, stepping through Levi's legs as she went.

In her bedroom, she grabbed her backpack from the closet floor, shoving her phone and wallet into its plastic front pouch. She stuffed in her pajamas and an outfit for tomorrow, a hand-me-down baseball tee from Ginger with an embroidered cheeseburger on the pocket. All the money her sisters made seemed to go toward their pitiful house or into Ruby's pointless college fund, and so with a bit of hemming and tucking from Dahlia, Ruby could fit into her sisters' old clothes.

She passed Ginger and Levi in the kitchen, him clearly towing her toward her bedroom. When only Ginger could see, Ruby fake-vomited into the fruit bowl that contained a single twig of withered grapes. Her sister scowled back at her before she was whisked through the doorway.

As Ruby grabbed her coat from the front closet, Dahlia poked her head into the living room. "Mac and cheese okay for dinner?"

"I'm actually going to Cece's."

"In this weather? You'll get soaked!"

"It stopped snowing two hours ago," Ruby informed her.

With her back to Dahlia, she plunged a quick hand into the pocket of Levi's jacket. Ginger must've hung it up, because her boyfriend wouldn't have bothered. She surfaced with the two crumpled twenties Dahlia had just handed him and another small baggie, all of which she slipped into her own pocket.

Fruit Street, where the Bakers lived, was a long row of well-kept colonials on the west side of Saltville only slightly smaller than the Colonials on Oak, the next neighborhood over, where the mayor of Saltville lived. Oak Lane had block parties in the summer, an Easter egg hunt in spring, a Halloween parade

in the fall, and carolers in winter. Fruit Street made do with
a Fourth of July cookout and an unofficial Christmas lights
competition.

Stone Road's only community event was a twice-a-year
spraying with repellent for its wasp problem.

Ruby parked in Cece's hedge-lined driveway—the Fruit
Street Block Association didn't like cars on the curb, especially not scabby lemons like the Malibu—behind Uncle Neil's
fog-colored Porsche Cayenne. A lighted stone walk led to the
Bakers' house, bright-looking even after the sun had set. There
were blue cedar shingles, butter-yellow shutters with hearts
carved out of the wood, and soft tulips in the flower patch.
The doorbell played the first few notes of "Auld Lang Syne"
when Ruby rang, because the Bakers changed their chime for
the holidays.

Aunt Annie answered with a curious, could-be-the-
neighbors smile. It became stoic when she saw Ruby. "Oh. I
forgot Cece mentioned you might drop in."

"Is that okay?" she asked, teeth clicking in the January
cold.

"No, of course." She stepped back to let Ruby inside. "You
know you're always welcome in this house."

Ruby knew she was something more like tolerated, but it
was enough.

The Bakers were in the middle of their own dinner, also
mac and cheese (these coincidences happened more often than

you'd guess) but the fancy sort made with crumbled bread-crumbs and truffle oil. Aunt Annie grabbed an extra glass bowl out of the cabinet, and Cece waved around a full mouth.

"Hey there, Ruby," Uncle Neil said, patting a cloth napkin across his mustache. "What's the word?"

"Not much." Ruby dropped her bag in the doorway. "What's been going on around here? Anything new?"

"Same old, same old," Uncle Neil said, the last word was cut off by Aunt Annie loudly clattering the silverware as she pulled a fork out of the drawer for Ruby.

After dinner, the girls went upstairs to Cece's room. To look at Cece, you'd think it would be plastered with concert memorabilia or posters for quirky French movies, with her tights strewn all over like rainbow-colored streamers. Maybe a Styrofoam head on the dresser, speared with funky ear-rings. In reality, the framed art on her delicate peach walls was of pleasantly innocuous items like sneakers, and star-fish. There was even a plaque that said: THINK HAPPY, BE HAPPY.

There *was* a composition book on her white wicker dresser, filled with song lyrics and poems she let Ruby read once or twice a year, peering through the fence of her fingers the whole time. Ruby had even less patience for poetry than for fiction, but anything Cece wrote was an exception, and Ruby was the only person in the world she would show them to.

Mostly, though, this bedroom resembled a page off the

Pottery Barn Teen website (carefully designed by her parents, in other words).

Ruby dropped her backpack and sat down on the crisp white quilt while Cece plugged her phone into the charger on the nightstand. She brought up Spotify and a song began. With a twinge, Ruby recognized the electric guitars, the ukuleles, the lyrics:

> *If I were a sea cucumber*
> *Beneath the briny waves I'd slumber*
> *No eyes to weep, no heart to beat,*
> *By sorrow I'd be unencumbered.*

"Why are you listening to this?" she asked, her stomach rolling.

"Dov made me a playlist."

"Who?"

Cece lowered her eyes, the same shadowy green as Ruby's, and climbed onto the bed beside her. "You know. Dov Mahalel. He sat with us at lunch today."

"You don't even like Creatures Such As We," Ruby pointed out, maybe a little too smugly.

"I'm learning to like them."

"Because you like Dov Mahalel?"

Her ears went pink. "Why wouldn't I? He's cute, right?"

Opting out of that conversation, Ruby scooted forward so

she could throw the quilt back, and Cece tossed her own side back. Together, they piled the pillows against the headboard, then lay flat, flinging the quilt up over their heads and across the pillows so that the blankets sloped up and away from their faces, just the way they liked it. Ruby turned her head to look at Cece, and Cece turned hers, bun mussed into a bomb mid-explosion.

"Hi, Bebe," she said.

"Hi, Cece," Ruby said.

They giggled in the close air.

"How was English?"

"Shrug. How was Levi?"

"*Ugh*. How was your weekend?"

"It was fine."

"Cece." Ruby watched her cousin in the filtered light. "Come on. You can tell me. We *promised*—"

Her cousin bolted upright, destabilizing their fort so that the ceiling collapsed onto Ruby's face, quilt and pillows and all. "Who even told you?" she asked sharply.

Ruby clawed her way out and brushed at the short strands of hair static-clinging to her face, trying not to feel wounded. "It's true, isn't it?"

Cece looked away, plucking fuzz off her tights with great determination until Ruby laid her hand palm up on the quilt, and Cece took it. They both stared at their interlocked fingers—Ruby's topped by rough purple polish, Cece's soft and clean. "Mom and Polina are already planning my party."

Ruby nodded, wishing fiercely that she'd smuggled the Stoli out of the house with her. They could both use the courage. She caught Cece's eye again. "It's your turn." *Finally*, she didn't say. *I've been waiting*, she didn't say. *I want to tell you mine*, she didn't say.

"I know, I just . . . didn't think it would be like this," Cece whispered, and it was in the older, wiser, stranger voice Ruby had been awaiting for three long years.

· FOUR ·

This was how Dahlia had explained the Chernyavsky "Gift" to Ruby.

One afternoon in early April six years ago, the breeze damp and cool and the clouds bone-bright above them, her sisters sat her down at a picnic table outside of the Cone Zone. Ruby remembered the year clearly, because both she and Dahlia had birthdays in April, and Dahlia had just turned twenty-two, while Ruby was about to turn eleven. She remembered *that* because their mother had left the morning after Dahlia's birthday, which was probably why Ruby received "the talk" so young. Not only to explain the curse, but to explain their mother, too.

The Cone Zone was a seasonal ice cream place in downtown Saltville. Their big attraction was something called the Danger Cone. Each week, they'd create some new unusual, ambitious, often foul flavor—spaghetti sauce, broccoli, fish-and-chips. That month it was garlic and mint, so when Ruby thought of the talk, she'd forever taste toothpaste and mashed potatoes. When she was younger, Ruby would order every strange flavor she could just to disgust Ginger, but she'd since realized that Ginger didn't care that much what Ruby did, so she was only hurting herself.

That day, she sat shivering as rivulets of her unappealing ice cream ran off the scoop and down her fingers—it really was too cold to eat ice cream outdoors—when Dahlia asked, "Ruby, what do you know about astral projection?"

"Um," she'd answered. "Is it about space?" On her nightstand was a library copy of *The Demon-Haunted World* in its battered plastic sleeve, and she was picking her slow way through it as best she could. Her first ever Sagan book, she'd borrowed it from the school media center after her fifth-grade science teacher posted a quote from it on their bulletin board: *Science is an attempt, largely successful, to understand the world, to get a grip on things, to get hold of ourselves, to steer a safe course.*

She'd already loved science books, and at the moment, getting a grip on things sounded good to Ruby. Their lives had flipped upside down in their mother's absence. Dahlia had left college and stayed home to take care of them, but she wasn't very good at it yet. The day before, she'd packed an entire sealed box of granola bars, no juice, and two pieces of bare white bread in Ruby's lunch, forgetting to spread them with peanut butter. But at least she was trying. Ginger, a senior in high school, would barely look at her sisters. She'd sit at the register counter in the closed tea shop in the front room of their house for hours every evening, reading one of her bleak and sophisticated novels, or swirling a finger through a pile of shredded peppermint leaves, or just staring out the window until the setting sun flared one last time over the pine trees, then sank.

"It makes Ginger feel better to be alone," Dahlia had said one night when she pulled Ruby away from spying at the shop door. That didn't make sense to Ruby, but the world didn't make much sense anymore. Maybe if she could decode the too-big words and ideas in her Carl Sagan book, it would again.

"No, space is astronomy. Right?" Dahlia looked over at Ginger, who sat on the opposite bench from them with a book propped open and a practical juice smoothie instead of a cone.

"Oh my god, Dahlia," she muttered, but never looked up from the page she was pretending to read. Her blond hair whipped in the wind, still natural back then.

"Right, okay," Dahlia continued, folding her hands atop the table. She hadn't gotten anything for herself. "Astral pro-jection is . . . it's kind of like a superpower. And it's a power the women in the Chernyavsky family have."

"You're lying," Ruby protested.

"Why do you think so?"

"Because superpowers aren't real," she said. "And neither are Mom's stories."

They had all grown up on their mother's stories of the Chernyavsky family, their gifts and their downfall, which were one and the same. How the Chernyavsky women had been powerful in the old country—healers, seers of fate, sources of great wisdom. How they'd helped the worthy people who sought them out in the deep woods, and punished the wicked. And how they'd been hunted for their abilities, and had all but abandoned them when they fled Russia, arriving in America with few possessions and fewer gifts left to them.

Ruby didn't really believe the stories—not when her mother told them, or their great-aunt Polina. At least, not all of them. She knew about the human brain and space and the periodic table of elements, but had never come across anything like the powers her mother had spoken of in her own books, books about *real* things, provable things. . . . Except that when her second cousin Alyona had died of breast cancer last year, she *had* felt the chill sweep through her; that icy premonition her mother had told her Chernyavsky women felt when a light among them was snuffed out.

Back then, she hadn't been so sure what to make of that.

"Believe me," Dahlia assured her, "it's something we all do, and someday you will, too. But only once."

Across from them, Ginger slapped her book shut. "You're doing it wrong. You're just going to mess her up! You'll ruin her for life if you tell her like that!"

"Well, who's gonna explain it better? You, or Mom?" Then Dahlia blanched, looking pained, as if she'd stubbed a recently broken toe, or slapped a fresh sunburn.

Ginger reopened her book, pretending not to care. "Be my guest," she said, eyebrows folded up beneath her blunt high school bangs.

"Thank you. Ruby, astral projection is this theory some people have, where you can leave your body. Because there's your body, right, and then there's whatever's inside of it."

"Your guts?" Ruby panicked. Pictures of intestines and blood and bones floating up from a rubbery pile of skin blossomed before her.

Ginger glanced back up, aghast.

"No, no, no, oh my god no," Dahlia hurried to say. "I mean, like, your spirit, you know?"

Ruby sort of knew. The Chernyavskys didn't attend churches or synagogues or mosques, but Saltville was the kind of place that put up a nativity in the town square each December, and piped not just "Rudolph" or "Frosty" but the heavy-hitter Christmas tunes over department store speakers; the slow, epic Jesus jams. So she'd gotten the gist. "That's real?"

"In a way. It's, like, your thoughts and your feelings and

your *energy*. And imagine those parts of you drifting up out of your body. Okay? Now imagine that you could be out of your body, but you can still move around. You can look down on your house, or your street, or you could land on the front lawn of Great-Aunt Polina's house, and nobody would see you or know you were there, because you're not in your body. But you could see everything. Are you imagining that?"

"Yeah." She stared at the table trying to picture it. By this time, her ice cream—named Cool Vampire—had been reduced to a minty, tangy puddle on the weather-bleached wood, with its cone like a ruined tower in the center.

"Good!" Dahlia bobbed her head. "So now imagine something else. You can't just travel from place to place, you can also travel in time. *But*"—she held up one long finger, stacked with silver rings—"you can only go forward into the future. And you can't go just anywhere. You can only go into your own body, wherever your body will be in the future."

This made no sense, and she was about to say so before Ginger added wryly, "Why don't you just call it time travel?"

"No, Ginger," Dahlia answered, her voice overly sweet. "Because that's you going into the future *inside* your body, so you're a whole person when you get there, and you can run into your future self in the mall, or wherever."

"Is time travel real?" Ruby asked, distracted, because in between her science books, she'd also been reading a book for history class called *11,000 Years Lost*, about a girl who, while hunting for Paleo-Indian artifacts near her school, wound up going back in time to the end of the Ice Age. And to be honest, that seemed like a much better power.

"No." Dahlia dashed her hopes. "I don't think so, at least. But the point is this: someday, probably when you're a teenager, you'll be standing in our kitchen, or watching TV, or taking a shower, and then all of a sudden, you'll blink and be in the body of your future self. And you could be fifty, or seventy, or one hundred. There's no way to know."

". . . Why?" Ruby dared to ask.

Dahlia sighed and fiddled with the clasp on her chunky bracelet, the one their mother had just given her for her birthday. "Because," she said, looking not in Ruby's eyes, but at a nonspecific spot on her forehead, "you're going to be whatever age you are when you die."

Here, Dahlia had fumbled the explanation a bit. For years, from their talk until the middle of a random gym period in eighth grade, Ruby had thought that when she saw her Time, as her family called it, she'd slough her body and slip into the future just in time to see her own demise. She then believed she'd pop back, like a video game restarting after a lost life, aware that she'd someday die in a plane crash, or clipped by a car, or falling off a ladder, or poisoned by Ginger when she'd mouthed off once too often. She thought that bitter kernel of knowledge was the whole point, and one could see, from

Dahlia's fumbling speech, how she'd gotten the idea.

But no. This was what actually happened.

When a Chernyavsky girl was old enough—maybe thirteen like Ruby was, maybe fifteen, maybe more—you didn't really see *how* you'd die. You could guess, a lot of the time, but you only saw who you'd *be* when you died. Who you'd be in the minutes or hours or some small, useless amount of time before the end.

There was one thing Dahlia did manage to get across that day at the Cone Zone, though: whatever Ruby saw during her one-time-only, nonrefundable trip into her future, it was inevitable.

"If you don't like your . . . your Time," Ruby had asked, "why don't you just change it? Like, if you're supposed to die on a roller coaster, you could just make sure you never go to Six Flags. Then you won't die."

Across the table, Ginger put her book down spine-up on the wood. She'd dropped the smug smile that had lingered throughout Dahlia's explanation and was instead pressing her top teeth into her bottom lip until the pink skin paled. "It doesn't work like that," she said.

Dahlia nodded in agreement. "Remember when Alyona died last year? She had seen herself having cancer treatment when she was a teenager. She never smoked a cigarette after that, or drank, or dyed her hair, or lived near power lines, or went outside without sunscreen. It didn't change anything."

"Okay, so why didn't she run away? Like, instead of going to that hospital for treatment, why didn't she just go to Japan or something? Has anyone tried that?"

"Somebody has," Ginger muttered at last.

"Mom?" Ruby guessed, a cold, fizzy feeling in her head as if she'd actually eaten her ice cream, gulped it down in one greedy bite.

"You don't know that," Dahlia said, glaring at Ginger.

"Polina basically told you—"

"No she didn't. That's your interpretation. We don't know why she—"

"Abandoned us?" Ginger cut in. "Maybe you don't want to believe it, but I know why. Anyways, *Ruby*," she said, turning pointedly away from Dahlia, "it won't work. Running away from fate won't change anything. It never does. It just makes everything worse, for everybody."

So that was that. Your Time couldn't be changed, and to try to alter fate wasn't the point. Good or bad, it was impossible to fight the future. Whatever powers the Chernyavskys had, that wasn't one of them.

At least, not anymore.

• FIVE •

Ruby: Strawberry or blueberry

Cece: ?

Ruby: Pop Tarts, can't decide

Cece: Have an apple

Ruby: OK got it, strawberry Pop Tart it is

Cece: Enjoy your delicious warm cardboard

Ruby set her phone down on the counter to pluck her already-burning Pop-Tart from the toaster. It was a Saturday afternoon in the first week of February, and Ruby had been texting her cousin constantly about everything *but* her Time. If she didn't pressure Cece, she hoped that it would become Not a Big Deal—though of course it was a Very Big Deal, the biggest—but to no effect. "I'm just . . . not ready," she'd told

Ruby the night of their sleepover. "This is *it*, you know? My whole future. I need time to, like, process." But it had been a month, and Cece was no closer to sharing. Not that Ruby could tell.

She'd just shoved half of the hot Pop-Tart into her mouth, when a familiar seed of a feeling sprouted inside her chest. It was small at first—the uneasiness of remembering the physics homework you never finished just as you pulled into the school parking lot.

But the feeling grew throughout the afternoon.

Restless, she retreated to her bedroom, plugged in her headphones and put on the newly published episode of *Solving for X-traordinary* as a distraction. After a relatively brief adventure, Kerrigan Black had left the Chalbi Desert behind two weeks ago, and had just landed in a seemingly suburban backyard somewhere in time.

I examine the grassy lawn crisscrossed with clotheslines before me, and the sturdy wood saltbox house peeking through the sheets. I drag myself to my feet, hurriedly shedding my bright red kanga and untying my braids. I stand shivering in the simple white shift dress in which I always travel, my hair unspooling across my shoulders, whipped up by the wind. I pat my pockets for my small field journal, exhaling in relief when I feel the familiar shape beneath the fabric.

*I get down to business determining my where-
abouts. I have resolved to gather materials from the
clotheslines, and then explore my surroundings, when
a racket from beyond the house calls me back to the
present . . . whenever the present is. I make my way
in my boots and shift through the side yard, and come
upon a crowd gathered in the street.*

*A plump middle-aged woman kneels in the packed
dust, twisting her long stained apron in her hands,
her plain linen cap crooked on her head. "I have been
falsely accused! Will no one help me?" The woman
cries, reaching out to no soul in particular, but to all
of us.*

*I stand shivering in my dress, surveying the angry,
appalled, shuttered faces of the crowd, searching for
pity. But none come forward.*

Ruby's attention drifted, her skin crawling inexplicably,
and the third time she had to rewind the episode, Ruby gave
up. Instead, she wandered the house in tight figure eights. She
stopped in the kitchen, where Ginger was banging around
beneath the kitchen sink, fixing a leaking joint in a pipe. From
the sound of it, everything was going wrong. "Son of a bitch,"
she swore, her voice echoing around the cabinet. Then came

the clang of Ginger's skull on the pipe. "Son of a *bitch*!" Scooting out, she glared at Ruby, one hand clapped to her head. Her hair color was fading, now like blue smoke, and it stuck to her forehead with sweat.

From her spot in the doorway, Ruby gave a *what are you gonna do?* shrug, meant to be sympathetic.

Ginger tossed her wrench to the tiles and grabbed for the roll of plumber's tape on the counter. "No, no, don't be *useful* or anything," she snapped.

"Don't be *competent* or anything," Ruby spat back, and moved on to the living room.

Dahlia sat on the couch, her own hair lightened from sky to cloud. For an hour, she'd been flipping idly through the *Plainsmen*, Saltville's weekly local newspaper. But she kept setting it down and gazing dreamily out the window into the early night sky.

"I'm going to the store," Ruby announced. "I need . . . something."

Slowly, her sister turned and watched her stuff her feet into boots. "Drive careful, okay?" The caution in Dahlia's voice blew wind across a spark of unease, flaming it up.

"I'll walk." Though it was frigid out, Ruby didn't feel like being boxed in.

"Be careful," Dahlia repeated, her gaze already drifting back to the window.

Outside, even the moon looked frozen when it peeked

through the clouds, a bobbing chip of ice in a sea-dark sky. The Saltville General Store was a mile trudge from the house. She walked up Stone Road and turned left on Church Street, creatively named for the century-old one-room United Methodist Church. Then right onto Elm until she reached the store, its lighted sign announcing BEEF, PIE, AND MILK in the window. The dented bell above the mantel gargled as she ducked inside.

Paul, the twentysomething cashier who she'd only seen emerge from behind the counter to wait on Dahlia, with whom he was clearly in love, nodded as she passed the counter. He tucked his beard into his chest and went back to reading *Game & Fish*, while she strolled the mostly empty aisles toward the grocery section. It was bomb shelter food; the isotopes in nuclear fallout would decay slower than the tins of ravioli and beans, vacuum-sealed jerky, and plastic-wrapped cupcakes.

From a lower shelf just beyond Paul's eye line, Ruby snatched a box of blueberry Pop-Tarts and stuffed it into her winter coat. She picked up a pack of toilet paper from the shelf behind, fingers jumping, and clutched it to her stomach.

The nerviness of the day dissolved all at once, and as she turned, she felt *good*. She felt powerful.

Until she saw boy's-name-that-started-with-a-D down the aisle, between her and the register. He had a full shopping basket slung over one arm and a box of saltines in his free hand, but he held perfectly still, watching Ruby. From the thinned line of his lips and the way his dark eyebrows knotted together below a gray ski cap, she knew he'd seen everything. The blood slipped from Ruby's cheeks.

Because there was nothing else to do, she picked up her chin and brushed by him toward the counter, waiting for the boy—Dov, she remembered—to call her out. She handed over one of Levi's twenties to pay for the toilet paper while Dov stepped behind her in line, but he said nothing.

It didn't matter. She'd won nothing, because she no longer had the power. And so while Paul was busy ringing Dov up, she pulled loose the waistline of her coat and let the Pop-Tarts tumble onto a stack of *Plainsmen* copies beside the door. Then she walked out into a wet, steady snow.

Another choked jangle of the bell, and Dov stood beside her on the sidewalk. He was taller than Ruby—everybody was—but not by much, a few inches at most, and she watched him squint up into the falling snow with her peripheral vision.

"You're Cece's cousin, right?" he asked, and without waiting, answered himself, "I thought so. She's my sister's friend."

Ruby said nothing.

Dov blinked as flakes melted on his eyelashes and salted his black hair and hat. "You want a ride?" He scratched his jaw. "I don't see a car."

What was worse, Ruby wondered, accepting a pity lift, or slouching pathetically off into the weather like Charlie Brown after blowing a baseball game?

In the end, she followed Dov to his shiny black pickup truck, too pristine inside and out to have ever gone mud-running. It smelled like fabric shampoo and something . . . sweet. Dov turned the key in the ignition, and they both jumped as a voice halfway between a moan and a scream blasted from the speakers, accompanied by a ukulele:

> *Love is patient*
> *Love is kind*
> *Unless, of course, it's poorly timed*
> *It might be deaf*
> *Or dumb*
> *Or blind*
> *Or require brief jail time*

Ruby snapped the radio off.

"Ahh," Dov said in protest. "That's a good song, though. 'Various Varieties of Love.' It's—"

"Yeah, I know who it is."

While the engine warmed, he pulled the box of saltines from his shopping bags, tore open the package, and held them out to her, flashing a lazy white smile.

"I'm not deprived," she informed him.

His smile wavered. "Good?"

"I know you saw me. But I'm not starving. I didn't do it because I'm poor." That was true enough. If the water at 11 Stone Road had been shut off once or twice, it was only because Dahlia forgot to send the checks before Ginger took over and put them on autopay.

"I didn't think you were," he said.

Though she knew she was angry at herself for being caught, for feeling weak, the low calm of his voice made her angrier. "Why not? Why couldn't I be? You don't know me."

"I guess I don't. I just . . . figured."

His nonanswer enraged her. "You *figured*? Okay, then. Masterful work, Inspector Clouseau."

"Who?"

"He's that famous detective, from those movies. It's not funny if I have to tell you."

"No, it's funny." Dov's voice was so deadpan, it actually *was* funny, and she laughed against her will. He gave her a shy grin, then pulled away from the curb into the deserted road, damp and glittering under the streetlights and the snow. He headed up Elm toward her house as she directed him.

They lapsed into silence, and Ruby could have let it stretch until they reached her house. But she surprised herself by breaking it. "You're in Cece's math class?" Not sparkling wit, but it was the only thing she knew about *him*.

"What, me? No way. I'm, like, remedial compared to her. And Talia. My sister will probably get a NASA scholarship to study on the moon, while I'm working on a chicken farm," he said cheerfully.

Ruby eyed the spotless, expensive leather interior of his spotless, expensive truck, doubting very much that Dov's future was in poultry. But she didn't point it out. "That's bleak."

"Not necessarily. Maybe it will be a fancy chicken farm in France."

"Right. One of those famous Parisian farms."

This time Dov laughed, one loud bark. "Exactly."

Was he flirting? Ruby wondered. Was *she*? It was hard to tell. She didn't have much to do with non-Chernyavskys, and since the family only ever had daughters, they didn't have much to do with boys at all.

It wasn't that they didn't like boys, or didn't want them—though, of course, some didn't. It was just that, except in strange cases like Aunt Annie's, they didn't keep boys around. Ruby didn't know her father at all—only that he was different than Ginger's, and Dahlia's—and she'd honestly never given it much thought. Chernyavskys didn't get romantic tattoos with men or move into small apartments with them or marry them. Sometimes they took promises and made promises. Sometimes they even ran away with them for a little while. But they almost always came back alone. It was why Ruby knew that however much Ginger liked Levi, he wouldn't last. Neither would Paul the cashier, if Dahlia ever glanced his way. And the thing about the boys: they didn't even seem that sad to be left. More like fishermen who thought they'd caught a giant trout, but upon reeling it in, realized it was a small dragon. And when the dragon broke the line and splashed back, they rowed home wondering whether or not it had all really happened. They were confused, disoriented, and willing to forget.

So why bother with boys, or with anybody at all, outside of family? Why pick up a book you'd never finish, or start a math problem you'd never solve? Why begin what you know is only destined to end, sooner or later?

Ruby was thinking about this while glancing sideways at Dov, at his profile stamped against the streetlights beyond the driver side window, when that frozen feeling crept through her again, stronger than it had been all day. Her ribs felt like windowpanes in winter, cold and fragile, frost embroidering itself across her bones as her breath hitched. In the next second, her phone went wild inside her coat pocket. Texts chimed in one after the other, and Ruby pried it out, fumbling it with nervous fingers. Without taking his eyes off the road, Dov caught her phone on the fall and handed it back.

"Thank you," she murmured, swiping at the screen. It was a group text between Ruby and her cousins.

Mikki: Did you guys feel it?

Oksana: Who was it?

Cece: Not me mom's here too

Lili: Me and Mikki are ok, obvi. Mom says Aunt P's not answering her phone?

And then a second thread lit up.

Dahlia: Ruby where are you????

"What's up?" Dov asked, shoving his ski cap back to keep his bangs out of his eyes. "Everything okay?"

"Can you please drive faster?" The words floated up from between her iced-over ribs. "It's a family thing."

"Sure." He put his foot down, and they lurched forward with the wet grind of rubber.

"Turn there," she told him, short on breath. "Stone Road."

"Which house?"

"This is fine." They were four houses up from her own, but she was impatient. "Thanks, for . . . for the ride." Grabbing her toilet paper, she left the warmth of the truck and tucked her head down against the snow. She heard the skate of his tires over asphalt as he turned to drive away, and looked over her shoulder. If Dov did the same when he paused at the end of the street, all he'd see would be the shape of her, getting smaller and farther away in the dark.

Behind their flimsy living room curtains, her sisters' silhouettes paced—Ruby could see them before she mounted the porch. She flung open the front door and they turned to stare at her. All at once, Dahlia melted onto the couch cushions with a shivery exhale of breath, while Ginger lurched forward, grabbing Ruby by the shoulders. "Why didn't you text us back?" she barked.

"I was almost home—" Ruby began, but lost her wind when Ginger crushed Ruby against her body.

"Always text back," she murmured into her hair, the afternoon's bickering forgotten.

Ruby tapped her elbows comfortingly; the only parts of her sister she could reach with her arms pinned. "Who was it?" she dared to ask.

Ginger shook her head.

Dahlia's phone buzzed on the coffee table, and she lifted it with careful fingers, as if taking a hot pan from the oven. Ginger peeled them apart but took Ruby's hand in hers, and they watched their big sister press the phone to her ear, white-knuckled. "Vera?" she answered, her usually serene voice brittle. Vera was another of the great-aunts, Polina's little sister. They listened while she listened, and then, "Yes, I'll tell them. Yes, we'll see you then." Dahlia ended the call, looking up to tell them, "It was Polina." Her green eyes shivered with tears.

Ginger squeezed Ruby's hand hard enough to grind the bones, then pried her fingers free and crossed the room to the kitchen, announcing, "I'll make tea."

"I'll make the calls," Dahlia said, though Ginger was already gone.

And Ruby? She stood frozen, waiting to feel anything besides numb.

· SIX ·

The night their mother left them, Great-Aunt Polina had been Dahlia's first phone call.

She came quickly, not waiting to be let in but barging through the front door of the big brick house. Though she had raised their mother from a young age, Polina hadn't rubbed off on her in any way that Ruby could see. Whereas their great-aunt moved powerfully through their halls, her mother was . . . soft. Ruby remembered exactly what she'd been wearing that morning: a ballet-pink sweater, loose high-waisted jeans, and wooly socks she'd padded down the driveway in to bring Ruby her forgotten lunch while she waited for the bus. In the morning cold, her cheeks were bright apples, her kisses light and her voice quiet as she murmured, "Be good, zerkal'tse."

Now she was gone—Dahlia, home visiting from college for her birthday, had opened the envelope that told them so—and Polina filled every abandoned corner of their home, like wind. Spying through the cracked kitchen door, Ruby heard her tell Dahlia in her harsh but comforting accent, "Ruby will live with me now." She said it matter-of-factly, as if solving the simplest problem in the world.

Dahlia sat at the kitchen table, elbows on the wood, hands knotted in front of her nose. "I don't know if . . . I should . . . she has friends here." At that time, Ruby had. "And Ginger—"

"She will come also," Polina hurried to say. Had she forgotten Ginger?

"They have school. We can't take them out."

"What's *friends*? What's *school*?" Polina set a steaming cup of tea down in front of Dahlia. It wasn't anything fragrant from their mother's shop, but something she'd brought along in her large purse, strong enough to curl inside Ruby's nose in the doorway. She'd also set a silver flask on the table between them, and poured a generous amount of its contents into each of their cups. "They must be with family. Where will they live when you go back to your college?"

"I don't know . . ." Dahlia repeated. "God, I have to call Ginger. She's sleeping over . . . somewhere. A friend's. She'll hate me just for telling her about Mom." Dahlia dropped her forehead onto her fists. "I need time to think."

"So think. You are still a child, and how can a child take care of children? You must be smart, kotyonok." The nickname, *kitten*, was kind, but from Polina, it might have been a reproach.

Ruby was not feeling smart. When the bus had brought her home from school that afternoon, she'd seen the envelope with Dahlia's name on it pinned with a magnet to the fridge. But she'd ignored it as she pulled out the bread to make a potato chip sandwich, believing it was a grocery list, or cash for pizza. It wasn't unusual to find the shop closed; her mother wasn't exactly flooded with customers during all daylight hours, pounding down the doors for herbal tea.

"You took care of your sisters when you were younger than me, didn't you? We've all heard the story," Dahlia shot back, sounding nothing like a kitten. In spite of everything, Ruby was proud of her.

"This is different. Even when I am young, I am not a child."

"Look, maybe we don't even have to move them. I could stay here a bit longer. Maybe she'll come back—"

"I love my Evelina," Polina interrupted. "You know this. But your mother, she is scared. So she makes her choice. We all make a choice," she said, curling forward in a way Ruby had never seen, as if bent under a heavy load. Then she straightened and scraped her skirt smooth, but said in her gentlest tone yet, "Family is everything. The most important power we Chernyavskys have. Your mother will find this out for herself, I think. I hope. If not, she will never come back."

· SEVEN ·

On Thursday, the sky hanging dark and low above them, Ruby and her sisters stood in front of 54 Ivory Road, squinting up. Ruby had always thought Polina's place looked like a huge gingerbread house. A gingerbread house that was left out in the yard for a couple of weeks for the deer and the birds to eat, but still. It was set a quarter mile back from the road by a sloped gravel driveway that sawed through the woods. Gray stone, with winter-bare tendrils of climbing ivy covering large patches. The tall windows were arced, the mossy roof tiles rounded like seashells. A tower on the left side, circled by a black-iron widow's walk, crowned by a weathervane. It was an old, old house.

Dahlia and Ginger clicked up the slate path in their heels,

and Ruby followed. The grand front door swung open just before they'd reached them, revealing Great-Aunt Vera—Polina's younger sister, though not at all young. Eighty-five years old, she'd grown up in the house just like Ruby's mother, but forty years earlier. Now she had five daughters still living (Alyona would have made six), fourteen granddaughters—some of whom were still teenagers, some in their late thirties—and six great-granddaughters. A black pillbox hat with a bow and a half veil was nestled in her blue-white hair. "You girls look lovely," she said, her accent much milder than her sister's.

Dahlia and Ginger wore matching black knee-length dresses with bell sleeves and sheer, floor-length overlays. Their hair was freshly dyed for the occasion, Dahlia's like lavender in spring, Ginger's striking violet. Ruby, too small for their Hip Witch aesthetic, wore a hand-me-down dress of Ginger's, a black satin shift dress with a high collar and a heart-shaped clasp at the throat. Dahlia had to chop half a foot from the hem for it to fit her. Ginger had smoothed and slicked her brown hair with bobby pins, and Great-Aunt Vera ran a plump hand over it before stepping back to let them in from the cold.

Except for bouquets of bright blue forget-me-nots on every clear surface, the house looked the same inside as it always had: the beet-red bubbling wallpaper, the dark hardwood floors, the lightly spiderwebbed molding. Past the foyer and down three steps was the great room. The ceiling here rose up two stories, the second floor ringed by a balcony, beyond which you could see door after door on the upper level.

The great room was full of women in black, some cradling babies or toddlers with demure dresses rucked up around their short, plump legs.

By the big marble fireplace, Cece lifted her arm and waved Ruby over to a cluster of cousins. They weren't *just* cousins, but second cousins once removed, though who could keep track of that? Except for Cece, they were all Vera's grand-daughters. There was twenty-year-old Lili, who looked more like Ginger than Ruby, only without the everlasting frown. Her sister, Mikki, was seventeen, stamped with the Cherny-avsky green eyes and her unknown father's black skin and dark, cloud-like hair. They lived with their mother, Aunt Mariya, an hour north. Then there was Oksana, Ruby's age, with ash-brown hair that dripped below her bottom and so many freckles, even her lips were dappled. Oksana went to ritzy Oakleaf Prep a few towns over; she and her friends wore their navy school blazers all the time, even when they were going out for ice cream. She wore it now, with its embroidered crest on the pocket, over her short black dress.

She slid over to make room, hooking her slim arm through Ruby's. "I knew it. Didn't you? I mean, I didn't know *who* it was when I felt *it*, but . . . And it was a heart attack, they said? Can you even believe it?"

"I thought she'd be around forever," Ruby said honestly. "She was so strong."

Mikki leaned her head on Lili's shoulder, but spoke to Ruby. "You must be so sad. You were her favorite, you know."

"I wasn't," Ruby protested, but weakly. *Ruby will live with me now,* she remembered her great-aunt saying, Ginger an afterthought. She had wondered . . .

"Mom just talked to her two days before it happened," Cece said in a small voice. "To plan."

"Oh, Cece, your party!" Oksana moaned sympathetically.

"We'll have it later. Maybe in March, Mom said."

"Remember Theo's party?" Lili asked.

Ruby did remember. It'd been about a year after her mother left. They'd all worn their fanciest, puffiest dresses and stuffed their faces with vatrushka, round buns filled with baked cottage cheese and sugar, and avoided the kholodets, the rectangular platter of cold jellied meat served at most Chernyavsky gatherings (paired with vodka for the aunts, though Ruby hadn't known it until she'd sipped from Dahlia's abandoned cup one New Year's Eve).

At night, when the aunts and big sisters gathered in the great room, all of the cousins who hadn't yet seen their Times but were old enough to be left on their own were sent upstairs. The five of them—Cece, Ruby, Mikki, Lili, and Oksana— claimed one of the bigger second-floor bedrooms. It had a king-sized bed with a fancy brass headboard, and they arranged themselves in a star on the quilt. On their stomachs, propped up on elbows, they faced the center of the star. "Truth or dare," Lili asked. As the fifteen-year-old leader, the game had been her idea.

Ruby had overheard the aunts murmuring about Lili, how she was old enough, how she was sure to see her Time any day now.

"Truth," Mikki picked.

"If the five of us were stuck on a desert island, who would you kill for food?"

"Oh, gross." She tugged on one black coil of hair. "But Cece I guess, 'cause she's the sweetest." Mikki giggled, then asked, "Ruby, truth or dare?"

Ruby chose dare. She usually did, and her cousins must've been counting on that, because it wasn't Mikki who spoke, but Lili. "You have to sneak out onto the balcony and spy on what Baba Yaga and everyone is saying down there, and then come and tell us," she ordered with a laugh.

It wasn't the kindest nickname for Great-Aunt Polina. Baba Yaga, according to the old stories, was a bony old woman with iron teeth and a nose so long it scraped the ceiling when she slept on her back. She lived in a magical chicken-legged hut behind a fence of stacked human bones, and gave tasks to the heroes who wandered up to the door of the hut, seemingly unwarned by the bone fence. If the hero succeeded, she gave them a gift. Fail, and she'd punish them, perhaps cook them in her giant stove. A scary story they'd grown up hearing, but only a story. Unlike legends of the old country, the

Chernyavsky glory and downfall, nobody pretended that Baba Yaga was real. It was like "The Death of Koschei the Immortal," "Vasilisa the Beautiful," and "The Giant Turnip": a fairy tale.

Out of loyalty to the woman who'd been to see them once a week since their mother had fled the family, Ruby never used the nickname. But she had to admit it wasn't unfitting. Their great-aunt had earned it with her oldness, her angularness—elbows and stockinged knees and cheekbones and even knuckles as sharp as arrows—and a few silver crowned teeth. If she caught the girls spying, she was unlikely to cook them, more likely to chastise their mothers (or in Ruby's case, sisters) in brusque Russian for raising children who snooped on their elders.

Grudgingly, Ruby peeled herself from the mattress, and to her surprise, Cece did, too. "I'll come," she announced. "I want to come."

Easing the bedroom door open and shut behind them, they crept along in their socks until the wall met the balcony railing that overlooked the great room. Dropping and flattening themselves against the hardwood floor, boards digging into the points of Ruby's hip bones, they did a dry-land breast stroke forward. Ruby peered down through the iron swirls of the railing, keeping her chin on the floor so that somebody would have to peer straight up and squint into the unlit hallway to catch pieces of them through the rails.

Cece squeezed beside her. "Look, they have the Recordings."

Their great-aunt was in her faded leather armchair, which smelled up-close exactly like her oversized handbag, and the headscarves she wore from September till spring. It was tobacco and strong tea and the perfume that sat in corked glass bottles on her dresser, shipped from her homeland. It was a Polina smell.

The middle-aged aunts sat on the squat sofas with wooden legs, the younger aunts in chairs dragged in from the kitchen. Ginger and Dahlia and the cousins sat on the floor, except for Theo, the youngest in the room, thirteen then. She stood right in front of Polina's chair, with her mother, Aunt Irina, behind her. In their great-aunt's lap was a book the girls knew as the Chernyavsky Family Recordings. It was thick and old and unlabeled, with a cracked leather binding. Ruby had never held it or seen it read from—when Alyona died two years before, Ruby had been sent off with the rest who hadn't had their Time, hadn't even gotten the talk that Dahlia and Ginger had already given Ruby at the Cone Zone. Theo had been with them then.

"What if I do it wrong?" Theo was asking Polina.

Aunt Irina reached around her daughter and placed a thick ballpoint pen in Theo's hand. "Don't worry about the spelling, baby."

"No, but I mean like . . ." Theo stopped, her voice shivery with almost tears.

Great-Aunt Polina rose from her chair. Even at ninety, she was strong, straight, her spine uncurved. "You will not. Write what you see. People, they waste a whole life worrying. 'Who am I?' But this is not your problem. You see yourself at the end, so you *know*. This is the gift. You know who you will be, so you know who you are." She pressed the book toward Theo. "This makes you strong."

Theo held it out from her body like something dangerous. "Will you read it when I'm done?"

Polina shook her head. "Not today. Not for a long time. Tell who you like, or tell no one. It belongs to you."

Tapping her on the shoulder, Cece swam backward up the hallway, and Ruby followed. Once they were beyond the wall, Ruby stood, brushing off her party dress, and trailed Cece toward the spare bedroom. But her cousin didn't go in. She kept walking to the far end of the hallway and the staircase that led to the tower. Narrow and uncarpeted, it spiraled up toward the door they couldn't see in the dark but knew was always locked. Polina said it was unsafe, rust and dust and old furniture teetering in stacks. Lili claimed it was haunted.

Cece dropped onto the bottom step, as far as she ever dared go, and Ruby sat below her on the floor. She couldn't see her cousin's face well, only the halo of her hair, frizzed out of its braids.

"What?" Ruby whispered.

"Aren't you scared?" she whispered back.

"We knew all that stuff already." Not that they understood it all, but at least the two of them had been told.

"Yeah, but what if, like, you get your Time and then you see you're in an electric chair when you die, because you robbed the Red Rooster and killed everyone, and everybody hates you? So then you figure out that you're an evil person, but you can't do anything about it?"

"If that's the thing you're the most afraid of, you're obviously a good person," Ruby pointed out.

"I hope so." In the dark she was just a rounded shadow, hunched and hugging herself. "Will you tell me?"

"What?"

"About your Time. When you get it."

"Oh." In the year since she'd been told, Ruby had come to believe Dahlia, and to believe most of the stories about their family. Still, it was hard to imagine small, skinny, unimportant, powerless her being a part of all that, even if it was much more about tea and tradition than actual magic these days. The stories were easier to accept than her place in them. "I guess so?"

"You guess?"

"Yeah, of course I will. Will *you* tell *me*?"

The shape of Cece nodded. "Let's tell each other together, after both of us see our Times."

They made their promises, and Ruby scooted up to sit on the same step as Cece.

"You're not afraid of it?" her cousin asked, leaning her head on Ruby's shoulder. "I am."

Thinking of her mother, she set her jaw and answered, "No, I'm not."

If it had been a lie at the time, she told herself that it wasn't anymore. When you knew your expiration date—or near enough—you knew what to expect out of life, what to hope for, and what not to hope for. As Polina had said, you knew who you would be, and so you knew who you were. Maybe it wasn't the death you would have picked, or the years you would have asked for, but you made peace with your Time. You looked it in the face, and you were stronger for doing so.

You certainly didn't run from it. As if you even could.

Even though she understood that she would never matter to the world—that she would never have the chance to—she mattered to her family. Ruby was a Chernyavsky, and that was everything. It was enough.

It had to be.

Now, as the afternoon passed and the aunts brought out bowls of pickles, fermented cabbage, platters of blini and the dreaded kholodets, and the cousins scrambled to speak over one another, and Great-Aunt Vera held court in Polina's old leather armchair by the fireplace, Ruby watched the clock. All she wanted was to go home, strip out of her dress and coil up on the couch with Dahlia and Ginger, half watching trash TV while they drifted through private memories of Polina. Like the time Ruby had gotten sick, and Ginger was still in high school, and Dahlia couldn't take off from whichever part-time day job she was working to keep the water on in the small house on Stone Road she'd moved them to soon after their mother left, having discovered how little a tea shop's profits had left them financially prepared. Polina came to watch Ruby, and instead of the NyQuil Dahlia left on the counter, her great-aunt had minced up garlic and onion, made Ruby stick her face over the bowl and breathe for hours or minutes.

"Without medicine, this cold lasts seven days," she'd said sternly as Ruby's eyes teared. "With medicine, it lasts a week." But then she'd fished through the compartments of her purse, pulling out the customary little bag of pastila.

That was Polina: garlic and onions, but with the unexpected aftertaste of sugar.

When the early evening light through the windows turned waxy and peeled away, leaving night behind it, it was time for the Reading. This was Ruby's and Cece's first, and they found seats on the floor among their cousins, facing Great-Aunt Vera in the armchair. Ruby supposed that was Vera's place now; the youngest of the three daughters of the supposed woman in the woods, she was the last remaining. The last Chernyavsky born on Russian soil, who spoke the old language fluently, and truly remembered where they came from.

Once Vera was gone, there would be nothing *but* stories.

"Thank you all for coming to celebrate our family matriarch, Polina Chernyavsky," she said in better English than her sister had ever spoken. Perhaps because she spoke so much of it; Vera was still a fountain of family gossip in her eighties. "The funeral will be next Saturday at the—" Vera paused, pressing her red lacquered lips together, blinking at a spot beyond the gathered crowd.

Heads turned—Ruby's too—and in the raised threshold between the great room and the hall, there stood a woman. Arms spread apologetically, palms up and empty, Evelina Chernyavsky said in the low but lilting voice lodged forever like a splinter in Ruby's chest, "I'm sorry I'm late."

· EIGHT ·

Ruby's memories of her mother were dusty with age and disuse, like the books you outgrew and never took off the shelf anymore, or the old photo boxes you stored in the basement so you could pretend your former embarrassing self had never existed.

But she'd never truly managed to forget Evelina Chernyavsky.

Ruby remembered the smell of her mint hand cream. Her long straw-blond hair, like Dahlia's and Ginger's, woven into crown braids or hanging loose, its tendrils alive on a windy day. Her fingers, slim and sure as they sewed Ruby's Halloween costumes, or stirred a pot of cabbage soup. Her voice, deep for a woman's but musical, even when she spoke, so her lullabies sounded like rumbling blues songs.

Most often, though, when she thought of her mother, it wasn't as the woman who'd smoothed Band-Aids over skinned elbows, or packed tiny origami beetles and butterflies and frogs in her lunch box, or let Ruby climb into her canopied bed during tornado warnings. It was as she'd seen her last: standing in their driveway in her thin pink sweater and too-big jeans, shoeless and shivering, diminishing as the school bus pulled farther and farther away from her.

Small.

Soft.

Scared.

Family is everything. The most important power we Chernyavskys have. Your mother will find this out for herself, I think. I hope. If not, she will never come back.

Now she realized her mother was even shorter than she'd remembered. And older, which she might have expected. Already twenty-eight when Dahlia was born, almost forty when she'd had Ruby, she must be in her midfifties by now. Her hair had salt in it, but it was still swirled into its familiar crown braid. In fact, she was dressed much as she always had, in soft summer colors. Light blue baggy jeans cuffed at the ankles above sheepskin boots, and a yellow cardigan buttoned all the way to her pale neck. Standing before a sea of black dresses and crisply tailored suits, she looked like the last sunflower in the field before the winter frost killed it, too.

Ruby turned back, searching for her sisters. They sat on

the couches with Vera's oldest granddaughters and *their* children, Dahlia holding cousin Zeny's very pink newborn, Ginger holding a vodka tonic. Dahlia's face was stone; Ginger's was glass.

She felt a soft hand slip inside hers, and wrapped frozen fingers around Cece's, squeezing hard.

In her armchair, Vera pursed her lips, then nodded once, releasing Evelina from whatever spell held her in the doorway. Her mother took the steps softly and tucked herself into the nearest corner of the great room, eyes on her boots.

"The funeral will take place next Saturday at the Mount Carmel Cemetery," Vera continued, slightly ruffled. "But today, we gather in the family tradition for Polina's Reading, as we someday will for all our daughters, our sisters, our mothers."

Ruby knew Polina had recited the same words at Aunt Alyona's reading; Ginger had described it to Ruby last night to prepare her for today. Next, Vera would read Polina's own account of her Time aloud to the family. Ruby tried to picture teenaged Polina, perhaps having just arrived in America, seeing herself as an old woman. Ninety-five would've seemed an eternity away. Had she been relieved, or scared despite the many years promised to her?

She wished she'd thought to ask her great-aunt, though she could imagine Polina's gruff response. *Why scared? Because I know I will die? This is not news, kroshka.*

As expected, Vera held the heavy Recordings aloft with slightly trembling arms and said, "Let us know Polina in death as she knew herself in life." She thumbed through the stiff yellowed pages of the book, and then she read aloud, translating the Russian to English as she went.

Entry in the Chernyavsky Recordings

April the 29, 1938
I am young, but not so young, perhaps thirty. In a small hard bed, my bed in my small house, I am giving birth. My sisters are around me, Vera's hand in mine, Galina at my feet. There is pressure and fire and so much pain, I myself am like a planet being born. But the child at the center of it all, I have always been waiting for. I am miserable and joyful and in such pain, and I am becoming who I am meant to be. Above all, I am in love. I have been waiting my whole long, short life to feel a love like this.
—Polina Chernyavsky, age 17

It was very, very quiet.

Ice chips floated in cold rivers through Ruby's veins. Cece sat unmoving beside her. Even Lili's freckles had turned pale.

Vera slapped the Recordings shut with a slight puff of dust. She seemed lost, as if when she'd opened the book she'd been sitting in a clearing, and now she'd looked up to find herself deep in the woods. They all might as well be.

Polina had lived to ninety-five. She'd died alone, in this house, without children. She might have raised Ruby's mother and Aunt Annie, might have loved them . . . but not the kind of love she'd described in the Recordings.

Their visions were never wrong. They never had been. This was the gift the Chernyavskys had taken with them. It was all they had left; that, and each other.

Ruby looked to her mother—for what, she wasn't sure— but Evelina still had not lifted her eyes from the floor.

Amid the hiss of whispered questions, Vera cradled the Recordings and stood. She waited until the room quieted, then said with only a small tremble in a voice strong enough to be heard from the back of the crowd, "You all know our story, my sisters and I. You know where we come from, and why my mother sent us away when I was too young to truly remember her. As the oldest, Polina watched over Galina and me on our long journey, and made us a home in this new country. She reminded us all the while that we were alive only because we had left behind our most perilous knowledge. Never again would we be hunted by those who desired it, for we did not possess the prize they sought.

"But if my beloved sister indeed brought my mother's secrets with her across that vast, cold ocean . . . If in her wisdom, she has kept them in silence all this time so that we might remain safe . . ." Vera gritted her teeth, then ground out, "then may they die at last, and be thankful that in her wisdom, she shared them with no one."

With that, she clapped the book closed and left the room without delivering the traditional toast. No tiny glasses of slivovitz were lifted in Polina's name, as they had been at Alyona's Reading. When it became clear that Vera would not return, the aunts and cousins began to drift away. One by one they climbed into their cars and vanished into the night. Aunt Annie fled with Cece almost at once.

If she had spoken to her sister before leaving, Ruby hadn't seen it.

Escaping the nervous buzz of the lingering women— they were like black bees in a threatened hive—Ruby snuck upstairs to sit with her thoughts for just a moment. Polina's bedroom was the first at the top of the stairs, and she placed her hands against the cold, heavy door that listed on its hinges, intending to push. But then she saw the slice of light below the dark wood and, when she held her ear to the door, heard the sobbing. It was quiet and compressed, as though muffled by a pillow. She backed away, leaving Great-Aunt Vera in peace.

Instead, she turned to the door opposite Polina's. It was her mother and Aunt Annie's childhood bedroom, and it was nothing she hadn't seen before when she slipped inside. Two antique-looking sleigh beds with curling headboards and footboards pushed against the worn, pale red wallpaper. There were no stuffed animals on the bench seat, or yellowed pictures or posters on the walls. It was just a spare room now.

Leaving the light off so she wouldn't be discovered, Ruby made her way by the moonlight through the drawn curtains and settled onto the floor between the beds.

She didn't mind the dark. She hadn't since she was ten years old.

There was a farm in Saltville that used to put on a haunted house and corn maze each Halloween. Ruby's mother took their family every year, until her sisters were too old. Then it was just the two of them. They'd gone for the last time the year she turned ten. In the apple orchard, they ran a haunted hayride that kids under ten weren't allowed on, so Ruby remembered standing in line for the very first time, and feeling her heartbeat in her ears. She remembered it beating, small and scared, but very alive. She had been waiting years, and she was ready.

But when the moment came to board the wagon hitched behind the tractor, she had frozen. Until, that is, her mother climbed the metal steps and stood in the hay. Her face glowed white under the stadium lights, hair rippling down under her yellow pom-pom winter hat. She held her hand out to Ruby, and a strange fire lit her eyes from behind. "Don't be afraid, baby. We're Chernyavsky women. The dark is scared of *us*."

Ruby breathed through the memory as if through chest pain.

That was when the bedroom light clicked on overhead,

and she blinked up at the figure in the doorway as her eyes readjusted.

"Oh, zerkal'tse. I was hoping that was you."

Even from across the room, her mother still smelled like mint. Ruby thought she would hold a hand out to help her up from the floor, but Evelina stayed almost inhumanly still.

"It's wonderful to see you," she continued, voice rough. "You look . . . you're beautiful."

Ruby held just as still as her mother, not trusting her own voice.

"Quite the Reading, wasn't it?" she continued. "And I guess I didn't help things. I suppose you weren't expecting me. But I—I felt the cold, and was sure it was Polina, and I knew it was time to come home."

Now, when Ruby spoke, she heard only disdain, thick as honey on a teaspoon. "You didn't have to. You weren't missed."

The fine lines around her mother's river-green eyes pulled tight. "I don't blame you for that. And I know this will be hard to believe, but I've always loved you, Ruby. I've always tried to protect you. It's why I left."

Years ago, when she'd still allowed herself to imagine her mother returning, Evelina would always give a speech just like this. And in her imagination, Ruby would launch herself forward, smash her face into her mother's sweater.

Instead, she stared at the toes of her mother's boots and tried to feel hatred. Mostly, she felt tired.

She stood, brushing dust from the seat of her dress as if that were her greatest concern. "I have to go home now."

"Zerkal'tse—"

"Stop calling me that. I'm nothing like you."

"Baby, I don't think you know who you really are. Not yet."

"I know for a fact that I wouldn't abandon my family," she snapped, surprised to hear Ginger in her words, but not regretting them "That's not what real Chernyavskys do."

"Real Chernyavskys," her mother repeated, laughing quietly. "I don't think you know who they are, either."

That was it. She wouldn't stand here and be laughed at by this stranger in her mother's clothing. Maybe the family wouldn't slam the door in Evelina's face—blood was strong, even if she was weak—but Ruby wasn't about to welcome her inside with a hug and a cup of tea. On unsteady feet, she strode past her mother to the door, determined not to look back.

"I don't have a phone yet—I've been out of the country for a while—but I'll be at the Molehill Motel in Hop River, when you want answers to your questions," her mother called out. "Room 113!"

Ruby kicked the bedroom door closed behind her, defiantly undignified in her anger, and trying to ignore the inevitability of *when*.

• NINE •

Snow began to fall as they drove home, first in slow fat flakes, and then faster. Loose snow slithered across the road like wisps of smoke in the dark, blotting out the center line. Dahlia steered them white-knuckled, while Ginger turned the radio up—the kind of club song her sister hated—until the bass rattled the seats. Probably so Ruby wouldn't try to speak to them from the back.

As if that could stop her.

"What do you think it means?" she shouted.

Ginger glanced up into the rearview mirror, where her glassy eyes met Ruby's. "What, Mom coming back?"

Her heart gave a sickening lurch. "No," she said flatly. "The Reading."

"What?"

"The *Reading*," she nearly screamed.

Defeated, Ginger turned down the music. "I don't know."

"You think Polina lied about her Time?"

"No."

"Then—"

"*No*, Ruby. Just . . ." Ginger swiveled around in her seat, and because the back of Dahlia's old watermelon-pink Mustang was the size of a picnic cooler, her pale face hovered inches from Ruby's. "Leave it alone."

"But—"

"You don't know what you're talking about."

"I *do* know. Am I a Chernyavsky or not?"

"You're a kid. You don't know anything about the world."

"Oh, sorry, I didn't know your daily fifteen-minute commute was so enlightening."

"If you two can't stop fighting . . ." Dahlia yelled vaguely.

Ginger's eyes nearly crackled with heat. "Maybe she did lie. Or Maybe Polina's Time was true, and she found a way around it. Maybe she knew more than any of us. But it's none of our business, either way."

"How can you say that?" Her voice edged into a shriek.

"Were you even listening to Vera? You know what happened to us the last time we had secrets worth dying for? We almost *died*, Ruby. We're safe now because we left all that shit in Russia."

"You actually believe those stories? Like some dude in a Cossack hat with a hunting rifle is gonna show up on our doorstep trying to steal some super-secret powers that are so secret, we don't even have them anymore? Come the fuck on."

Dahlia slammed the horn, though the glittering, shifting road ahead was empty. "Stop it, okay, you guys? We can't talk about this now. Any of it. Everybody's sad tonight. Everyone's scared. Let's just keep it together."

Besides the radio, the rest of the ride was silent to the bone.

They stayed quiet until they ducked inside the house, frozen from the dash to the front door. Dahlia hung her keys on the wall hook, then an extra set beside them; one Ruby had never seen before, dangling from a brass chain, the worn medallion stamped with a cursive *P*.

"What's that?"

"The house keys. Vera gave them to us in case we need to get in."

"To Polina's? Why?"

Ginger rushed away to the kitchen to make tea, leaving Dahlia behind to answer her questions. "We might need her documents to get things settled, or to call a plumber if a pipe bursts, or there might be a break-in, or . . . I don't know, Ruby," she said tiredly. "Things happen. Somebody needs to take care of the place, and we're the closest." Again, Aunt Annie wasn't a consideration, despite being a nearby grown-up with no job.

"So is it ours now? Like, are we going to live there?" Ruby wasn't sure how she felt about the possibility. Polina's home, one of the oldest in Saltville, was a palace compared to their place on Stone Road, crooked doors and rippled wallpaper and all. But her great-aunt had filled up the huge old house. Without her, wouldn't it be like living in a library with no books?

"No," Dahlia said after a pause, looking uneasy now. "She wanted . . . she didn't leave it to us."

The teakettle shrieked through every tiny room.

After they'd all changed into pajamas, the sisters curled up on the couch, Ruby's feet under Ginger's butt, her knee pressed into Dahlia's shoulder. They watched reruns of *Finding Bigfoot*, a show where *not* finding Bigfoot was confirmation of his existence ("We scoured these woods all night and found no trace of the beast sighted just days ago, but bigfoots don't linger around a single hunting ground, so it only makes sense that he's moved on by now"). After two episodes, Dahlia headed off. She had a morning shift at 'Wiches and Wings. Then it was Ruby and Ginger and their cooling mugs of tea, the silence suddenly deafening.

Ruby shattered it first. "Can I just ask—"

"I don't want to talk about the Reading," Ginger cut in without looking at her.

"It's not about that. Mostly. I was just wondering . . . did you, um, talk to Mom? After?"

"No." Her sister's face didn't twitch in the blue light of the TV, but something dangerous simmered in her voice. "And I'm not going to."

"Oh."

"She can't just fucking . . ." Ginger continued, her rage fanned to a crackling flame. "If she really thinks this family will take her back now . . ."

"Vera didn't exactly kick her out," Ruby muttered.

"So? She didn't run out on Vera."

Hadn't she though? Hadn't she committed the deepest betrayal possible for a Chernyavsky and left all of them?

Ginger did turn then, studying her. "Did she talk to *you* at the Reading?"

"Not about anything important. Do you think Dahlia will talk to her?"

"Doubt it. Not after Mom stuck her with us. That's a lot to forgive."

It was a bleak thought, but Ruby couldn't deny it.

Her sister's phone vibrated between them where her feet were still wedged against Ginger. Shifting, Ginger pulled it from the pocket of her yoga pants. All at once her rage dripped away, replaced by a syrupy grin.

"Levi?" Ruby guessed reluctantly.

The grin spread, unbearably sticky-sweet.

"Ugh. Why are you with that guy?"

To Ruby's surprise, Ginger considered this, and seemed to answer honestly. "Because . . . he's easy. He's safe. He makes me laugh."

"You're too good for him."

"Am I?" Ginger asked blandly.

"He makes you laugh, and that's enough for you?"

"It has to be." Her sister turned back to the TV. "When I was your age, I'd had my Time, but I still thought I was gonna leave Saltville, be a famous poet or journalist or I-don't-know-what. *Something.* I was gonna go to college in Boston, and wear turtlenecks and men's suit pants to poetry slams, and travel to every country alone. Then Mom . . . she did what she did. And I learned."

"Learned what?"

Ginger pressed her fingertips together in thought. "How much . . . pain you can cause, when you run from your fate. To other people, and yourself."

"Your fate is to be Levi Dorgan's girlfriend?"

"Maybe. You're a kid, Ruby. You think a small, happy life is this terrible, wasted thing, like I did. But you'll grow up. You'll learn, too."

Ruby swallowed, dry throat clicking. "What was your Time, then?" It wasn't the first time she'd asked, but maybe here in the dark with Ginger in honesty mode, the outcome would be different.

Ginger's lips twitched once, and she smiled distantly. "Don't stay up too late—back to school tomorrow." She got up and went down the hall to her bedroom, leaving Ruby alone.

For a while, Ruby watched the hunters bumble around the woods with no intention of discovering their prey. Then she muted the volume, got her headphones from her bedroom, and sat back on the couch. Kerrigan Black would distract Ruby; she always did. Kerrigan, and her belief that anything could be explained, given enough time and access to the right science.

Ruby liked thinking that someday, somebody armed with the full knowledge of future science might look back and understand the Chernyavskys. Maybe a century from now, they would make sense.

And if someone wanted to travel back to 2019 to explain Ruby to herself, she wouldn't hate that.

She sat with the TV on, still muted, and the lights off, staring idly at the new key ring on the hook in the wobbling blue glow from the screen and listening:

Because nobody else moves to do so, I force my way through the circling crowd toward the woman collapsed at its center. I hear some gasp at the inappropriateness of my dress (or at my undress) but I push through to kneel and look her in her tear-streaked face, aged by hard winters more so than years. "What is your name?" I ask simply so I won't betray that I don't belong here.

"I am the widow Harrison, and I am not guilty of that which my neighbors accuse me. I have done

no murder or shape-shifting. I am no witch! I am not guilty!" she cries.

I don't know if she's innocent of murder, but certainly, she isn't a witch. I've seen it in every time, and I've seen it in my time: a speck of dust catches in a camera lens, and suddenly, a manor is haunted. Cows die of natural causes and bloat in the field, and thus, a satanic cult roams the farmlands. Myths and legends—they've always grown around some tiny seed of mundane truth.

And who better to dig down and uncover that seed than I?

· TEN ·

Because the twenty-four-hour Red Rooster Diner was only three blocks over from Fruit Street, Cece was already seated at a booth in the back when Ruby came in on Friday morning. "No fries?" Ruby asked her, sliding into the bench across from Cece.

"I ordered hash browns. It's six a.m." Her cousin yawned. She might be tired, but Cece looked perfect, hair tamed into two neat braids, her orange Dirty Birds T-shirt clashing expertly with her electric blue skirt. Then there was Ruby, with her too-big skinny jeans tucked into heavy boots, her once-sleek hair inflated with wind and icy rain.

"I didn't know you were so particular about your potatoes."

"What's the Super Actual Emergency?" Cece asked, slightly impatient. Ruby had used the Super-Actual-Emergency emoji code—bomb + fireball + poop stack—because it was the most extreme code they had, guaranteed to pull Cece from her bed an hour before school, and some things you just couldn't say over text. Such as:

"Why doesn't anyone want to talk about what happened last night?"

Cece softened. "You mean your mom? Ruby, are you—"

"I'm fine. That's not—I want to talk about the Reading."

Cece stirred nervously in her seat, glancing around as though spies might be listening in, but Ruby pressed forward.

"I know they're scared," Ruby said. "Your mom. My sisters. All the grown-ups."

"It's like Vera said, right? The stories—"

"Are stories. Bad guys hunted Vladlena and her daughters in the woods in Russia one hundred years ago, so now we have to keep our heads down and get good grades and brush our teeth before bed and blah, blah, blah."

Suddenly, Cece sat upright, smiling politely at an approaching waitress. She kept smiling even after the woman plopped her paper basket of hash browns on the table and stalked away to fill Ruby's order of an ice water. Then she leaned in. "If you don't believe the bad guys are real, why do you believe any of the stories about us?"

These were not new questions between the cousins, but

very old ones: Do you believe? How much do you believe? In *magic*? How can you?

Ruby had been trying to figure that out in earnest since she'd picked up *The Demon-Haunted World* in its plastic jacket the first time around, and with every Sagan book since, and each late-night Wikipedia binge, and even with Kerrigan Black, who believed that the legends, myths, and monsters people feared had a scientific truth at their center. *Pearls form around a speck of grit to protect the oyster, and so to protect us from what we can't yet understand, stories grow around a grain of truth* was one of Ruby's favorite Kerrigan quotes.

And so, after years of careful consideration, Ruby had decided that she had no fucking idea.

Maybe Kerrigan Black was right, and everything in the world really did break down into water and salt and the periodic table of elements. There were a lot of mysteries left in the world: Why did the sun's corona blaze hotter than the fiery neon photosphere of the sun itself? Why did perfect ice circles form over slow-moving water, like glass mushrooms sprouting from the cold surface? What caused a hurricane on Saturn, where there were no oceans? And if monarch butterflies only lived long enough to migrate one way, how did their children find their way back to a home they couldn't remember, but must somehow have felt in their small bodies, in their blood? Science had yet to solve these puzzles, though presumably, someday, it would.

There were people, too, lots of them out there, capable of strange and "scientifically impossible" feats that were, nevertheless, *possible*. Ruby had looked for them, read all about them, collected them. Akira Haraguchi could recite the first 100,000 decimal places of pi from memory. Henrietta Lacks was the first known person whose "immortal" cells could divide forever outside of her body. A Dutch man named Wim Hof could control his autonomic nervous system to survive extreme cold through meditation—he'd climbed Mount Kilimanjaro in shorts—and a group of Tibetan monks could raise their body temperatures with meditation, enough to dry large towels soaked with ice water and draped around their shoulders within an hour. A karate expert, Masutatsu Oyama, had once killed three bulls with one punch each.

And then there was magic.

Ruby had done her research, read about voodoo and Santeria and the Vlach women of Serbia—witches who lifted black curses and told the future (or, depending who you asked, poisoned their enemies with coffee made from water used to bathe dead bodies). Common sense said they were just sharp, perceptive women who served as counselors in their small villages. Their advice was solid, and when people took their advice, their lives improved, which fed rumors of the witches' powers.

Wasn't that exactly what her sisters did, under Polina's tutelage?

Still, if their great-aunt really *had* been holding on to some sort of ancient knowledge, family secrets that only she, as the eldest child of the woman in the woods, had been privy to . . . then maybe the stories weren't just fairy tales, after all. At least, not totally.

"'We wish to pursue the truth no matter where it leads,'" Ruby quoted Sagan to her cousin.

"What does that mean?"

"It means I believe," she said slowly, "that I don't know exactly what to believe. But it can't hurt to try and figure it out."

"Assuming there are no bad guys?"

"I didn't say there never were. And maybe they murdered the woman in the woods and drove out Polina and her sisters—fuck, women get driven out of their homes for having periods, never mind for magic. But this is America. This is *Saltville.* I don't see any villains around here. Nobody worse than our Republican mayor and that religious guy who screams at women outside the Popeyes. So what exactly are we hiding from? I just . . ." She collapsed against the seat back. "I get that you have the *normal* family—"

"I'm not—" Cece started, pink and indignant.

"It's fine, but you are, and you do. You get the mom and the dad and the two-syllable last name and you never have to fight the wasp uprisings. And your Time was probably awesome, and your future is, like, bouncy castles and champagne forever, and you die when you're ninety, while boning one of the

Hemsworths. Or both, and that's great, 'cause you're my best friend and I love you, and I'd be really, really happy for you. But that's not what I—" Ruby drummed her boots against the booth in frustration. "If there's even a little tiny particle of you that wants to be someone slightly different, why not try to find out how? So the rest of the family is too scared, but I think . . . maybe . . . we're supposed to know. I think Polina would want us to stop being afraid." Ruby wasn't at all sure of that. Their great-aunt had never said as much. She'd only repeated the family lines: stay hidden, stay safe. But believing so made her next suggestion easier to say aloud. "I think we should go back to her house."

"You want to break into Polina's house?"

"*Break in?* No." A touch dramatically, she slid the heavy key ring out of her pocket and slapped it onto the tabletop. The brass medallion with its curled *P* glinted under the diner lights.

Cece shook her head. "I love you, and I'm not saying that you're being sociopathic. But our great-aunt *just* died in that house. And you want to sneak in and root through her stuff for, like, *clues*?"

It did sound sociopathic when a nice, normal person said it aloud. "It's not like that," Ruby protested weakly.

Screwing her eyebrows up, Cece stared at Ruby in a way she rarely did. "Your Time wasn't bouncy castles and champagne, was it, Bebe?" she asked.

Deep inside of Ruby, something rattled. It was the truth, she knew, caged for three long years, but never peaceful in captivity. Awake and wild, it crashed against her ribs like a zoo animal mangling itself on the bars of its pen to break out.

"Bebe," Cece repeated softly.

Bursting through in a spray of bone shards, the truth clawed its way up her throat, swollen and raw-feeling in its wake.

"Bebe, come on!" Cece's foot nudged hers below the table. "Forget the deal. Just because I can't . . . Because I'm not ready . . ."

Impossibly heavy on her tongue, now it pounded against her teeth, and if her cousin said one more word—

"You don't have to keep the secret. You can tell me anything."

She let her mouth fall open, and the truth broke free.

• ELEVEN •

February 11, 2016

I'm in Ginger's car, the Malibu, except I'm driving. I'm young, maybe seventeen or eighteen? I can feel it. Plus there's a Physics 2 textbook on the floor of the passenger seat with a badger sticker on the cover, and that's the Saltville High mascot. So unless it's seriously overdue, I'm still in high school.

It's morning, and the sun is coming up through the windshield, but I know I'm not driving to school. I'm on a street I don't recognize, and I'm drinking gross coffee out of a foam to-go cup from a diner I've never heard of, so

I don't think it's in Saltville. There are empty ones just like it stuffed into every cup holder and side pocket, and crumpled up turnpike tickets, too. Like the kind we got that summer Mom took us to Pennsylvania on vacation, when it was my job to hold onto them for her between the tollbooths.

This okay band, Creatures Such As We, comes on the radio, and I turn it up. Somebody's waiting for me. I'm singing along to this song, even though it's not my favorite, but I'm really excited to get where I'm going and see them.

Then I don't see anything else.

—Ruby Chernyavsky, age 13

· TWELVE ·

She'd expected Cece to fling herself across the tabletop, scattering hash browns in her haste to comfort Ruby.

Instead, her cousin retreated, shivering right down to the tips of her braids as she pressed herself against the seatback. "Oh, Ruby . . ." Cece said, her name an almost-soundless exhalation, a wisp of breath.

"It's okay," Ruby lied.

"Do Dahlia and Ginger know?"

"I never told them."

"Why not?"

"Because they couldn't change it," she said. But that was a lie, too, or at least it wasn't the whole truth.

Despite the new lightness in Ruby's chest, she already

regretted telling Cece. Though she'd wanted her cousin's help, needed it—this was too big a mystery to solve alone, and how could Cece deny her now?—she'd never told her sisters because she hadn't wanted them to look at her for the rest of her life like she was dying. She didn't want them to treat her like she was . . . weak. To look at her with trepidation, as though inspecting fruit in a bowl for signs of rot, or watching for a tiny crack in a glass to star and shatter, the way she knew they would.

Why had she thought her cousin would be different?

"We should tell your mom," Cece whispered.

"What?" Ruby hissed in return. "Why?"

"She grew up with Polina. Maybe she knows something. She might—"

"If she thought Polina could change Times, why would she have run away from hers? She would've just asked Polina for help. She doesn't know anything," Ruby insisted. She was scrambling to justify herself, but as she spoke, she knew the logic was sound. "Evelina can't help us, and we can't trust her."

"Okay, I get it. I just don't know what we can find out by ourselves."

"Let's go there and see!"

"We can't go now," Cece said, aghast. "We have school."

Ruby rolled her eyes. "Tonight, then."

"Maybe . . . I promised Talia I'd come over."

"So? Is that really more important?"

Cece blanched and flushed at the same moment, her round cheeks marbled. "No, of course not," she said quickly, quietly.

Ruby paused to take a breath. If she didn't want Cece treating her as if she were dying in the next twenty-four hours, she probably shouldn't act like it. "Sorry, that was rude. What if . . . we could go together?" she suggested as sincerely as possible.

"To the Mahalels'?" Her cousin's eyes widened.

"Yeah, why not? It's not like you're on a date. We could, like, watch a movie or something. You're always asking me to hang out with you guys, right? So I'll come, and then we'll go to Polina's."

Cece's mouth fell open while Ruby drank her ice water as casually as possible.

It was true that Ruby had little use for non-Chernyavskys. But right now, she very badly needed a Baker.

• THIRTEEN •

That evening, Ruby tried to smuggle herself out the door before her sisters asked too many questions about her plans, but was stopped by a puzzling sight: Dahlia, cleaning the kitchen. She knelt in front of the refrigerator, from which every rotten lettuce head and flat soda can and jar of long-expired mayonnaise had been exhumed. In elbow-length rubber gloves, she scrubbed at the drawer that had been sticky with spilled syrup since Ruby could remember. Even Ginger wouldn't touch it. She'd claimed the middle shelf for her fancy Icelandic yogurts that were twice the cost of American yogurt—her one indulgence, and not an exciting one at that—but had washed her hands of the rest after the Great Maple Syrup Spill of '17.

"What are you doing?"

Dahlia sat back on her slippers, rubber-gloved hands held up like a surgeon's. "Chores. You look nice."

Ruby wore a slouchy black sweater, one of Ginger's old ones, with embroidered skulls the size and colors of candy hearts, and her own scuffed black skinny jeans. She meant to say *thanks*. Instead she asked, "Why?"

"Why do you look nice?"

"Why are you doing chores?"

"Because that's my job, Ruby." Dahlia wiped an elbow across her sweaty brow, lilac bangs plastered to her forehead. "I take care of things. Who else will do it if I don't?"

By her sister's uncharacteristically barbed tone, Ruby guessed *Ginger* wasn't the correct answer. "Sorry, I was just . . . surprised." Though the way to the door was clear and the night beyond beckoned, she hesitated, even as Dahlia dove back into the refrigerator. "Hey . . . are you okay?"

"Of course," her big sister's voice echoed around the vegetable crisper.

It was rough, and Ruby suspected if she were to turn around again, tears would hover in her eyelashes, sand-colored without makeup. But Dahlia didn't turn, and Ruby didn't ask the next question on her lips: *Is this about Mom?* If Ginger was wrong, if Dahlia had reached out to their mother or planned to, she hadn't told Ruby about it.

Instead, she rushed to the hook beside the door and grabbed

her keys, and Polina's where they hung beside them.

She'd have to wait to use them. The plan was for Cece and Ruby to meet at the Mahalels', since Dov and Talia lived only a short walk from Cece on Oak. Ruby parked outside a tall red saltbox house with an antique plaque that read 1886 beside the door. She'd seen the place before, driving through the nice part of Saltville a few months back to look at Christmas lights with her sisters. All the houses around them were decorated with classy white string lights and bushy evergreen wreaths, while the saltbox had been a glitterless island. That made sense now. Ruby knew they were Jewish—Talia had been talking Hanukkah plans around the lunch table when everybody else had been obsessed with Christmas—but even so, the Mahalels' still looked like a gingerbread house. One in good condition, with its round shrubs, and neat stone path, and the warm golden squares of the windows. She parked against the curb just as Cece came strolling up to the driveway.

Although she'd only admitted her Time this morning, and they'd seen each other at lunch like always, Cece had somehow found time to text her between classes all day, each message more painfully heartfelt than the last.

Cece: Hey, how are you?

Cece: Are you okay?

Cece: Thank you for telling me

Cece: About your Time I mean

Cece: How are you feeling?

Cece: Sorry, you don't have to answer that

Cece: Don't worry, like you said, we'll figure it out!

Cece: I love you Bebe

Now Cece held her arms out to Ruby, gloves grasping and sympathy in her eyes.

Ruby raised her own cold hands to slow Cece's approach. "I have a proposal."

Her cousin stopped in her tracks. "Okay?"

"I will allow this one hug, and it can last as long as you want and I won't even fight it. But after that, let's just . . . press pause on the whole 'Ruby's dying' deal. We don't have to ignore it"—she hurried to speak over Cece's objections—"but could we just . . . not talk about it or act like it's happening in any way, unless whatever we're doing is directly related to it?"

After a moment, Cece nodded. "I can do that." Then she wrapped herself around Ruby. At least she didn't hug delicately, as if Ruby's bones were paper and might fold under the slightest force.

When she'd gotten her fill, Cece backed away, though she held Ruby's cold fist in one fuzzy gloved hand as they crossed the lawn side by side.

It was Dov who answered the doorbell, shivering in the gust of cold wind that accompanied them. He tugged down the sleeves of a baggy henley, crisp white against his tan skin, and swooped the unsettled hair back off his face. Cece wasn't wrong—he had a good face. Features you'd call "fine." Better than Levi Dorgan's, which was all teeth, his dull blue eyes trained always on Ginger's ass, like a crocodile watching an innocent zebra as it approached the water to drink. Dov's big brown eyes flickered between the cousins, so it was hard to tell which of them his smile was meant for. Probably Cece, whose pounds of hair rippled free around the shoulders of her pristine white wool coat, her lipstick bright and glossy so her lips looked like dewy peach slices.

Ruby's heart betrayed her without warning, pumping bitterly. All the hot blood in her veins—red cells and white cells and plasma and platelets—vibrating with one poisonous thought: Why not me? The feeling passed just as quickly. But she clutched Cece's hand even tighter, disgusted by the small, secret, sour chamber of her heart that wanted to take something, some boy she barely knew, from Cece. As if anything or anybody mattered more than family.

Cece squeezed back, probably mistaking it for nerves. "Where's Talia?" she asked Dov.

He stepped back to let them inside the mudroom, neatly lined with sneakers and boots and very tall heels. "Basement. You guys can go down. I'll tell you guys when the pizza gets here."

"You're not watching the movie?"

"Oh, hell no. I don't do horror." As Cece went in, he turned back to Ruby, still shuffling out of her snow boots. "What's up, Sir Charles Lytton?"

She paused, standing in a single boot. "Who?"

"He's the thief. The Phantom. From those movies. I looked it up." Dov blushed through his tan but finished bravely, "It's funny if I don't have to tell you."

You went home and looked up my stupid Pink Panther reference so you could make an equally stupid reference the next time we met? Ruby could have asked. *You were at home, after you saw me, still thinking about me?* she wanted to ask.

"Where's your bathroom?" she asked instead.

She needed a moment to collect herself, let the strange flush fade from her cheeks. But as Dov deflated a bit, she deeply wished she hadn't been such a nerd about it.

He led her down the hallway, jewel-purple walls lined with family photos. A man with smile lines cut like dried riverbeds around Dov-ish eyes, his skin a shade darker than his children's, and a pretty, pale, blue-eyed woman with long auburn hair. There was a constellation of pictures of Talia—in long black pigtails on a park swing; as a skinny tween, angular limbs poking out of a pink princess dress; in a sleek gown at a high school dance with her arm slung around a girl in a tux—but only two of her brother. A baby portrait of him and Talia in matching white onesies; and a teenaged Dov sitting astride a Jet Ski in a short-sleeved wetsuit and life vest, beaming beneath mirrored shades, hair wet and messy, the ocean vast and sequined with light behind him.

Maybe *his* family took down embarrassing photos upon request.

He pointed her toward the right door, and she ducked inside the bathroom.

All she had to do was make it through a movie, she told herself as she turned on the sink and ran her hands—then, still feeling overheated, her wrists and elbows—under cold water. It was early enough that they could leave right after, get to the north side of Saltville and back again before Cece's curfew.

And they would see . . . whatever there was to see in the house where their great-aunt died.

Polina would want them to, Ruby told herself once more. She wasn't like the aunts or cousins or—or Ruby's mother. She wasn't afraid of anything, or anybody. If she'd kept quiet about her secrets, she'd still kept them, hadn't she?

Too nervous to sit in the seashell themed bathroom any longer, Ruby jumped up and flung open the door—running smack into the woman from the Mahalel family photos.

"Crap, I'm sorry!" Ruby yelped.

Blue eyes wide, the woman stumbled backward into the hallway, her polka-dot bathrobe flapping around thin white legs.

"Wait," Ruby tried again, reaching out, but then Dov was there, his arm around his mother, guiding her away.

"Mama, you didn't have to get up. What do you need?"

"I was th-thirsty . . ." she stuttered weakly, letting Dov help her up the stairs with one arm around her thin shoulders, one hand at her elbow.

Ruby waited in the hallway while their footsteps sounded overhead, trying to remember whether Cece had said anything about Mrs. Mahalel before, if she'd mentioned that Dov and Talia's mother was sick. It seemed serious. The woman hadn't just looked unwell, she'd looked scared. Haunted, even. Just like the clients who came to see Ruby's sisters.

After a minute or two, Dov clomped back down the stairs and sighed. "You, um, want something to drink?"

Because he seemed as if he was genuinely offering, and because she was in no great rush to join Talia and Cece, she nodded and followed him to the kitchen. It was half the size of Ruby's house, vast expanses of marbled countertops and stainless steel all reflecting points of light from a crystal-drop chandelier overhead. It tinkled gently as Dov yanked open the door of the fridge and peered into the depths. "Water? Ginger ale? Something purple with antioxidants?"

"Anything is fine. Is your mom okay?" Like it was her business.

Dov answered anyways. "She's fine. She just gets sick for a day or two sometimes. Kind of runs in the family." Turning back with a bottle of ginger ale, his lips—full like his mother's, only hers had been so chapped they looked serrated—pressed into a tight line. "Bad blood."

"I'm sorry."

"It's okay. I'm sorry about your aunt."

"Who, Polina?"

"Cece told Talia why you guys were out of school. I just wanted to say, you know, I'm really sorry."

"Thanks." And then, because it felt strange to take his sympathy when he must be picturing a typical aunt—ten-dollar bills in birthday cards and funny family stories at Christmas—Ruby wanted to explain. "She's actually my great-aunt. But she babysat me a lot when I was a kid. And she raised my mom, so she was more like my grandmother."

He nodded, unscrewing the bottle cap to a brief burst of fizz and pouring three glasses he'd lined up. "Cece said you were her favorite?"

First Mikki had said so, now Cece. "Sometimes it was hard to tell," Ruby answered honestly. "She wasn't exactly grandmotherly. She was . . ." Ruby thought. "She was a silver-toothed Russian hard-ass in a hair kerchief for as long as I've known her. But I loved her." She shrugged. "We were family."

"Family is complicated," Dov said, squatting to dig something out of a low cabinet. He surfaced with a golden-brown bottle of Bushmills and tipped a bit into one of the glasses, skipping the second. "Spicy or mild?" he asked, poised over the third.

Ruby raised her eyes to the ceiling, as if she could see Dov's mother through the plaster and beams.

"The spicy one's for her," he laughed. "She never drinks

when she's healthy but swears by it when she's sick. Says it cleans the blood."

Because he hadn't poured any in his own glass, Ruby passed with a wave of her hand. "Is your family? Complicated?"

"Kind of. My dad was born here, but his parents were born in Israel, and he has an older brother who's lived there his whole life. Like twenty years older, actually. My grandparents were super old when I was born, I didn't really know them. My uncle does something in engineering, super smart like my dad. And like Talia—she got it all," he said, again without bitterness. "We've visited a couple of times, but him and dad are, like, I don't know, uncle and nephew instead of brothers. They get along okay, though."

"Is your mom Israeli too?"

"No," Dov said, something like a laugh in his voice, but not in his eyes, trained intently on the soda. "We don't talk to her family. Or, they don't talk to us. They don't like Mom's *choices*."

"That sucks."

He shrugged lightly and slid her glass across the counter, looking up at her as he did. "It really doesn't matter. It's just blood, you know?"

Ruby didn't know. Family was everything, the only thing—where you came from and who you were—and it felt blasphemous to speak of it otherwise.

And to turn your back on family . . .

The old splinter in her chest pricked at her, and she pushed it down, suspecting she was doing more damage than if she'd plucked it out cleanly to look at it.

She liked Dov, she realized. Even if he was a bonfire smoking, snowmobiling slacker bro, he was also a good talker, with a good face, and good, slightly crooked teeth, and good hands. But . . . that was where it ended. Maybe the Chernyavskys were something out of a storybook, but Ruby wasn't foolish enough to believe every story out there. She knew that kisses did not break curses. It hadn't been True Love that kept steely Polina going past the Time allotted to her. Which meant that Dov, however good his face, could not grant her a life.

"I should go down," she said.

He nodded and grabbed two glasses in one hand, so they clinked between his fingers. "I should go up." His brown eyes hovered on Ruby's and he scrubbed at his smooth jaw. "It's Ruby, right? I realized I never asked."

"It's Ruby." Stung, even though she'd only just learned his name, she asked, "And yours starts with a *D*?"

He laughed, sincerely this time. "Dov."

The *o* was just a little longer than Cece pronounced it— closer to *dove into a pool* than *dove*-the-bird—which made it feel like he and Ruby shared a secret her cousin didn't. And *that* made her feel like a traitor. Her cousin might be shy about boys, but if she'd admitted Dov was cute, if she was listening to his terrible music and blushing about him, she must have a thing for him.

Though how much could she really care if she didn't know his name?

Ruby sat for a moment after he left the room, staring into her glass before dumping it down the sink. She had important things to do, and couldn't afford to be drinking soda some boy had poured for her, thinking about him. He didn't even know your name, she reminded herself.

But, a still smaller part of her shot back, he knows it now, doesn't he?

· FOURTEEN ·

It was nearly nine when Ruby and Cece stood in Great-Aunt Polina's foyer, stomping the crust of snow from their boots. It was warmer inside than the bitter night outside, though it wasn't *warm*. The heat had been turned low since the Reading. They kept their coats on, but kicked their boots off automatically; Polina may have been mortal, but her rules were eternal.

"Have you ever been in here alone?" Cece asked, her voice very small, a snowflake on the edge of melting.

"Yeah," Ruby said too loudly. "Once. Remember that big ice storm, like, five years ago? Dahlia's car got stuck at the bottom of the driveway coming to pick me up after work. Polina went down with the cat litter to help, and made me stay in so I wouldn't slip."

"Ten minutes doesn't count."

"It felt like it counted." Ruby had looked out the window beside the door, watching Polina heft her heavy plastic pail down the slope of the driveway, strong even at ninety. She'd vanished into the trees, their limbs glass-blown by the storm, and Ruby swore that all at once, the whole house stirred. Suddenly the worst thing imaginable was being stuck there all night, even though nothing bad had ever happened to her in this house. With Polina inside, it had felt like one of the safest places to be; without her, the house felt . . . disloyal.

So where did its loyalty lie now that Polina was gone forever?

Ruby shivered.

"Where first?" Cece asked quietly.

"Her bedroom."

The girls passed through the great room. Cece headed right for the stairs, but Ruby paused beside the table set up from the Reading. The food had been cleared away, of course, but Polina's samovar sat there still. Cold and empty of tea for once, it was shaped like a pint-sized potbelly stove, its spigot in place of a door. Beside it, Polina's gold-plated tea glass holders, washed and waiting.

She picked one up—a podstakannik, it was called. Delicate-looking, but heavy for its size, it felt like family in her palm. Without thinking, she shoved it into the deep pocket of her coat. Then she reached with both hands for the familiar round glass bottle of slivovitz beside the samovar. A plum brandy the Chernyavskys drank at family funerals and birthdays and Readings, it smelled like jam-flavored jet fuel when she unscrewed the cap. She knew it tasted the same, much stronger than the Stolichnaya, but Ruby took a long pull to remind herself.

"Pah," she gasped, her nose raw and her throat on fire.

She shoved the bottle back onto the table, turned away—

—and smacked into Cece. They shrieked identical shrieks.

"I looked back and you weren't there!"

"I'm still here," Ruby rasped, throat aflame, and took her cousin's hand to lead her away.

With Cece behind her, Ruby eased open the heavy door to Polina's bedroom. The room looked . . . well, it looked like Polina. Everything ironed and orderly, from the dark wood furniture that hadn't had time to gather dust, to the big four-poster bed, with thick blue curtains hanging closed. Cece gave a shudder that Ruby felt up her own arm and down her whole body. Ruby let her go to edge into the room, trailing her hand along the dusky blue wallpaper patterned with black roses on winding black vines.

"What are you looking for?"

Maybe she hadn't realized until now, but when Ruby answered, she was sure of it. "The Recordings." She slipped around the curtained bed, scaring herself by imagining a pale old hand parting those drapes from the inside. Cece peered nervously at it, too, perhaps picturing the same.

We're Chernyavsky women, and the dark is scared of us, Ruby told herself. As always, it made her braver.

It didn't look as if the aunts had taken anything, yet. The room was as it had been. There were Polina's sharply cornered reading glasses on the nightstand. Her clothes were still in their drawers when Ruby peeked inside the bureau, smelling of her particular perfume, like old books and strange dried flowers. On top of the vanity, a neat row of crystal bottles twinkled in the lamplight. Even her jewelry remained; Ruby opened the lid of a little wooden box to see the small locket she remembered Polina wearing, an inartistic pattern scratched into the dulled gold.

There were no Recordings, though.

To be sure, they did a sweep of the rooms on the second floor, even their mothers' childhood bedroom. They looked in Polina's library, the last room at the end of the hallway, but it didn't hold much. Two shelves of books, some in English, worn paperbacks with corny titles like *No Shirt, No Pulse, No Problem*; some in Russian, identifiable by the cover illustrations of men in tuxedoes or military suits, and women in white gowns both slinky and fluttery, all of them holding smoking pistols. There was another leather armchair mottled with age, much like the one in the great room, beside a stained-glass floor lamp. It cast its buttery light on the wall of framed family photos.

Still no Recordings. On the floor of the closet, there was

a small black fire safe, but Ruby wasn't the kind of thief who could crack open a combination lock. Besides, it was barely the size of a small briefcase, and couldn't possibly contain the Recordings. It was probably all banking information and spare keys.

With a sick feeling in her stomach like the slivovitz roiling back up, Ruby sank into the armchair where she and Cece used to fit side by side. If the aunts had cleared out . . . whatever paperwork grown-ups felt important enough to protect from fire, then the chances that they'd left the most prized possession of the Chernyavsky line behind were very small.

Cece slid a yellowed book with ravens on its cover back into place, then squeezed herself onto the cushion beside Ruby. They didn't really fit together anymore, so the sharp point of Ruby's hip bone ground into the meat of Cece's, and her cousin had to twist her spine to lay her head against Ruby's. "Now what?" she asked.

Ruby shifted to make them both more comfortable, but winced as the key ring in her coat pocket jabbed her. She pried it out and twirled it around her fingers, letting the keys clap together on every spin. "I don't know," she admitted.

"Hmm," Cece murmured, and then, gazing at the many portraits on the opposite wall, "I guess no one's gonna change those pictures now. Too bad, I really hate my sophomore photo."

All of the cousins' latest school pictures were mounted in

plain wooden frames. Mixed in among them were photos of the aunts and great-aunts graduating from nursing school, or serving cakes at family parties, or posing soberly in Polina's own great room at more serious family affairs. All of them arranged in precise rows and columns, organized in chronological order. Cece and Ruby were grouped together near the bottom right, while the first and oldest black-and-white photo in the upper left corner showed Polina and her sisters, Vera and Galina.

It was taken in 1938, the year before Ruby's great-grandmother sent her daughters to America to escape their enemies (Great-Grandmother Vladlena, the trunk of their strange family tree, stayed behind, having seen from her Time that she would die in the dark pine forest where she'd been born). The sisters were lined up in front of a crooked little log house, shortest to tallest. Vera would have been five; Galina, nine or ten; and Polina, fifteen. The girls wore blouses with puffy sleeves and high collars, the plain tips of their boots peeking out beneath full skirts. Their faces were pale ovals inside dark knotted kerchiefs, dead-faced in the way of old colorless photos, their green eyes unremarkable in a black-and-white world. Each held a plate in front of them, heaped with what might be berries, but could be rocks or dirt for all that anybody could tell.

The picture had been payment from a traveling photographer in exchange for Vladlena's services—her gifts—and was one of the few possessions that made the trip over, in a single steamer trunk with precious family heirlooms. Like the pod-stakannik weighing down her left coat pocket, the Recordings, brass candlesticks, embroidered skirts, and a few other trea-sures Polina had said were stored in the tower for safekeeping . . .

Ruby closed her fist around the keys mid-swing.

Almost every key on the ring was labeled in Polina's bold, spiked handwriting—Vera's House, Front Door, Bathroom. There was the key to Polina's old Volvo in the garage, and then a fifth, small and tarnished, unlabeled. "Is this the key to the tower?" she guessed aloud, as though Cece would know.

Cece stiffened, the leather crackling beneath them. But when Ruby leapt up and ran for the spiral staircase at the end of the hallway, she followed loyally.

At the top, Ruby stooped down to squint through the key-hole in the heavy door.

"What do you see?" Cece breathed down her neck.

"I see . . . a keyhole."

Which fit the little unlabeled key perfectly.

They hadn't turned on the hallway light below, so after they swung the door open, while they fumbled with their phones to see into the yawning dark, Ruby reminded herself: *The dark is scared of us. We're Chernyavsky women, and the dark is scared of us.*

Their screens illuminated a pull cord dangling by Cece's head, which she tugged so sharply, Ruby worried it would drag the ceiling down on their heads. She relaxed when the beams didn't cave, and then they were gazing into the tower for the very first time.

It looked clean. Cleaner than she'd imagined a ninety-five-year-old woman would keep a creepy attic tower. Dust motes sprinkled the air, very cold and stale—unsurprising, given the single shuttered window—but the floor was swept. The storage shelf that stood awkwardly against the circular wall was neatly arranged, as was a thick, squat wooden worktable below the window. It held a pile of candles, probably for power outages during winter storms, and a stack of metal bowls. Ruby crossed to it and unlatched the shutters, pulling them inward with the groaning of old wood and a great puff of dust. Curiously, she peered out of the window, which looked down on the driveway where it melted away into the black trees.

CRASH.

Ruby spun around to find Cece standing beside the table. She looked extremely guilty, even in the low light.

"Sorry, I bumped it," she whispered. Her cousin bent to pick up an old clock, the small kind that usually sat on a mantel. The glass face must have cracked in the fall, and the spiderwebbed pane crunched delicately, though miraculously, the second hand still ticked on.

"Do you think it's expensive?" Cece asked, a little teary-eyed, turning it to show Ruby.

"I don't think anyone will miss it," Ruby assured her.

"At least it fell faceup." She set it gingerly on the table, as if it was a wounded animal.

"Why is that a good thing?"

"Why is it a bad thing?"

Aside from the table, the only other furniture in the room was a cabinet covered in chipped black paint. It held rows and rows of tiny drawers with brass handles, their faces the size of playing cards, and a bottom drawer that ran the length of it. She'd seen one like it in the antique store where Dahlia had worked for about three months of Ruby's freshman year: an apothecary cabinet. She remembered the name on the tag, because she'd pretended to read the price while slipping a cloudy silver tea ball into her pocket. Not to keep, because what was she going to do—pull out a precious-looking tea ball to make Twinings in front of Dahlia or Ginger? Instead, the next afternoon, she'd taken the plug out of one of the ceramic piggy banks on the little souvenir shelf in the General Store, the kind with the state of Maine stamped on the side, and stuffed the tea ball inside.

It wasn't really the having that made her feel powerful. It was the taking.

Ruby pinched one of the knobs and pulled, wrinkling her nose at a pile of dull dried leaves, and the bitter smell the drawer coughed up.

Cece pulled open her own drawer, which held a small mound of rust-colored dirt.

They tried others and found the sharp tips of feathers, string and frayed scraps of cloth, kernels of corn dried as hard as teeth, clear white pebbles, black seeds, and the withered remains of berries.

"Did Polina have a garden?" Cece asked.

"Yeah, she was growing those heirloom pebbles everyone loves so much." The idea of Polina gardening was hard to believe. For one thing, the land behind 54 Ivory Road was wild, a plot of earth being digested by trees, overrun by creeping thistle that grew taller and more tangled every year. For another, Ruby had never seen their great-aunt in anything but her high-collared shirts and wool skirts and thick brown stockings, even in summer, when cooking over the hot stove. So the idea of her in gardening gloves and a big brimmed hat and jeans with soiled knees was ridiculous.

"What then, she was a crafter?" Cece snapped back; she was only short-tempered when she was very nervous.

"Maybe." Ruby slid closed a drawer of strange dried cones the length of matchsticks that smelled a bit like pepper.

Cece spun slowly around, scanning the tower, while Ruby tugged on the long bottom drawer. The warped wood had to be coaxed along centimeter by centimeter. After a moment, the peeling paper corner of a book appeared. Her chest flamed with excitement, but she quickly stomped it out—the Recordings were as thick as the giant fancy dictionary Ginger kept pretentiously on her nightstand, and this drawer was as slim as the rest, even if it was longer. Slowly, Ruby worked it open to reveal a cloth-bound book with a golden-haired princess on the cover, its title in Russian.

Ruby pried out the book, a film of grit and dust slipping from the cover, and turned carefully through delicate yellowed pages. The neat Russian text was punctuated with painted color illustrations she had never seen, but which still seemed familiar. An old man with a wizard's beard and staff in a wintry forest, a white duck on a dark blue pond with a palace in the background, a young woman with no arms caught in a thorn bush.

"The Armless Maiden," Ruby realized. A fairy tale she'd been told when she was little. Maybe by her mother, or Polina, or by anyone of the aunts at a cousin sleepover. Though she couldn't read this version, she remembered the plot. An orphaned brother and sister had wandered the countryside until they settled in a village, where the brother was married. His wife, jealous of his sister's beauty, caused all kinds of trouble—broke their furniture, spoiled the food in their pantry, killed their horse—and blamed the sister. When the wife gave birth to a baby, she killed it, and accused the sister. Finally, the girl's brother took her for a ride in their carriage, shoved her out into the bramble, and cut off both arms at the elbow in revenge.

Not the nicest story, but then, Russian fairy tales weren't famous for their humor. This one had a happy ending, though.

The sister was married, and gave birth to a boy whose arms were gold, who had stars on his ribs, the moon on his forehead, and the sun in his heart. When the wife found out and tried again to cause trouble, the brother eventually realized her lies, tied her to the tail of a horse by her braid, and slapped its haunches. The horse returned that night with only the wife's braid, the rest of her having been trampled into the fields.

Well. It was a happy-ish ending.

By now, Cece had come to peer at the book over Ruby's shoulder. "That's Polina's?"

"It must be." Ruby turned to the title page, expecting more unreadable script. Instead, she found Polina's spiky black handwriting slanted across the paper, its inscription in her questionable English:

Remember this, Evelina: if time is a prize you want to win, you must prepare to lose.

Her heart stuttered, then quickened at her mother's name. She flipped forward, searching for more, for any notes in the margins. The paper was faintly splotched by age, but it was clean and unmarked.

Except for pages twenty-five to thirty, which were not disfigured; they simply weren't there.

After page twenty-four and before page thirty-one, a whole chapter had been ripped away, jagged white scraps poking out of the binding like exposed bone. She turned to what was presumably the table of contents to find the missing story, but of course, she couldn't read the titles.

Suddenly, Cece grabbed at Ruby's sweater and nodded toward the battered clock on the worktable, still ticking. "We have to go!"

She was right. It was quarter to ten, and they'd only just have time to deposit Cece at her front door if they left now. "Yeah, okay." Swiftly, Ruby tucked the book down the front of her coat.

Cece watched, wide eyed. "So we're not just breaking and entering, we're stealing, too?"

Ruby brushed a patch of dust from the shoulder of Cece's bright white coat before heading for the attic stairs. "Calm down," she said, pulling the light cord so that her cousin scrambled to keep close to her in the fresh dark. "You have to break something for it to be 'breaking and entering.' And anyway, it's just a book." Which was true. It wasn't much, but the feeling that it was *something* prickled at her. Maybe it was the only clue they could ask of the old house, seemingly emptied of the Recordings.

Besides, if the fairy-tale book had once belonged to her mother, as Ruby suspected, then taking it wasn't really stealing.

It was more like . . . inheriting.

• FIFTEEN •

The story of how Evelina and Anfisa had come to live with Polina was just one tiny, twinkling speck swallowed up inside the dark nebula of the Chernyavsky family history.

At the very end of the 1930s, three sisters—Polina, Vera, and Galina—disembarked from a boat at Ellis Island and made their way north, their hearts only comfortable in the woods and the cold. By day they took small jobs in the small towns they traveled through, sewing skirt hems, cleaning homes, collecting eggs from henhouses. By night, they told fake fortunes and read tea leaves in Russian accents that only added to their mystery.

When they reached Maine in the early '40s, Polina decided

that that they would stay. She found permanent work as a cook for an old widower who lived in a large stone house in the small town of Saltville, with a big kitchen where nobody had lit the stove since his wife, years before. The widower let the sisters sleep together in the tower and share his food, as long as Galina and Vera, still children, kept out of the way.

There was talk in town when the sisters went to the shops. By then, Polina was eighteen, and she wasn't beautiful—her mouth was thin and sharp, her nose hooked and sharp, and her eyes the sharp, cold color of a pond beneath treacherously thin ice. Still, she had a quality. People looked up when she passed by, and hugged their bags to their bodies even though she was immigrant thin. Despite the fact that she took up little physical room, she filled the space around her.

Maybe that was why, when the widower died and left Polina his large home after ten years of loyal service, Galina and Vera still moved away. Vera went a little ways north, but Galina stayed in town with her oldest sister. She lived alone until her thirties, when she had two daughters of her own. For all that anyone had seen men around, she might've spelled them out of air, or brewed them like tea. Evelina was born calm, self-possessed for such a little girl. Anfisa, two years younger than her sister, was bony and nervous from the start. It was not strange to see them in the small park blocks away from their house, playing together as the sun set. Nobody bothered them, or brought them back to their mother despite the dark. People had a better sense for these things back then, and they sensed not to meddle with the Chernyavsky girls.

One early fall afternoon in '72, the sisters walked home from elementary school arm in arm. The lights in the house were on, but their mother wasn't home. It wasn't strange—Galina spoke to her own sisters almost every day, and often dropped everything to visit. The fact that her car wasn't in the driveway meant she'd probably run over to the north side of Saltville to see Polina, or even an hour away to Abbot to see Vera.

They left a note and went to the park, stayed until the sun was a golden crown just over the treetops, and then all at once . . . they felt it. The sudden bone-deep freeze, the shortness of breath like they'd been running uphill in the cold instead of playing in the sand beneath the slide. The way that time seemed to stop and stretch painfully before snapping back into place. Neither Evelina nor Anfisa had experienced it before—what it feels like when a branch of the Chernyavsky tree withers and dies—but they sensed something was wrong.

The sisters ran home to nothing. Galina was still gone, the house growing cold because nobody had turned on the wood stove once the mild day faded. The phone rang, and it was Polina, who had felt it and knew.

The police found Galina's car parked along Route 201 almost fifty miles away, not far from Vera's home. She sat upright in the driver's seat, stone dead, but without a mark *on her, without a clue as to why. Nothing was revealed by the autopsy, and while her Reading confirmed she'd gone right on schedule, as usual, there was no mention of how.*

So nine-year-old Evelina and seven-year-old Anfisa moved into the house on Ivory Road with their aunt Polina, and became who they were always meant to be. They learned a little more Russian than their mother had taught them, though Anfisa never had a gift for languages. They learned how to cook dumplings and shuba—herring under a layer of grated beets, onions, mayonnaise, and boiled vegetables—and vatrushka for family parties. They learned how to brew tea over logs on the fire, and to rely on garlic and onion in steaming pots of water for every sickness.

And, of course, they learned about Time.

· SIXTEEN ·

If her life were a TV show about two spunky teens trying to unlock their family secrets, Ruby would've found an English version of the book on eBay or Amazon with a little mild sleuthing. But she couldn't. Of course there were Russian fairy-tale collections that included "The Armless Maiden," and "The White Duck," and "Father Frost." Those were popular stories. But not any book with this cover, published in 1936 (the copyright date was readable, at least).

Or she could've brought it to a conveniently local professor of Slavic languages at the community college to decode the text and tell her she'd been right, that there was something special and unique and meaningful about this particular collection. Unfortunately, the college's only foreign language courses were Spanish and Italian. Ruby had checked that in a moment of desperation, too.

She could've brought her cousins in, but they didn't know any more Russian than Ruby. None of their mothers were anything near fluent. The only Chernyavskys who truly spoke the language were the three who'd been born on Russian soil, of which Vera was the only sister left alive, and Ruby couldn't imagine her as a willing accomplice.

She could have driven to the Molehill Motel, knocked on the door of room 113. . . .

But what had changed since the Reading? She still didn't trust her mother. She could've told Ruby anything she wanted to when they were alone, but all she'd done was make weak excuses for her long absence. And so the book had her mother's name in it—how meaningful could it really be to Evelina, if she'd left it behind?

So the month rolled on. Cece was waiting for her rescheduled party, roped into weeks of preparations with her mother and Vera, and Ruby was waiting to have Cece's full attention once more.

One night after school, Ruby sat on her bed, smoothing her fingers across Polina's lightly impressed handwriting for the hundredth time. It wasn't fair. These stories belonged to her—just as this language belonged to her—but unless the letters magically rearranged themselves into a known alphabet, she would learn nothing from them.

Remember this, Evelina: if time is a prize you want to win, you must prepare to lose.

To lose *what*?

Her phone vibrated on her nightstand beside a library copy of *Pale Blue Dot*, a week overdue already, but the fairy-tale book was the only one she cared about these days. She picked her phone up to read the text.

Cece: Uuuuugh I need a break. Is Dahlia working the register tomorrow? Could she get us in?

She meant at 'Wiches and Wings, where Dahlia mostly waitressed in the café, serving Bug Juice and sandwiches with bug-based names (like the Antuna on Rye), but occasionally sold tickets at the register in front of the butterfly house, wearing glittery costume wings. Even if she only applied for the job because Ruby had been going through a serious entomology phase a little while ago and made her sister take her every free weekend she had, it actually wasn't the worst work she'd had. In the six years since she'd taken legal custody of Ruby and Ginger, Dahlia had bounced from one low-skill job to the next. Last fall had been Party Monster, the seasonal Halloween shop. Over the summer, she'd manned a frozen lemonade cart by the city pool, where she got a 5 percent employee discount on top of her minimum wage. Before that, Ruby lost track. Maybe it had been the paint-your-own-pottery place called the Clayroom, where she was fairly certain Dahlia got paid in weed alone.

Ruby: Us who?

Cece: Talia and me. And you???

Somebody knocked, and she dropped her phone so she could lean down and slip the fairy-tale book into her backpack, where it lived whenever she wasn't cradling it. "Occupied!" she huffed, mysteriously out of breath.

"Ruby?" Dahlia's voice floated through the bedroom door.

"Yeah, okay." She grabbed the Sagan book and spread it on the bed before her.

Dahlia entered, blackbird-and-vine-patterned skirt swishing. Her sisters were preparing for a client, which meant Ginger was actually home for once; she'd been spending more time at Levi Dorgan's than ever, sometimes days at a time.

Ruby was pretty certain her mother's return was the reason for Ginger's absence.

"How's the homework coming?" Dahlia asked.

"Fine. Are you at the register or in the café tomorrow? Cece wants to know."

"The register. That reminds me, I have to lint-roll my wings later."

Before she could stop herself, Ruby snorted.

"We can't all be gastroenterologists." Dahlia shrugged with half a smile. Cece's father's profession was something of a Chernyavsky punch line. Which was funny, because any other family would be thrilled to have a respectable doctor in its ranks. In her family, *gastroenterologist* was code for *normal person*, and that was not a compliment.

"No, but . . ."

"But?"

"You could have a job where you don't wear wings." Ruby threw her hands up. "Or monster horns. Or a beret with a big plastic lemon on it."

"Maybe." She twisted her opal ring around her thumb, one of many she wore. As always, she was extravagantly bejeweled for the appointment. "But I'm not my job. So none of that bothers me, and I'm sorry if it bothers you."

Ruby hadn't meant to start a fight. But with every day that passed since the Reading, she'd felt the breath of time on the back of her neck, felt it squeeze her heart in its iron fists. Meanwhile, Dahlia had all the time in the world to become *something*. And yet, like Ginger, she had no plans to do so, content to be small and safe and ordinary. Ruby herself had always obeyed the Chernyavsky law—believed that her Time could not be altered or escaped—but everything was different since Polina's Reading. Didn't her sisters understand that? Didn't they care? They claimed to be paralyzed by a fear three generations old, just like Vera. But for all Ruby could tell, the Russian boogiemen who had allegedly hunted them eighty years ago were just another excuse not to try.

And suddenly, a fight was exactly what Ruby wanted.

"Who are you, then?" she sneered.

Dahlia crossed Ruby's room in two slow strides and sat

beside her on the bed, spreading out her skirt. "I guess . . . I'm your sister, and Ginger's. I take care of you. At least I try to. That's who I'm supposed to be."

"That means Mom was supposed to leave us."

Dahlia winced. "None of us knows why she left, because she didn't tell us. You know that. You read the letter."

That was true. Dahlia had shown it to her the morning after their mother vanished. She was a part of their family, Dahlia had said, and had a right to see. It was also true that the letter, scribbled on a harmless-looking piece of stationary with a border of cartoon coffee cups from the pad they'd kept in the junk drawer, contained no actual explanation. "But Ginger said—"

"She doesn't know, either. Polina told me that Mom was scared, and I probably shouldn't have repeated that to Ginger. I thought it would help. But she believes what she needs to. It's easier for her to tell herself that Mom was weak, that she betrayed us all, than to wonder . . . why else Mom left her."

"She was," Ruby insisted. "She *did* betray us." Family was power, and her mother's fear, her weakness, had made them all weaker. She must have known; Polina must've taught her that when she was young, as surely as she'd taught Ruby.

"Maybe. But we don't know what she was going through."

"So what, you forgive her?"

"No. I don't know, it's complicated. I think I'll always be angry at Mom. But . . . I can't hate Evelina Chernyavsky. Because I never really knew her."

"They're the same person," Ruby said through gritted teeth. She was already furious with Dahlia for pretending that Polina's death hadn't changed all the rules and turned over the game board, and now, for pretending it was some harmless stranger and not their mother holed up a mere twenty-minute drive away in Hop River, waiting to be let back in from the cold. Waiting for one of her daughters to weaken just enough to open the door.

Well, it wouldn't be Ruby.

Dahlia cocked her head to the side, maddeningly Zen. "If you say so."

Once her sister had gone, Ruby grabbed for her phone, jamming her thumbs at the keyboard.

Ruby: She is working tomorrow, and I'm going too

Cece: Really?? Yay!!!

Ruby: But ask Dov to drive us, I don't want to pay for gas

Cece: Will do!

Maybe her sisters were perfectly fine with their little lives, but Ruby wanted more. She wanted so many things for herself, and though she wasn't sure if she would get any of them, here was something she could have right now: she could spend an afternoon staring up at Dov's good face, feel that shameful but addictive rush of superheated blood through her whole body, and do a little pretending of her own. She would imagine that, if she were guaranteed a future, a boy like Dov Mahalel could somehow be a part of it.

· SEVENTEEN ·

When Dahlia waved them by the ticket counter the next afternoon, she did so with a dramatic double take. "Well, this is a surprise. I wasn't expecting my beautiful little sister," Dahlia said while smiling at Dov, who just happened to be walking next to Ruby.

Glaring, Ruby tugged her sister's sparkly pink wings askew as they walked past the register and into the butterfly house.

Beyond Dahlia's register was the little antechamber with mirrored walls, a brisk fan blowing, and a sign that read CHECK FOR HITCHHIKERS ON YOUR WAY OUT! Through the doors and into the garden, the hot, humid air weighed ten pounds at least and smelled of soil and ripe bananas. Cece peeled off her faded Coney Island Bowling

League sweatshirt from over her T-shirt and tied the sleeves around her waist. Dov shoved up the sleeves of his thermal, and Talia scooped her long hair into a lush black waterfall of a ponytail.

Ruby's vision adjusted slowly to the butterflies, the way it would in a dark room after standing in sunlight. There were hundreds of them. Some, she recognized from her entomology phase. Tiny glass-winged butterflies, the transparent panes of their wings revealing the flowers behind them. Tiger swallow-tails, their black-and-yellow-striped wings tipped with long black points like the nibs of calligraphy pens. Blue morphos, her favorite, with spotty brown wings that flashed bright aquamarine on the insides, like fluttering chips of sky.

Cece and Talia kept stopping to laugh and whisper, though they'd spent the entire car ride laughing and whispering, so Ruby wasn't sure what they had left to say. She'd thought Cece would be in the passenger seat when they picked her up after school. But as she'd crunched across the fresh snow on her driveway to the gleaming black truck, she saw her cousin tucked into the back beside Talia, leaving the empty seat beside Dov for Ruby.

With the girls behind them once more, she and Dov moved quietly down the winding path through the garden. There was wildlife beside butterflies. Koi shone like large gold coins in a dark little pond. A quail and its train of chicks darted through the underbrush. On a tree trunk by the path, there was a giant winged beast twice as big as Ruby's hand, with a sign pinned below that read: I AM SLEEPING. PLEASE DON'T DISTURB ME. THIS IS MY WORLD.

"This is a particularly epic butterfly," Dov appraised.

"It's an atlas moth, actually," Ruby said, and felt her cheeks flush. She wanted to slap herself—why was she embarrassed to know this? Why shouldn't she correct him?

But Dov simply said, "Oh, nice!" as he leaned in to look, finger-combing his hair back off his forehead. It stuck in position, like a black wave before breaking.

Ruby leaned in, too. She felt warmer than she should, even in the tropical air. There was a kind of electricity around them that pricked the back of her neck, the hair on her arms. She was charged, like if she touched Dov's hand—perhaps the hand shoved into his jeans pocket, with barely enough room for hers to slip in beside it—there'd be a blue-white static shock, sharp and painful and exhilarating.

She leaned away "So . . . how's your mom doing?"

Ruby could've slapped herself. What a brilliant conversation starter—asking the boy she liked about his mother.

Smooth as fucking ice.

He looked surprised. "All better, thanks. Like I said, we get sick easy, but we bounce back quick." As he turned away from the atlas moth's tree, a butterfly landed in his hair. She couldn't identify this one. Like panes of stained glass lit from behind, its wings were incandescent green segmented by black, even deeper than Dov's soft-looking black hair.

Ruby reached up to touch it—the hair, or the butterfly—but pulled away, pointing instead. "You have a hitchhiker."

He froze and rolled his eyes skyward, peering through long black eyelashes, also soft-looking.

"Here." Taking a picture with her phone, she held it at an angle he could see without moving his head.

"Is that its tongue?"

Ruby bent a bit closer to examine the long pink straw-like thing probing his hair. "It's the proboscis."

"Pro-bos-cis." Dov tasted the word. "Can you send that to me? Maybe we'll use it as an album cover and rename ourselves Proboscis. If we ever learn a third song." He gave her his number.

She typed it in. "You're in a band?"

He nodded slightly so as not to dislodge his passenger. "We call it a band. But it's just a couple of us from school, playing whatever we had in our garages from middle school music lessons."

"Are you good?"

"We're . . . loud." The butterfly took off, and he looked at Ruby. Or looked down at her—Dov wasn't tall, probably no taller than Cece, but he still had nearly a head on Ruby. "We practice, though I don't think it helps much. We're not too ambitious. Right now, we've only played at that bowling alley in Skowhegan. They pretty much pay us in fries and shoe rentals."

"Are you a good bowler, at least?"

"No." He laughed. "Maybe a loud bowler. I don't know. We're playing tomorrow night. And bowling. You could come and judge us." He said it offhandedly, peering down the path, but then he snuck a look at her, his teeth denting his bottom lip.

Ruby's heart must have spent the last few years asleep inside a chrysalis, because all of a sudden it burst through the brittle casing and emerged damp and fluttering behind her ribs.

"I might," she said bravely, and then made herself turn down the path, walking back the way they'd come to hide a ridiculous smile before Dov saw, or Cece. . . .

Her stomach swooped violently as she thought of Cece, and that was when she knew she wouldn't go see Dov. She had no business hanging around a bowling alley with the boy her cousin wanted, however she felt about him. Were pleasantly crooked white teeth and long black eyelashes all it took to betray her best friend, her blood? Ruby took things, true, but they were things nobody would miss. She didn't *steal*. She wasn't a thief.

Was she?

As she rounded the corner behind the fairy-lit gazebo, Dov shot a hand out. Though her sleeve lay between his fingertips and her skin, her arm crackled with heat. What the hell was wrong with her? Why this boy? Why now?

"Let's just go this way," he said. His touch was light, but he sounded anxious to steer her away, to keep her from moving forward.

So of course that was the direction Ruby went, peering through the broad leafy branches of the plant right in front of her, through the butterflies that zoomed across her field of vision, to the purple tips of Talia's ponytail, which she first confused for one of the colored pods of sugar water staked out among the foliage. Then she saw Cece behind the greenery, too. And the beaded bracelets that slid up Talia's arm as she brushed away a white-blond strand of Cece's hair, stuck to her pink skin. And the way her cousin's cheeks flushed butterfly-bright. . . .

"Come on, Ruby," Dov said gently, but let her go and walked away.

Without his anchoring grip, she stumbled sideways into a branch, swearing. Talia's eyes snapped forward. They were lighter than her brother's, Ruby realized, big and amber and blazing angrily as she caught sight of Ruby.

Ruby rushed down the path after Dov. "Did you know?" she asked, her voice fuzzy.

He frowned, and one eyebrow disappeared beneath his fallen bangs. "Didn't you?"

"Cece, come out."

Her cousin moaned, voice rusty and muffled by the quilt—they had gone to Ruby's house to talk because it was empty, but now, burrowed under Ruby's sheets, Cece wouldn't let her in.

"No, I promise, that wasn't a pun! Just . . . look at me. It's not that big a deal. I mean it is, it's a deal, but . . . it's also not!"

She flipped the covers back, and her eyes were pink, her round cheeks splotched, her hair wild on the pillow. "I'm so fucked."

Ruby grabbed the quilt to keep her from retreating. "No, Cece. Maybe . . . maybe it feels that way. But this isn't like a bad thing. And Talia, she's . . ." Ruby scrambled for details about the girl she'd sat across from in the cafeteria for an entire semester, but never paid much attention to besides her obvious nearness to Cece. "Her hair is amazing. Are you guys, um, officially dating?"

"No . . . not officially. Like, I'm not sure what Talia's told her family. I mean they know she's gay, and they know me, but we don't talk about her parents much."

"Well, I would never tell anyone, you know that, but there's nothing wrong with liking, you know, a girl. I just—I kind of thought you liked Dov." She felt giddy with relief that she wasn't in danger of stealing from her cousin, but felt guilty for being happy when Cece was so unhappy.

Cece sniff-laughed, wiping her nose on the quilt. "I wish."

"You wish you liked him instead?"

"I don't know. No. I think this is just who I am. I like girls. But I'm not . . . it's not who I'm supposed to be."

Ruby bunched the blankets in her fists to keep calm. "Are you talking about your Time?"

Pulling viciously at a loose thread, Cece nodded.

Ruby held her breath for a few heartbeats, then set it free so she could say, "If you don't want to talk about it, that's fine. I get it if you're still not ready—"

"I think I am," Cece said, but was silent for a long moment before she spoke again. "I was married to this man. I mean, I will be, when—when I die." Her swollen green eyes darted up to catch Ruby's.

Was that why Cece was so upset?

Ruby tried to keep her face compassionate, when what she really felt was frustrated. She'd sat on her own Time for years, keeping her fairly imminent demise a secret until Cece caught up with her, and *this* was the great tragedy awaiting Cece? This was the terrible secret she'd had to pry out of her cousin? That Cece wasn't still with Talia, her high school sort-of girlfriend, in her Time?

What the hell? How was that even comparable?

"Right," Ruby said carefully. "That . . . really sucks, that you guys aren't together. You must like her a lot. But . . . you still shouldn't feel ashamed about it or anything. Dahlia is bi, you know that. I mean she hasn't actually been with anyone in . . ." She tried to count. Dahlia had brought a few high school boyfriends over, and her girlfriend Nadine came home with her for Thanksgiving one year in college, but since their mother had left? Nobody, Ruby realized. "Maybe you can talk to her."

"I'm not bisexual," Cece mumbled. "I don't think so. But it doesn't matter, 'cause I don't love him. My . . . husband. In my Time, I don't want to be with him, and I even kind of hate him for that. We were, um, in our bedroom." Cece's cheeks flushed nearly maroon. "We were old, and we'd been together for a long time. We had daughters, and they were grown-ups. There were pictures of them above the bed. He went to . . . touch me, and I felt . . . like I wanted to die, I was so miserable. And tired, like I was really, really used to feeling that way. I was mad at him, and at our daughters for, like, trapping me in this life, and at myself. And that's—that's all I saw. I don't think he was a bad guy. Like he wasn't abusive or anything. He was just a guy, and I was miserable, so now I know I'm gonna have a long miserable life. . . ."

"Oh," was all Ruby could say.

She had truly never considered the curse of a long life.

Cece scraped her hair back from her face, held it too tightly in both fists, and tugged. "I'm just like my mom."

"Aunt Annie loves your dad! And she's, like, the über-mother. She lives for the PTO."

"Does she?" Her cousin's eyes were pinched with tears. "Maybe she's just pretending. She and Dad don't touch each other when we're alone at home, you know. They never hug or hold hands or anything. Dad doesn't even sleep in their bedroom—Mom says he snores, but I never hear him. She didn't move away from the family to be with him, like every other

Chernyavsky who really falls in love. Sometimes I think . . . She, like, decorates for dances and organizes fundraisers for the school computer lab and petitions the Fruit Street Block Association for a new playground every other year, but she doesn't *enjoy* any of that.

"Once, she took me up to her old bedroom at Polina's, after Alyona's Reading. I think Mom was a little drunk. More than a little. She was talking about Alyona, how when they were kids they promised each other that someday they'd go to Tokyo together and wear awesome clothes and eat sushi in the park every night. Obviously they didn't, though when Alyona found out she was stage four, she did go to Japan that same week. Mom couldn't go, because I was scheduled to get my tonsils out. At the Reading she said—she said she'd always regret not going away with Alyona when she had the chance."

"I'm sure she wasn't blaming you—"

"Oh, I know," Cece said quickly. "I'm pretty sure she meant the first chance, when she was young. I'm pretty sure she meant that she wished she'd lived that life instead." She exhaled, and it snagged, momentarily, on a sob. "So I really think . . . maybe she only had me in the first place because she was supposed to. She was doing her Chernyavsky duty. And then because she's Mom, and she's always cared what the entire fucking world thinks about her, she didn't do it like the rest of the family— just find somebody for a night. She got a husband, and she joined the PTO. And because I'm just like her, and I'm always scared what everybody thinks about me, I'm going to do the same thing."

This was a lot to take in, so Ruby began with the simplest question: "What do you mean, her Chernyavsky duty?"

Cece sniffed. "To have daughters, you know? To pass on the name, and the stories, and the traditions, and whatever. My mom always says so, even if she doesn't use those words."

Ruby had never considered this her duty. Before seeing her Time, she'd thought of children as the inevitable problems of grown-up Ruby. Like a career, or scheduling your own dentist appointments, or the gas bill Ginger always sighed over. And after she'd seen her Time, it hadn't been an issue.

"You know, when we were little," Cece continued, "one of our cousins once told me she wasn't a girl? I thought she was kidding, so I laughed and called her a boy. But she said she wasn't a boy, either, and she wasn't joking."

"Which cousin?" Ruby asked, more sharply than she'd meant.

"I can't tell you that, Bebe! But I asked her about it again, like, years later, after she'd seen her Time. She got really quiet and teary, and said it hadn't meant anything. I know it did, though. I think she just couldn't imagine telling her mom and the aunts and grandmas who she really was."

Ruby's head was buzzing. "Okay . . . but that's not you. You don't have to be straight to have daughters. You don't even have to *have* daughters to have daughters."

Unbelievably, Cece looked at *her* with pity. "It's about the blood, Bebe. It has to be Chernyavsky blood for the line to survive. And that's not the whole point. It's not like I don't ever want kids, but not with some man I can't—" Her voice wavered, and she stuffed the quilt over her mouth.

"But . . . but Polina didn't have children," she pointed out. "Remember her Time? She was supposed to, but somehow she didn't. She never got married, either, whether she was supposed to or not. And she definitely didn't die in childbirth."

Cece sniffed again, but her shoulders stilled. "Her Time was wrong."

"Or she figured out a way around it."

"Right." Her cousin rubbed the tears out of her eyelashes. "I'm sorry. I know it's nothing like your Time."

"So? That doesn't make it less important," Ruby hurried to say, even though she'd thought so mere moments ago. Now she wrapped her arms around her cousin fiercely, blanket and all, and they tumbled sideways onto the mattress, heads knocking together. She didn't let go. "So we'll figure out exactly what happened with Polina. We're already working on it, right?"

"Okay, Bebe."

"You believe me?"

"Yeah," she sighed wetly, shuddering.

That was good. Ruby wanted Cece to believe her. She wanted to believe herself, too.

But . . .

She thought of Aunt Annie, the most normal among them, all alone in her big bed on Fruit Street; of her mother all alone in a strange motel room; of Galina, who'd died alone on a highway; of Ruby's great-grandmother Vladlena, who'd sent her daughters away and died alone in the dark woods, besieged by her enemies. In the coldest little corridors of Ruby's heart, she wondered: If the Chernyavskys were really so wise and powerful, then why did it seem they were cursed?

• EIGHTEEN •

Ruby spent most of that weekend in her bedroom, feeling extremely sorry for herself.

She lay on her bed with the lights off, watching the sunset slowly tint her walls. She slipped out to eat only when Dahlia and Ginger weren't around and, in the dead of Saturday night, snuck into the kitchen and scaled the counters to steal a teacup full of Stoli, and then another, sloppily pouring water into the bottle to hide her crime. When Dahlia knocked on Sunday morning, Ruby groaned that she was getting sick, and she looked so gray and miserable that her sister brought her tea and left her alone.

It was Sunday night before her mood—and her hangover—cleared enough to wriggle fishlike out of bed and flop toward her backpack, where her phone had been in the front pouch since Friday. There were texts from Mikki in the cousin chat about her new French-Canadian boyfriend, and one from a number she didn't recognize, but could guess when she opened it and saw the butterfly suspended in Dov's black hair, the first message in a thread. The second was a short video, presented without caption or comment. A bowling ball rolled leisurely down the gutter to plunk harmlessly into the pit at the end of the lane.

She mustered the strength to send back an applause emoji, but a little smile curled across her face without her meaning it to.

The only other message, the one she'd been avoiding, was from Cece. With a shuddering breath, Ruby opened the thread, expecting some bleak or terribly sad text she didn't have the strength to answer, not even with a sparkling heart emoji.

Cece: I was investigating, or like, I was looking around my mom's stuff for clues, and I think maybe I found something!!! Come over when you can. Dad's out and Mom's at MoM

That was Meeting of Moms, a loosely ruled group of mothers who gathered at Saltville's one coffee shop every Sunday morning to put together petitions, demanding more crosswalks downtown or a wooden fence around the park to replace the rusted metal cage. Aunt Annie had invited Dahlia to join once, and she'd gone to be polite. But she'd had to run over from her job at the lemonade cart by the pool, and had shown up sweating in her yellow bikini and sarong and the beret with the plastic lemon bigger than her head perched atop it.

Ruby smiled at the memory, but it slipped away as shame rushed in. She and Cece were supposed to be searching for leads together, and yet she'd wasted the whole weekend, hiding in a fog of vodka and misery, thinking only of herself. Meanwhile, Cece had kept her shit together.

Now it was after nine, past Cece's Sunday-night curfew. (Ruby wasn't sure if she had a curfew; it had never come up, since she was unlikely to be out anywhere her cousin wasn't.) Quickly, she answered.

Ruby: Sorry, just saw this! Meet before school tomorrow?

Cece: Finally!!!! Yes, Dad leaves early and Mom leaves at 7:30 for PTO

Ruby: I'll be there

She followed this with an unnecessary number of sparkling heart emojis, still squirming with guilt that in her wallowing, she'd completely forgotten about her cousin, whose fate might be the opposite of her own, but it was no happier an ending.

If Cece's bedroom looked like a picture from a furniture store, Aunt Annie and Uncle Neil's was even more so. It was all flowered bedding, and white pillar candles with wicks that had never been lit, and blown-glass bowls of dried coral or polished river rocks. There was a hope chest at the foot of their bed with a fancy brass lock, modern but made to look antique, and Cece shocked her by opening the little jewelry box on her mother's dresser and pulling out the key.

"You little thief!" Ruby cried. She'd never seen her cousin take so much as an extra ponchiki at a party or Reading, but maybe the habit ran in their blood.

"No, I'm a borrower," Cece said, tightening the mushroom cloud of her sloppy bun defiantly. "Now come look before we have to leave for school."

She dug down through the chest, to a layer of personal flotsam. An old wooden rattle with fading pink paint, and a knitted dress for a little girl with graying lace, and a baby doll, its unlikely '60s-style bouffant frizzed and blue eyes cloudy—Cece's childhood things, or Aunt Annie's? The way they were buried beneath folded quilts and tablecloths made them seem like Aunt Annie's true Chernyavsky self, beneath the PTOs and MoMs and the Baker name.

At the very bottom was a manila envelope, the clasp sealed. Eyes sparkling, Cece opened it and carefully poured out a thin stack of papers, yellow and rippled with age, ragged along the left side.

"Wait, is this . . ."

Cece's eyes sparkled. "Pages twenty-five to thirty."

The illustrated chapter header on top was a version of a painting Ruby had seen in her online searches: a young girl in traditional Russian peasant dress, her long braid bound with blue cloth. She stood in a dark forest, the floor thick with toadstools and weeds. Behind her, a log hut perched on chicken legs was just visible through the trees, bordered by a fence of human bones and skulls. She held aloft one skull on a stick, white light blazing from its eye sockets. This was "Vasilisa the Beautiful," and the mean house in the distance belonged to Baba Yaga.

The pages were in Russian, obviously, but she already knew the story from the many, many retellings she'd read.

Once upon a time in a far-off tzardom, there was a lovely girl named Vasilisa whose mother lay dying, as they do. Before the end, she called Vasilisa to her and gave her a wooden doll, which her own mother had given her. When Vasilisa was sad or scared and needed help, she was to feed the doll something to eat, and it would tell her what to do.

When her father remarried, as they do, it was to a widow from the village with two daughters a little older than Vasilisa. While her father was around, the woman was kind, but whenever he left for the village, the stepmother proved herself to be a bitter old shrew, and her daughters, bitter young shrews. They sent Vasilisa to work in the fields, where they hoped she would become scrawny and sun-leathered, but she only grew more beautiful as the stepsisters grew hard and horrible. So the stepmother decided to get rid of Vasilisa for good.

While her husband was away on a long trip, the stepmother sent Vasilisa into the forest on some new errand each day, hoping she wouldn't come out again; everybody knew that Baba Yaga lived there, and that the old crone devoured people as birds devour worms. But the doll spoke words of comfort to Vasilisa to keep her from losing hope, and Vasilisa always came home safely.

One night, all the lamps in the house had been extinguished except for one, in the room where the women sat spinning and sewing and knitting. The elder stepsister put the last candle out, pretending it was an accident, and they all ordered Vasilisa into the forest to bring back a light from Baba Yaga. Taking the doll, she walked all night and all day and into the next night through the trees, and came at last upon a hut perched on spindly chicken's legs. It was surrounded by a fence made of bones, topped by grinning skulls with bright, burning eye sockets that lit the clearing.

The trees began to groan, the branches creaked, and along came Baba Yaga, trailed by howling spirits until she reached her gate. Then she thrust her long nose into the air, sniffed, and declared, "I smell a Russian bone or two! Who is it? Show yourself!"

Trembling, Vasilisa came forward and told Baba Yaga that she had been sent by her stepmother and stepsisters to get a light. Baba Yaga promised her one if she would work for it—otherwise, she would eat Vasilisa for supper.

That night, Vasilisa brought Baba Yaga food from the oven, watching as the old witch tore apart the meat and crunched *large bones between her iron teeth. The next day, Vasilisa cleaned the hut, weeded the yard, and picked the bad grains out of the wheat from the storehouse with the help of the doll, whom she fed scraps from Baba Yaga's table. The next day it was the same, and she cleaned the poppy seeds from the storehouse one by one, which she managed with the doll and her mother's blessing. Angry that she couldn't eat the girl, Baba Yaga was nevertheless an honest dealer, and gave Vasilisa a burning-eyed skull from her gate, stuck on a stick. "Here's fire," she said. "And I hope your stepmother and stepsisters enjoy every bit of it!"*

Vasilisa walked all night and into the next, when at last she cleared the woods and approached the house on the edge. Inside, her stepmother snatched the skull from Vasilisa, complaining that they had waited for so long in the dark. Suddenly, the eyes burned brighter, boring into the stepmother and stepsisters with a white-hot light, until all three were burnt to ashes. Untouched, beautiful Vasilisa dug a hole in the ground and buried the skull, and then sat to await her father's return.

Unexpectedly, Ruby's heart dropped. Whatever she'd been hoping for—maybe an obscure story with some seed of truth that spoke to her, as Kerrigan would say—this wasn't it. The story was in every Russian collection. The fairy tale was neither special, nor unique, nor meaningful. Even if she couldn't read the Russian, she could follow the illustrations enough to know that the telling was a traditional one.

"Is this it?"

Cece shook her head, bun bobbling. From the envelope, she pinched out yet another piece of paper—the handwriting on this one familiar—and with the look of somebody delivering news that might be good or bad, she passed it to Ruby.

That evening after dinner—two bowls of Cheerios in front of the television, eaten dry because Dahlia had forgotten to buy milk—Ruby leaned against Dahlia's open doorway. Her sister sat cross-legged on her bed. She held a beautiful glass pipe in one hand, and her homemade sploof in the other, cobbled together with a toilet paper tube and a dryer sheet. It was supposed to catch the stench of the weed when she exhaled through it. Dahlia felt no guiltier about smoking than she did drinking a glass of wine with dinner. But she never left evidence behind—she wouldn't set her wineglass in the sink before washing it, even if she'd let bowls of pasta sit for days.

It was probably a habit formed while Dahlia was filing for legal guardianship. Because you couldn't just take over custody of your minor sisters without a little paperwork, or a home visit from a calm but intimidating court representative, who it seemed could sniff out bad behavior from their driveway. At least their mother had made it easy on them, or tried to. Her note of consent was folded up in the envelope on the fridge the day she'd left.

As her sister breathed smoke into her sploof, Ruby asked the question she'd spent all afternoon working up the nerve for. "Can I, um, can I look at Mom's letter?"

Dahlia coughed. "Why?"

She'd also spent the afternoon trying to craft a convincing lie. But what could she do, claim it was for school? What kind of class project required your estranged mother's goodbye note? And she couldn't pretend away its importance.

So she simply said, "Because I need to."

Her sister looked at her. Then she inhaled deeply from her pipe, as if drawing in breath before plunging underwater, and let out a bluish cloud. Finally, she stood and walked to her closet, riffling through shoeboxes of all sizes to find the right one. She carried it by her fingertips to Ruby, held well away from her body. "Just . . . be careful with it, okay?"

"I'm not gonna hurt it."

Dahlia frowned. "That's not what I meant."

Shut safely away in her bedroom, Ruby had thought she was prepared to open the box, sufficiently braced against a ten-year-old's longing. It wasn't real pain, she told herself, only remembered pain. Not love; just its ghost. But when she lifted the lid and saw the envelope inside, Dahlia's name printed delicately across it, she rocked backward, battered under the wave of it. She could look down on Dahlia for pretending, but every story she had told herself about a girl who never really knew her mother, and had always lived happily with her two big sisters in a charming little wasp-infected house on Stone Road, watched over by their strong, surly great-aunt—all of that was just a fantasy. A fiction riddled with plot holes, built upon a terribly shaky foundation.

None of it held under pressure.

With sweat slick fingers, she opened the envelope and took out the letter. Missing the form that had granted Dahlia custody of herself and Ginger, it was only a few lines, written on their junk drawer stationary. Happy cartoon coffee cups smiled up at her from the border while she reread the words that had been carved into her hippocampus six years ago:

I'm sorrier to leave you than you'll ever know, though I hope to see you again soon. Until then, my beautiful daughters—

Solnyshko, be strong.

Zvyodochka, be kind.

Zerkal'tse, be good.

Love, Mom

In those first few months after, she'd written letter upon letter of her own, with nowhere to send them. She'd scream at their mother in print, using every swear word her young brain could conjure, and in the next paragraph, beg her to come home. But as the days and weeks and months passed with no further contact, she realized the full truth of Polina's words.

Family is everything. The most important power we Chernyavskys have. Your mother will find this out for herself, I think. I hope. If not, she will never come back.

If she hadn't yet figured out what every other Chernyavsky seemed to understand from birth, she never would. And Ruby didn't need a mother she would never see again. Better to believe she'd never had one.

Swallowing roughly but determinedly, she reached into her backpack and pulled out the book of fairy tales. Folded inside was the unreadable story of Vasilisa the Beautiful, scanned and printed on Neil Baker's home office computer that morning. Also, a copy of the sheet of note paper, which she placed on the bed beside the letter. As if the happy dancing coffee cups weren't proof enough, the sloped *n*'s and precise little *o*'s matched exactly. It even seemed they were written with the same thin-inked blue pen.

In her mother's handwriting, the note read:

Remember the story. This is the price, Annie.

Ruby's first instinct had been right, of that she was certain; the story meant something. Fairy tales weren't just important to her family, they were history. They were legacy. And this one had made its way from Polina to Evelina to Annie, falling into Cece's and Ruby's hands years later. Like the Chernyavskys, it, too, was trying its hardest to survive. There must be a reason for that.

And then there was Polina's inscription.

Remember this, Evelina: if time is a prize you want to win, you must prepare to lose.

Time was exactly what she was after. She'd felt a secret clock ticking inside of her since she was thirteen, but what if it *could* be stopped? According to stories, the Chernyavskys had been powerful enough to do just that, once. And if Ruby could be strong enough—and smart enough—then she could save herself and Cece, too. She could take back what belonged to her, because judging by Polina's thwarted fate, it had never truly been abandoned.

And there was nothing she wasn't prepared to risk to find it. She didn't have much to lose in the first place.

Suddenly, Ruby could no longer sit still in this quiet little house, which was overwarm because their thermostat was acting up again, and thick with the smell of Dahlia's weed despite her sister's best efforts. Shouting that she was going for a walk, Ruby was out the door before her coat was zipped.

Fresh powder shifted under her boots, the frozen air heavy with the promise of more to come. The temperature on the electronic sign outside Saltville Hometown Banking read 13 degrees—no wonder her bones felt like thinly blown glass, like they'd shatter if tapped upon. Hunching down in her coat, she shuffled toward the General Store, though it was closed by now. And while she knew she shouldn't, she couldn't help but glance around for a big black truck glittering under the streetlights.

So it seemed like a kind of magic when her phone chimed, and she pried it out with stiff fingers to find a text waiting.

> **Dov: Hey, there's a bonfire behind Keebler's Saturday night. Interested? No band. Probably no bowling. Can't make promises**

A smile threatened to split the cold skin of her lips.

> **Ruby: What's a Keebler?**

> **Dov: You don't know Keebler??? You are missing . . . probably not much, he's kind of an ass**

> **Ruby: Then why are we going to his bonfire?**

> **Dov: Touché**

Emboldened by possibility and alive with *wanting*, she wrote back as new snow drifted silently down around her.

> **Ruby: Maybe we should just have our own bonfire**

Three eternal minutes later, an answer arrived.

> **Dov: We could do that**

• NINTEEN •

Dov had instructed her to park in the Mahalels' empty driveway at 6:00 p.m. that Saturday, and from there, search for the trail in the snow.

The drifts around the driveway were three feet deep at least, but there it was: a neat pathway carved through them, leading toward the backyard. Shivering, she shoved her mittened hands into her coat pockets and stomped forward. The backyard was wide and deep when she reached it, disappearing at the far end into a thicket of gray trees rising up out of the white.

Through their leafless branches, Ruby saw the flicker of fire.

She followed the path toward the flames until it spit her out into an unexpected clearing, surrounded by trees and dunes of snow. In the middle was a squat black fire pit, the earth around it scraped nearly down to the grass, dark blades poking through the crust here and there. Dov sat in one of two camping chairs in full winter gear, gloved hands tucked beneath his armpits. He beamed proudly up at her, a shovel leaning against the snow wall nearby. Clearly, he was the architect.

Ruby's mouth fell open, breath steaming out, but she tapped a mitten against her lips to hide it. "How long did this take?"

"Not that long. Well . . . I started at noon," he admitted. "Then I had a minor heart attack, but now I'm super rested."

Ruby nodded as though beautiful boys built snow forts in her honor all the time. And even in his puffy coat, Dov looked beautiful, with the orange glow of the fire splashed across his skin, his gray beanie pushed carelessly back over his black hair, and his dark brown eyes lit like candlewicks.

At her silence, his forehead wrinkled. "We don't have to stay out here. We can go in, or to a movie or something—"

"No, no, this is fine. This is good." She settled into the chair beside him, positioned so they were both staring into the fire pit. They were close enough that with their elbows on the canvas armrests, their coats swished against one another. Every noise was made louder, every hint of contact electric, by her growing certainty that this was a date.

According to Cece, of course it was a date. "He's inviting

you to a private bonfire," she'd said on the phone when Ruby had called her, just after the text exchange. "Obviously he likes you."

"But why?"

"Why not?"

"I don't know him. He doesn't know me."

"So? You're pretty and funny and mysterious. Of course he wants to get to know you." She sighed, as if explaining simple math, then said, "You don't have to go, Bebe. But if it makes you happy . . . I think you deserve to have fun." Cece's voice was soft with what Ruby could only interpret as pity.

To stop herself from following that downward spiral of thought, she nodded to a box of organic graham crackers in Dov's lap. "What's that?"

He offered it to her. "This was the best I could do, s'mores-wise. I forgot to go out and pick stuff up, with all the shoveling. But here." He bent over and picked up a mug and a thermos from the ground by his feet. "I made tea."

"Spicy or mild?"

He laughed, then from a pocket on the side of his chair, he fished out an almost-full bottle of Canadian Mist. "That's up to you." He had his own mug nestled in his chair's cup holder, she noticed.

Glancing back toward his house, she took the bottle. "Your parents are . . ."

"Mom's working out of town, and Dad's chaperoning

Talia's ski club trip. They went up to Eaton Mountain, and they're staying in town so they can hit the slopes early."

She'd known that Talia was in the ski club, and the French club, and mock trial—she moved quickly, for a new girl. But Ruby had been paying extra attention, now that Talia was important (and not just in an integral-cog-in-the-vast-and-unfathomable-machinery-of-the-human-race way, but important to Cece, and thus, to Ruby). She'd been observing them at lunch. Yesterday, Cece had blushed down to her T-shirt collar and smiled shyly when she saw Ruby watching, and Ruby had smiled back. But the one time Talia met her eyes, Dov's sister had cocked an eyebrow challengingly and looked away in her own sweet time.

"Your sister seems . . . nice."

"I don't think I'd call her that. I don't think she'd call herself that. But she's a good person. She's a good sister. It's not her fault she's brilliant. I think it's probably really tough, actually. Because everyone expects that whatever she ends up doing after high school, she'll be mind-blowingly great at it. Like, change-the-world kind of great. That's a lot of pressure, if you think about it. And Mom . . . she has, like, really strong ideas about what she wants Talia to do. Following in her noble footsteps and everything."

Ruby filled her mug with steaming tea and a thick splash of whiskey. "What about you?"

"Not so much."

"Sorry."

"No, it's cool! It's good. I'm not really great at any one thing, especially not my mom's thing."

"Why, what's *her* thing?"

He took a sip from his own mug, and by his wince, she guessed there to be a good amount of whiskey in it. "She's . . . into helping people."

"Like, she does charity work?"

He laughed. "Definitely not. More like, uh, holistic medicine."

"Ah." Ruby said. "Crystals and candles and stuff? Dahlia— my sister—she's into that."

"Not you?"

"I would say that I am firmly science-based."

"Yeah, I'm not really into it, either. Or, I don't know, it's not into me," he corrected, though that made little sense to Ruby. "And I know Mom's sad about that sometimes, even if she never says so. But it's okay. It kind of means I can do anything, you know? I could be in a band that sells three whole albums on iTunes, ever. I could go teach English in Morocco. I *could* work on a chicken farm in Paris, and I wouldn't even have to be a brilliant chicken farmer. I could just *be*." The way he said it, he seemed in awe of the idea.

Ruby was envious. She would never feel that kind of freedom.

Unless . . .

"What about you?" he asked. "What do you want to do after we graduate?"

She didn't want to lie. That seemed wrong, when he'd just given her something personal. So she hedged. "When I was a kid, I wanted to grow up and be a scientist. Just a generic scientist in a white lab coat I guess—I didn't know how many fields of study there were, or even what a 'field of study' was. But I was Carl Sagan for Halloween when I was eleven. Like, I combed my hair over and wore a tan suit from Goodwill that my sister chopped up, and a turtleneck, and I carried around a library copy of Carl Sagan's *The Cosmic Connection*."

"I'm shit at science, but that sounds fantastic."

"It is. He wrote it to try to get people back into science in the seventies, after the Apollo missions didn't find life on the moon and everyone peaced out. I have this part memorized . . . wait." She gulped her tea for courage. "'There is a place with four suns in the sky—red, white, blue, and yellow; two of them are so close together that they touch, and star-stuff flows between them. I know of a world with a million moons. I know of a sun the size of the Earth—and made of diamond. There are atomic nuclei a few miles across which rotate thirty times a second. There are tiny grains between the stars, with the size and atomic composition of bacteria. There are stars leaving the Milky Way, and immense gas clouds falling into it. There are turbulent plasmas writhing with X- and gamma-rays and mighty stellar explosions. There are, perhaps, places which are outside our universe. The universe is vast and awesome, and for the first time we are becoming a part of it.'"

Dov whistled, and in the cold, steam billowed from his lips. "I kind of meant little you in a suit and comb-over, but that's pretty fantastic, too. I was probably just Batman when I was eleven, because I dressed up as Batman for, like, three years in a row. For Purim, too."

"Purim is like Jewish Halloween?" Realizing that might be a terrible or offensive question, and that she might be a little drunk already, she wished she could take it back. "Sorry, sorry, forget I said that."

But Dov laughed again. "No, it's fine. I mean there's a whole long story behind it, but it's not a big holiday. We're not even that religious. We had to convert when we were little and everything, since my mom isn't Jewish. She's . . . kind of complicated. But mostly we did it because our saba and safta, Dad's parents, wanted us to. I don't even know if I believe in any of it." He chewed thoughtfully on a graham cracker. "I believe in things I don't absolutely understand, though. That doesn't mean they aren't real. I don't know if anything's impossible."

A shudder ran up Ruby's spine.

Dov slid his arm across the armrest and took her free hand. "Cold?"

There were layers of Thinsulate and fleece between their palms, certainly too much fluff to feel the heat from his skin. And the air just outside the globe of the fire was freezing. But she didn't feel cold.

She felt electric, and powerful.

They sat for a long while, watching the fire burn up the fuel on the logs. Sometimes they talked—Dov about the dozen or so places he'd lived, his favorite being St. Petersburg, Florida, where they rode Jet Skis instead of snowmobiles all winter long. Ruby, about being a Maine native, and about Cece, and the one time she and the cousins had convinced her to go snowmobiling, when she'd crashed Mikki's ride within seconds.

Sometimes she and Dov sat there, glove in mitten, silent, watching the flames crackle down, diminishing in the pit.

When they were low, she snuck a glance at Dov, his face flickering in the dark. Emboldened by their nearness and, probably, by Canadian Mist, she broke the pleasant silence. "Can I ask you something?"

He leaned forward to set his mug down but didn't drop her hand, instead pulling lightly on her arm until he'd righted himself. "Sure."

"Why'd you want me to come over tonight?"

Swiveling a bit, he looked at Ruby, full lips parting, eyebrows folding. "What do you mean?"

"I'm not talking, like, ulterior motives or anything. Unless you have those. And that's cool. But you don't even know me," she said, repeating what she'd tried to tell Cece. "You've been here for six or seven months, and we've never talked before. So why now?"

Rubbing his chin with his glove, Dov squinted into the fire.

"I guess because you haven't been around. I never saw you out, even with Cece. Maybe we would've talked, I don't know. I wish we had. And I thought . . . if we were alone, this could be our chance. Because there's some stuff I wanted to tell you, before we hang out again. I mean, if you wanted to. Hang out again."

The soft hope in his voice, and the solid feel of his hand, sent another shiver through her.

His fingers contracted around Ruby's. "*Now* you're cold. Come on, we can talk inside." He dropped her hand at last to put out the fire, which took a while—long enough for her to top off her mug with Canadian Mist and drink it down. He poked through the logs with the shovel, thinning the flames into almost nothing. Then he spread the remains around, picked up a small bucket of water and poured it slowly over the bowl. The ashes steamed, and he added more water until nothing billowed from the pile. By the time he was done, he had to reach down and pry Ruby out of the camping chair— her limbs were frozen stiff, though at her core she was warm and fluid.

Maybe it was Dov, or maybe it was whiskey. Probably it was both.

Back up the snow path through the pitch-black yard, they surfaced under the glow of the lampposts along the drive- way. They started for the front door, but Dov held her back. "Damn, I forgot my keys out back." They had left their chairs, taking only the bottle of whiskey with them. "It's fine, this one's always open." He let them in through the garage, and they spilled out into the bright kitchen. He set the bottle, its contents considerably emptier than it'd been a couple of hours ago, on the counter beside a tall glass vase of roses the exact blue-violet of the Orion Nebula. A plastic tag speared through their middle read *Get Well Soon!*

Flowers for Mrs. Mahalel?

Peeling off coats and gloves and boots, shedding half their bodyweight in winter layers, Ruby nearly moaned as the blood came back into her fingers and toes.

He winced sympathetically. "Can I get you a blanket?"

"I'm fine," she said, teeth chattering in her skull. She tugged off her hat and freed her trapped hair, which fanned out around her face with static.

Dov laughed, his own skin flushed. He reached out and smoothed the strands from her face, and then—

There was a natural phenomenon Ruby had read about, completely unexplained and so rare that until the sixties, scientists believed it was a myth: ball lightning. It appeared in stories throughout history, tales of luminous electric spheres, from pea-sized to meters wide, spit from the sky during storms. Of fire that chewed through stone and smashed wooden beams, that split ships' masts, that singed the earth as it rolled slowly along, that sounded like cannons and smelled like sulfur.

As the warm pad of Dov's thumb swept her icy cheek, she

could swear that electricity rolled from his fingertips, a bright ball that sparkled and singed and sounded like gunfire in her ears. It should've hurt. It should've been terrifying.

She wanted more.

Ruby wrapped a hand around his forearm, fingers pressed into the ropey muscles beneath.

He slid his palm around the back of her neck.

She ran her fingers across the shoulders of his oversized plaid button-down and along the collar, skimming her fingers through the hair at his nape. He shivered under her touch, and leaned down, eyes bright and unfocused. Then they were kissing.

Ruby had kissed boys before. But her few samplings were limp things, dry lips and surprise tongue and misaligned noses, and no real thought behind it but *Is this all?*

Not this kiss. This was something else.

They traveled from the kitchen, down the hall, to the bottom of the staircase that way—tangled in each other, hands moving and lips crushing. There was a warm bud inside her chest like the cherry on a cigarette, bright in a dark room. It burned hotter as they stumbled up the stairs, pausing to kiss on the third step, the landing, and by the time they reached Dov's bedroom right at the top, it was a star going supernova. It was wonderful and horrible, like the death of Ruby's heart foretold by one last, awesome explosion.

Maybe this is real kissing, she thought as he fumbled at his doorknob, back pressed into the door, every part of her body pressed into his. Everywhere and not enough. *Maybe this is wanting,* she thought. Maybe this is love.

She slid her hand up, playing at the hem of his shirt and just under, the skin above his jeans smooth and hot.

Suddenly, Dov grabbed for her wrist. "Wait." His dark eyes refocused a little, panic surfacing. "We shouldn't . . . we can't do this yet." Ruby didn't have time to feel slighted, because that was when she heard the voices.

They were braided together into one low chant, but still recognizable. There was Polina's voice, steely and gruff; there was her mother's voice, velvet and gravel and fresh in her mind; there were great-aunts and great-grandmothers and cousins separated by generations. Voices she'd never heard, but knew they belonged to her. They spoke Russian, and though she didn't know the language, she somehow knew these words:

Prinyat' vse.

Take everything.

She shoved off from Dov's body and stumbled away, the impossible lightning gone, her vision clearing, too. But she didn't remember the edge of the staircase behind her until she realized she was falling.

Dov grabbed for her at snail speed as she teetered backward.

He missed.

Ruby had too much time to look up at him while she floated

slowly away. She saw the horror on his face, the way his reddened lips shaped around her name, the breath too tangled up inside his throat to make a sound. She wanted to answer him, but the collapsed core of her heart was lodged inside her own throat.

It took forever to fall, and then, no time at all.

• TWENTY •

Nothing cleared the mind like a broken bone.

Whatever electric fog she'd been lost in at the top of the stairs, Ruby was awake by the time she smacked into the landing, rolled, and crashed to the bottom. She heard the sound, like a nut splintering inside a nutcracker. Lying flat out, the wind knocked from her lungs, she felt it even as she gasped for air. Her right ankle was *wrong*. Not painful, but promising pain.

Then it arrived, like a deep bruise but so much worse.

Dov thundered down the steps, jumping over her twisted body. "Shit, shit, shit, shit," he said, coming to rest beside her on the floor, his careful hand on top of her head.

It's fine, she tried to say—a silly promise to make after

hearing the celery snap of your own bones—but she hadn't got her breath back, and all she could do was lie there, wheezing.

"What hurts? Is it your back?"

It was a little hard to concentrate, and by the time she shook her head, he wasn't looking anymore, patting around in his pockets instead. He pulled out his phone, already dialing. Maybe it was 911—he was calling an ambulance to come and get her and her ankle-that-was-not-an-ankle—but then he swore, and hung up without speaking.

Is 911 out to dinner? she thought stupidly.

Dov's eyes burned down on her. "Just wait here, okay?" he said, suddenly calm.

Ruby tried to laugh, and it vibrated through her body, kicked up a dark cloud of nausea. Then she was alone, until his face swam into view once more, jaw tense.

He was holding the vase of purple roses from the kitchen.

"Ffffuck?" she managed to gasp, because it seemed he'd left her on the floor to bring her a *Get Well Soon* gift.

Then, instead of handing them to her, he did something insane. With force, he smashed the vase into the hardwood. From her strange angle, Ruby watched the water puddle across the floor, glass glittering among the flowers. Kneeling down, Dov pressed one hand into the mess, swearing under his breath as he ground his palm into thorns and shards and petals, until blood wisped out into the water like red ink.

She gaped as he wrapped his raw, blood-slick hand around

her wrist. There was heat coming off his skin, and suddenly it wasn't just in her wrist but in her leg. Not so different from the fire in her chest moments before, but this time, no dead ancestors whispered to her. She heard only the whoosh of blood, a heartbeat in her ears, in her throat, in her bones. So loud, it took her a moment to realize she was shouting at Dov while he murmured to her—or to himself, she couldn't tell—and her whole leg was aflame beneath her jeans, and then . . .

It wasn't.

She was herself, perfectly fine, folded over on the floor. Her ankle was an ankle and not some hinged, busted thing. She wasn't even out of breath.

Ruby sat up in time to watch Dov slump to his side, his face a horrible shade between brown and gray.

"What . . . just . . ." Ruby began.

Braced with one elbow, Dov turned and vomited on the stairs.

Resisting the urge to scramble backward in revulsion, she crawled forward, careful to avoid the glass. Tentatively, she cupped one hand around the back of his neck. The skin felt hot and clammy. Where moments ago, she couldn't stop herself from touching Dov, she now stopped herself from pulling away. There was no lightning this time, but a faint crackle, like the last heat of a dying fire. "Dov? What did you do?"

He dragged his unbloodied hand weakly across his mouth and rasped, "You okay?"

"Am *I* okay? Yeah, but—"

"Okay," he sighed, then tipped forward.

That was how his mother found them: at the bottom of the stairs, Dov resting his cheek on the floor and breathing hard, Ruby crouched awkwardly over him on her good-as-new leg, patting his damp back through his overshirt. Ruby looked up at the thud of the front door, and the click of heels, and then there she stood in the hallway.

She surveyed the scene. "What happened?" she asked quietly.

Even with her head swirling, Ruby saw that Mrs. Mahalel was now the picture of health.

"I fell," Ruby managed.

"I see." She nodded, as if this was explanation enough. Dropping her purse, she shoved a thick wave of auburn hair away from her face and sighed. "And he helped you? Oh, Dov . . . I really wish he hadn't."

"I'm sorry." Ruby swallowed something sharp.

His mother knelt beside them, grabbed Dov by the shoulders, and rolled him gently over, with Ruby's somewhat ineffectual assistance. He helped them feebly, his eyes open but fevered.

"No," Mrs. Mahalel said as she lay a hand on her son's forehead. "I mean he should have waited for me. I could've done it myself."

● ● ●

"He'll be all right," Mrs. Mahalel said, "in a few days. Maybe a week or two."

They stood in the kitchen, an island of marble between them. Mrs. Mahalel had taken a Tupperware of soup out of the fridge for Dov, something oily and brown with vegetables and bones bobbing in it that nevertheless smelled wonderful. She poured the contents into a pot on their shiny stove and turned the burner on, a click of gas and the whoosh of the flame.

All the while, Ruby braced against the countertop, legs tensed, ready to . . . to what? To run? To fight? To throw up on the tiled floor?

But Mrs. Mahalel seemed perfectly collected. Gone was the polka-dot bathrobe. Her crisp white jeans and a white silk T-shirt had somehow escaped without a spot of blood or vomit. Even her necklace, strung with amber and gold and dark red beads, rested perfectly across her collarbone. Not a single hair sat askew.

Ruby didn't know how she looked, but she felt like a stray cat, cornered and trapped in a crate.

"He's a special boy," Mrs. Mahalel continued. "In fact, our family is special. I suppose you've picked up on the fact that we have . . . gifts."

"Who doesn't?" Ruby asked flatly, very possibly in shock. Realizing this, she tightened her grip on the cold stone to pull herself together. She was not just anybody who'd stumbled into an upside-down corner of the world they couldn't fathom. She was a Chernyavsky, and the dark was afraid of *her*. "You heal people," she said in a calmer voice. Holistic medicine was her thing, Dov had said.

Well, it certainly wasn't science-based.

Mrs. Mahalel weighed the truth in her manicured hands. "We can fix what's broken. Among other skills."

"Is that so different?"

"My mother would say it is. And her mother, and hers."

"I thought . . . your family didn't talk to you."

Mrs. Mahalel's left eyebrow twitched before she smiled. "My son's been whispering our secrets, I see."

"Not really," Ruby answered nervously, though she couldn't say exactly why. "We just met. We don't really know each other."

"Well, now you know us a little better." She turned away to stir the pot, then looked down the hallway toward the staircase, flinching as if her son still lay at the bottom. "He should have waited for me," she said, this time to herself more than Ruby. "It wasn't his place. He knows he shouldn't be practicing."

"Why not?"

Giving the pot another stir, she shrugged. "Dov might tell you, if you ask. If you really want to know. He certainly seems to like you. Maybe he even thinks it's love, now that he's felt the Spark." She turned back to look at Ruby, and said dryly,

"You felt it when you touched, didn't you? I assume you and my son weren't headed upstairs to play checkers."

A bright ball of energy, rolling up and down her body, crackling in her ears, catching fire . . .

Ruby's ears burned.

Mrs. Mahalel nodded, satisfied. "It really is something. It's like a . . . what do you call it, when particles collide with their opposites?"

"An annihilation event," Ruby mumbled. When an electron collided with a positron, it created new particles but destroyed the originals. That was the law of conservation of energy: creation required destruction.

Nothing without a price.

"Right, thank you." Mrs. Mahalel looked pityingly at Ruby. "But it isn't love. That feeling? It's just what happens when power meets power." Then she tipped her head, as if paying Ruby her due.

A seed of unease blossomed suddenly into fear. Ruby's face felt bloodless, her tongue packed with ice. "You know who I am?" But that wasn't right. She couldn't possibly matter to a woman like Mrs. Mahalel, unless it was the Chernyavskys themselves who mattered. "You know who we are?" she guessed again.

"Better than you do, I assume, or you wouldn't be here. I should have known you were one of them when I met you— that was my mistake. I was off my game. But I recognize you

· 181 ·

now." Mrs. Mahalel took the bubbling pot off the burner. "And I know your people are very good at . . . surviving, whatever other skills you might possess. So I think you'll listen.

"I don't intend to hurt a harmless child. I don't *like* the taste of blood." She ladled soup into a bowl, perched it on a wooden tray. Then she looked up at Ruby, and her eyes were no longer pitying. They were the dagger tips of icicles, cold and piercing and very Polina-like. "But if you believe nothing else, believe this, and remember it: if you get in my way, you'll learn our gifts *aren't* harmless."

Ruby couldn't understand what was happening, couldn't wrap her mind around it, but that Dov's mother was dangerous, she did believe.

Somehow, she scraped together the will to ask, "Did you come to Saltville to . . . did you come here looking for us?"

Mrs. Mahalel gave a little shake of her head, glossy hair shifting. "Lisichka, you're here because of *us*." Then she set off to bring the tray upstairs. "We'll be seeing you," she called without looking back, leaving Ruby to show herself out.

Ruby stumbled out of the Mahalels' house and down their driveway with half of her winter clothes bundled in her arms. The cold cleared her head a little, and by the time she'd reached her car, thrown herself inside, and locked the doors, she could think again. She had to go to Dahlia and Ginger. She had to tell her sisters about the Mahalels. That somehow, somebody had come looking for Chernyavskys, after all. They'd call

Aunt Annie and all of the nearby family. They could . . . what?

Death premonitions weren't exactly defensive. And when Mrs. Mahalel hinted at more sinister gifts, Ruby didn't doubt her.

I don't like *the taste of blood,* she'd said. But something in her voice suggested that she knew it well, all the same.

So they could pack up and run.

They *would* run, Ruby knew in an instant. It was what Chernyavskys did when they were scared. When they were threatened.

Her heart pulsed.

Almost before she'd decided, she'd thrown the car into reverse and screeched out of the driveway, heading not toward Stone Road, but out of town. She *would* tell her sisters. She'd do her duty as a Chernyavsky.

First, though, she desperately needed answers. Because there were certain truths about being a Chernyavsky that she'd always accepted. She'd believed that their powers were all but forsaken, and their fates inescapable.

But either Polina's Time had been wrong . . . or she'd found a way to change it, buying herself decades. There was no denying that, no matter how stubbornly the family tried to pretend it away. Polina could have saved Ruby, she was more sure of it by the day—maybe their great-aunt could've helped Cece, too, found a way to free her from her own painful fate—but Polina was gone, and her sisters and aunts weren't talking. And they never would, not with one of the bad guys they'd long expected on their doorstep at last, one who claimed to know more about the Chernyavskys than Ruby did.

Ruby needed to know . . . whatever it was that she didn't. She couldn't count on some perfect clue hidden away in Polina's house to tell her, any more than she could count on her family. And she couldn't keep waiting, not with her Time on the horizon, and Mrs. Mahalel at her heels, and Dov—

Stopping to sort through her feelings for Dov was another thing she had no time for.

Yes, what she needed was answers.

And as it turned out, pride was the first thing she was willing to lose to find them.

• TWENTY-ONE •

Evelina Chernyavsky answered the door to room 113 in a powder-blue bathrobe sprinkled with little pink flowers, her hair braided into a blond-and-gray corona. She wore no makeup, and blinked heavy eyes in the light filtering through the clouds.

It was barely eight o'clock at night—had she been in bed?

"Ruby." Her mother blinked and looked beyond her, as if she'd been expecting somebody else on her doorstep. Finding no one, she shuffled back to let Ruby in.

Though the air outside was freezing, Ruby didn't rush across the threshold, but stepped cautiously over it. She could tell on sight that the Molehill Motel wasn't a mints-on-the-pillow place, more the vending-machine-for-dinner-except-the-vending-machine-is-busted sort of accommodations. Maybe there was a "continental breakfast" in the lodge, if they preferred boxed cereal and a pitcher of room-temperature milk on the continent. Inside the fairly barren room barely lit by a flickering bulb, there were two twin beds with two papery-looking pillows apiece. There was a mini fridge, a small TV on a bureau, and a single-serve coffee maker surrounded by boxes of assorted teas she must've accumulated over the last month. The closet door gaped open, her mother's things spilling out. Worn, loose jeans, soft sweaters, milky-colored scarves. A yellow knit winter hat faded and pilled with age, a giant pom-pom perched on top.

She recognized that hat.

Don't be afraid, baby. We're Chernyavsky women. The dark is scared of us.

There was a tug in Ruby's heart as something ruptured, some seal puncturing, letting loose six years' worth of little-kid need, mindless and pure. The sort Dahlia never elicited, no matter how hard they pretended that she was the "mom." But this woman who smelled the same as she remembered? Ruby wanted her to promise again and again that it was going to be okay. She wanted her mother to take care of everything and be in charge of everything. Of Ruby's hunt for the truth, of Ruby's future, of Ruby.

And that was no good at all.

"Bathroom?" she gritted out. It was becoming her go-to move.

Without waiting for an answer, she tracked snow and road salt into the carpet, headed for the closed door beyond the closet. Ruby hurled herself into a bathroom the unhealthy green of an overripe avocado, locking the door, sitting on the toilet, trying to breathe through what felt like pounds of gravel clogging her throat. Still, she wasn't far enough from her mother, so she shoved back the plastic shower curtain, tucked herself into the dry bathtub, and pulled shut the curtain.

That was a little better.

She needed to approach this scientifically, unemotionally. Create hypotheses, ask questions, gather information.

She needed to get her shit together.

Crawling back out of the tub, her eye caught on the sink top. Among travel-sized bottles of shampoos and creams, hairpins and coiled cast-off jewelry, a familiar necklace winked. Polina's locket, the one she'd seen in the little wooden box on her bedroom vanity. Her mother must've gone back to the house and taken it.

Ruby doubted any of the aunts or cousins felt particularly sentimental about the locket—her mother and Aunt Annie were the closest Polina had to heirs, and as far as she could tell, Cece's mother had wanted nothing from the house on Ivory Road. Still, something in Ruby wanted to take it just so her mother didn't have it. Because she shouldn't be able to come back after all this time and claim whatever pieces of the family she believed belonged to her, not after leaving it behind for years.

Her fingers shook as they skimmed the cool gold.

Instead, she reached into a pile of lipstick tubes, plucking one from the bunch. It was a sleek black Chanel tube labeled *Insatiable*, a bright poppy red when Ruby pried off the cap. She couldn't picture her mother wearing it—whenever Evelina put on lipstick in her memories, it had always been sweet, girlish shades like Peach and Primrose. But the stick was smudged and softly dented from use.

Ruby slipped it into her boot, where she felt the shape of it against her skin. Once that was done, she felt stronger.

She burst from the bathroom and announced to her startled mother, still hovering by the door, "Here's how this will work. You said after the Reading that I didn't know who the Chernyavskys really were, and to come find you when I wanted answers. Well, now I do, and maybe you think I'm too young or stupid to hear them, but I'm not. That's the only reason I'm here. I want to know what I don't know, no matter how *complicated*." Ruby paused, a bit out of breath, and finished hoarsely, "Okay?"

Emotions flickered across Evelina's face like the flare of passing streetlights on a dark road, too many and too fast for Ruby to name. "I'm . . . I'm so glad you came, zerkal'tse, really. I've been so hoping you would, but . . . this isn't the best time."

"Not the best—" Ruby broke off, feeling suddenly small again. She shifted her foot until the uncomfortable but comforting pressure of the lipstick tube against her ankle bone reminded her that she had the power. "Why not?" she demanded. "Your Tinder date is on his way?"

"No, it's . . ." Her mother's eyes darted to the clock on the nightstand. "Never mind, we've got a little while." Her mother sat down on one stiff twin bed. "Where do we begin?"

Although Ruby was swimming in questions, their dark shapes bobbing all around her as she tried to tread water— crowding her, threatening to drown her—she'd prepared for this on the drive up. From her backpack, she pulled out the book of fairy tales she kept with her always, the torn pages of Vasilisa's inscrutable story tucked inside. "Here," she ordered. "Tell me what this means to you." It wasn't her most pressing question, but that made it manageable. It was a small, solid place to start.

Her mother turned the book over in her lap, face distant. Ruby sat down on the other bed, legs crossed, feigning patience, though she felt time trickling through her fingers, moment by moment.

"This was a gift from Polina," her mother said at last, brushing her fingertips across the yellowed pages. "She brought it with her from Russia when she and her sisters emigrated, and gave it to me when my mother was—after I came to live with her."

"What was it like?" Ruby asked. Her whole life, Polina had been there, but lately, she'd been wondering whether she ever actually knew her.

Wasn't that just what Dahlia had said about their mother,

that the woman who'd waved to Ruby as she ran to catch the school bus was a totally separate person from the real Evelina Chernyavsky? She'd been furious with Dahlia for suggesting it, but maybe, sometimes, it *was* complicated.

"What, growing up? Well. My mother, Galina, had been a shy woman. Kind, but not one to command attention. Vera would talk your ear off about anything, and Polina was . . . not quiet." The way she said it seemed affectionate, but there was a flattened expression on her face, like a map of mountains rather than the jagged earth itself. "So it was different, growing up in my aunt's house. Her rules were strict, but strange. When we were teenagers, she didn't care if Annie and I broke into the vodka supply to get silly in our bedroom, or snuck out to meet neighborhood boys by the pond in the woods behind Ivory Road, or lied to our teachers when we hadn't done our homework—though Annie almost always did hers, she was too scared of authority figures.

"If we lied to *Polina*, on the other hand, we got long lectures, half in Russian, and had to peel vegetables until bedtime. Annie called her Baba Yaga."

In spite of herself, Ruby laughed. "Sometimes the cousins did, too."

"It was a good name. She wasn't cruel but . . . she had her opinions, and wasn't one to blunt them to spare us. We knew exactly what she thought of us, even as girls. Annie said I was the favorite, and I guess I was. Polina showed me things she never tried to teach my sister. I ate it all up. It was never enough. Annie had a thirst to please, but no real ambition. Polina loved us both, I suppose, in her way. I do believe she tried to make up for . . . what happened to our mother. Still, she was no Galina Chernyavsky." Evelina's eyes glittered sharply, as she said this, then dulled when she saw Ruby staring. "Anyways, she taught me more than my mother could have, though I always wanted to learn more."

"What exactly did she teach you?" Ruby asked, hope flaring bright and hungry.

Her mother picked up the fairy-tale book again. "She told me stories. This book was one of her prized possessions, and I practically had it memorized. It was written by a man your great-aunt knew back home, one of the people her mother helped. And that's a story, too."

Polina Chernyavsky grew up knowing little about the cities across the river, their factories and power stations and processing plants. All her early memories were of the quiet forest, of her mother, Vladlena, and the sister born when she was five. Galina's fiery-red curls, her cloth diapers and rag dolls. Galina, tied to their mother's back with a knotted blanket while they worked in the garden, pulling berries and mushrooms and roots as Vladlena pointed them out. Polina was put in charge of her sister whenever their mother went up the mud path, crossing the river to bring back supplies they couldn't grow or weave themselves . . . and whenever someone from the cities crossed the river and made their way into the forest to see Vladlena. From the time Galina was old enough to be shushed, the sisters would spy on their mother's work through the uneven door slats of the room where all three slept.

It wasn't until Vera was born and little Galina set to the task of watching her that Polina was allowed to help her mother with her work, though only to a point before she, too, was sent away.

One day, a young man walked out of the trees and up the path. One of the refugees seeking food and safety, her mother murmured to her in the doorway. This was during the Famine, which burned through the Soviet Union when Polina was ten. Peasants from the countryside had settled just outside the cities in temporary slums. The young man swam inside his ragged coat and black cap, his square beard tangled and damp. He arrived on their doorstep, and without asking his purpose, Polina's mother knew.

"The braziers, kotyonok," Vladlena commanded.

Polina, twelve years old now, lit the brass bowls of coal hanging in the four corners of the front room the way she'd been taught, setting pots on top filled with river water and herbs, saxifrage and juniper berries and others. Once the water boiled, the room became warm and humid, and smelled bitter and sharp. But even despite the heat, it felt like winter again when Polina glanced up at the man.

Vladlena took his coat and hat, revealing flesh stretched over bones. He was a writer, the man said, who'd been traveling by train when the famine struck, going into the countryside to collect folklore and fairy tales. Starving alongside the farmers, he migrated with them to the settlements outside the city, where he gathered their tales still. But—here, a coughing fit wracked his brittle frame—he needed time. Time to finish his work, which he believed was vitally important. How can a people know who they are, but through their stories?

Besides, whispered stories were how he'd learned about Polina's mother.

"When I am done, you will have strength enough to do what is needed. But to finish your work, you must complete the ritual. You know how?"

Here, the young man nodded—he had heard this in whispers, too.

It was there that Mom fell quiet.

Ruby waited, but only for a moment. "That's the end? But . . . what did she do?" Though Ruby was never certain what she believed about the woman in the woods, she'd sometimes imagined her welcoming women into her home, pouring them tea, giving them counsel and support the way Polina and her sisters always had. This was not what she'd pictured. "What was the ritual? What was it for?"

"You can't guess?" her mother asked.

"You can't tell me?" she snapped.

Her mother searched her eyes for an uncomfortably silent moment. Then, it seemed she came to some decision with a slight nod. "What if, instead, I show you?"

". . . How?"

"I have someone coming here, tonight." She checked the nightstand clock again. "Soon. I thought maybe you were them, arriving early."

"They're coming to the motel?"

"Sure. I need to pay for my room somehow. Ruby, I want you to stay and watch."

Ruby's phone chimed in her backpack—probably her sisters summoning her—but she didn't answer. "All right," she said hesitantly.

She would text Ginger and Dahlia when she left that she'd fallen asleep watching a movie on Dov's couch—was it just hours ago that she'd sat beside him by the fire?—and while they'd assume she was lying, they'd never dream it was to hide a truth like this.

· TWENTY-TWO ·

O ver the next half hour, her mother's cheap motel room
was transformed.

Evelina spread a black cloth over the nightstand
between the beds, cleared off the lamp and clock, and carefully arranged objects on top like a strange table setting: A
bowl of brown eggs. A pile of dried corn kernels on a white
handkerchief. A tiny clay teapot, and a plate of blini, the same
ceremonial food they ate at parties and readings, which her
mother took from the mini fridge. How she'd prepared them
without a kitchen, Ruby couldn't guess. There was also a glass
jar of water with bits of what looked like chopped roots bobbing inside it, a black candle, a coil of red yarn, and an electric
soup pot.

Her mother put on no makeup, only went into the bathroom to change into jeans and a sweater. But when she emerged just before their guest was due to arrive, Polina's locket winked dully around her throat.

Before Ruby could mention it, there was a knock at the door. Her mother looked to her and placed a finger against her lips. "Questions later. I'll handle everything. You only need to watch."

Evelina ushered in her mystery guest, a short, square-shouldered woman with a halo of white curls that must've turned early, because she wasn't all that old, even though Ruby could see the knobs of her bones through her withered skin. It was as if her bones were bigger than her body. The woman leaned on her mother, mouth drawn thin with pain as Evelina guided her to a bed and eased her gently down.

The woman glanced over at Ruby, who'd shoved herself into the corner between the closet and the bathroom.

"Nell, this is my daughter," Evelina said in a hushed voice. "She's here to learn. Shall we begin?"

The client—Nell—nodded once, then looked to the spread on the nightstand. "You know I can't . . . can't keep much down these days."

"It doesn't matter," her mother said. "It's only the ritual that's important."

The "ritual" began with the pouring of tea. Evelina sipped from a Styrofoam coffee cup, then passed it to Nell to drink.

She handed Nell a blini from the stack with her fingers, which Nell took and nibbled warily, grimacing as if it were baked of ash. It was barely bitten when she dropped it back into Evelina's palm.

Her mother spoke then, the words meaningless but the bled-together sounds familiar, rich then soft, then harsh.

She could've sworn her mother didn't speak fluent Russian.

Busy listening for any stray word she might recognize, she nearly missed it when her mother asked in clear English, "You brought the offering?"

"Yes." Nell nodded weakly. She reached into her large purse, and Ruby thought she was about to pull out her wallet. But she drew out a hand towel crusted in something dark, splatters and spots of black in the dim light.

Ruby wouldn't have touched it, but her mother took the towel with both hands and draped it over the bowl of eggs, like a cloth napkin over a bread basket in a fancy restaurant.

Next, her mother lit the black candle and sifted through the pile of corn kernels with her long fingers as if searching for . . . something. The candle smoke and its familiar, peppery scent grew in strength and presence, a coiled snake slithering through the motel room. It was a wonder it didn't trip the fire alarm, Ruby thought.

She realized that she'd smelled something like it in Polina's attic, in the little drawers full of odd plants and pebbles. And before that, even—the candle she'd once found in Dahlia's room.

Nell swayed slightly on the bed, eyes glassed over, and Ruby felt like she was swaying, too, dizzy with confusion, head stuffed with smoke. She pressed herself tighter against the wall.

It might have been the flickering light, but as she watched, Nell began to . . . *change*.

First it was her eyes, like cups filling slowly to the brim, where before there'd been dregs. Her skin, sagging and pale, grew firmer and pinked. Her hands in her lap ceased to shake. It was like watching paper curl in a candle flame, but in reverse.

Evelina lifted the lid from the little soup pot and, to Ruby's amazement, pinched something from the boiling water inside with her fingers without flinching. A lump of coal, it looked like. It hissed as she plunged it into the jar of water, screwed on the lid, and wrapped it with the red yarn.

She handed it to Nell, who tucked the jar inside her purse. "Is it done? It feels . . ."

"It is." Evelina leaned in and kissed Nell's now-pink cheek. "Make good use of it, moya dorogaya."

As Nell rose on steady feet and handed her mother a sealed envelope stuffed to the seams, she didn't look happy, exactly. More like grimly satisfied, as if she'd gotten what she came for, and not a penny more.

The Molehill Motel had a little square pool, tarped in winter. It was bordered by a gate, but the padlock had rusted through, so Evelina took Ruby from the still-smoky room to sit on poolside plastic loungers under the flickering security lights while she explained. "Nell is very, very sick, Ruby. You could see that—you could probably sense it, anyway. I didn't give her much. A good week, maybe three. Enough to do what she couldn't have done without me. Put things in order, spend a bit more time with the people she loves."

Ruby felt as if her brain had been packed in ice, each thought chipping its sluggish way to the surface. Her mother had warned her—she'd told her the stories—but hearing them was one thing, and seeing, another. "But how—how can we do this?"

"It's what we do," her mother said simply. "What we've always done. Our Times, they're just a bit of the tree root that pokes aboveground. They say we ran from our true gifts, but they're all connected. The way we recognize the presence of death, the way we feel it when one of us dies. It's all about time. We sense it. We speak its language. And if we know exactly what to ask of it and how, time obeys us."

"Time isn't, like, a being. It's just a fundamental quality. That's *science*. How do we make it *do* anything?"

Evelina turned up her palms helplessly. "You want me to tell you the exact mutated gene or chromosome that makes us who we are? I can't. Some things you just have to believe, Ruby—there can't ever be a perfect explanation."

Kerrigan Black would beg to differ. "Fine, say we can

control time. You couldn't give Nell more than a few weeks?"

"Not for the price she was willing to pay."

"But if she *was* willing to pay it . . ."

"Then that's a different story."

Ruby's blood quickened inside her. "So what *is* the price?"

"First, tell me: Why is this so important to you?"

Her mother's eyes were green seas, and Ruby felt herself sinking as Evelina stared into hers. She took a deep breath, trying to stay afloat. "I just don't get it. If we still have this power, why do our Times always come true? Why hasn't anybody tried to stop it besides Polina? Like, okay, maybe Alyona didn't know how, but Galina must have known *something*. She was only a couple of years younger than Polina. Why didn't your mom—"

"There's always a choice, Ruby," her mother said, so softly it barely stirred the air. "We make our choices, and we face the consequences. That's the way it works, even for Chernyavskys. I made a choice when I left you. I was trying to do the right thing by you. I know it's hard to . . . I thought I knew about right and wrong. But now I'm back, and no matter what, I will never leave you again. You and I, we're going to fix what I broke six years ago."

"It's too late for that," Ruby said, angry at the wobble in her own voice. Angry at herself for not being angrier with Evelina.

Her mother cupped a hand over her cold cheek, and it

smelled like mint. "Well, I'm not going anywhere. We've got time."

"Maybe you do. Or Dahlia, or Ginger. But I don't."

And then she told her mother about her Time.

"Zerkal'tse," her mother said, the nickname a low moan. She reached between them and pulled Ruby closer over the arms of their chairs, into the pillowy shoulder of her coat. "My baby girl. I—" Evelina cleared her throat and tried again. "I won't promise I can fix this for you, because you're not a child anymore. You grew up while I was gone, and you're strong—I knew that as soon as I saw you. You're so important to me, and to this family, in ways you can't even imagine. You're more powerful than you realize. You can fight this. There's a way to fight. And if you'll trust me, I promise we'll do it together."

It shouldn't have made Ruby feel better, but it did, even as she sensed her carefully bricked walls crumbling, falling away. On the side of the dark highway where her grandmother had winked out of existence, Ruby hugged her mother hard against the loss of them.

When she pulled away at last, she felt colder than she had before. "Okay. Okay. So . . . how? How exactly do we fight?"

"You asked about the fairy tales. There was a missing story—"

"Vasilisa the Beautiful. I know, we found it at Aunt Annie's."

"I'm surprised she still has it," her mother said dryly.

"You gave her those pages, didn't you?"

"Yes. We were . . . we'd had a fight. A disagreement. And I wanted to remind her who we were. Where we came from."

"The story tells us that?"

"In a way." Then her mother closed her eyes, reciting the tale from memory.

As with any story, the details changed a bit between tellings. In some versions of the tale, there were riders on horseback in red and white and black, or talking mice, or scheming cats, or disembodied hands to work the corn. But the bones remained the same.

Not the version Ruby's mother told then. That one was different.

When Vasilisa the Beautiful was stricken with the same wasting sickness that had killed her mother halfway through, the story changed.

Not wanting to catch the sickness themselves, her stepmother and stepsisters—who weren't kindly anyway—sent her into the woods while their father was gone on business. "Seek Baba Yaga in the forest," her stepmother said cruelly as she barred the door behind Vasilisa. "Perhaps she can help you, if she does not eat you up."

Terrified but having little to lose, Vasilisa did so, though her legs shook with every step. Once she reached the chicken-legged hut and Baba Yaga had sniffed her out, she did not beg for a light. She asked for a cure so she might live to see her father again. Baba Yaga made her the usual deal—if Vasilisa worked for her, she would give her what she needed. If not, she'd eat her. Vasilisa warned the witch she would catch a fever if she did, but Baba Yaga only cackled. "Bah! I am the Bone Mother, and death is afraid of me."

Vasilisa worked hard, sorted grain, scrubbed poppy seeds. Again, Baba Yaga gifted her with a fiery skull perched on a stick. "Here is your cure," she cawed. "Take it to your stepmother and stepsisters, and may they enjoy every bit of it!"

"But I am scared," Vasilisa pleaded. "What if they will not let me in? What if they open the door only to rid themselves of me for good and bury my bones in the garden?"

Baba Yaga sent her away despite her tears. "Time is a costly prize, child, and to win it, you must be prepared to lose."

So, gathering her courage, the girl marched on through the dark woods, and when she reached her father's gate, used all of her cunning to convince her stepmother and stepsisters to let her in, so that they might see the wonder of Baba Yaga's miraculous cure.

The skull burned them up alive.

Vasilisa stood on their ashes, healthy again, restored to her youth and glory. She wept at what had come to pass, but the next morning, she swept the ashes into the garden, buried the skull, and sat down to await her father's return.

• • •

In her chair, Ruby shivered, the plastic slats squeaking beneath her. "So Vasilisa risked her life to find the cure for death. That's what she was prepared to lose, right? Like Polina wrote in the front of the book. That was the cost for time."

"I wish I could protect you. You're my daughter, and I wish I could wrap you up and keep you safe forever. That's all I've wanted since the day you were born. But that's not the way this works. It's not how the world works. I'll be here with you the whole time, helping you, but . . . if you want a life, Ruby, then you'll have to fight for it. And you need to decide what *you're* willing to lose."

She'd known the answer to this question since Polina's Reading. She knew it when Cece confessed her own Time—

"Cece," Ruby said aloud.

"What about her?"

"Her Time. She's not dying anytime soon, but she doesn't exactly have a happy ending. Is there a way to change it? I promised . . ."

Her mother considered this. "Perhaps. Polina didn't only add years to her life; she changed it. She unbound herself from her own fate. If we work together, we can figure out how. I truly believe we can."

It would have to be enough; as she'd said, Cece wasn't in imminent danger, and with time, they could help her, too.

"So, Ruby. What are you willing to lose?" Evelina repeated the question.

"Anything," she answered at once. She'd felt it when she

looked into Dov's eyes across the fire. There was nothing she wouldn't risk.

"Good," her mother said, pride in her voice.

"Okay, so, where do we start?"

"I think you should get home for now. Your sisters will be worrying. And I'll still be here tomorrow." She spoke up over Ruby's sound of protest. "I told you, zerkal'tse, I'm not going anywhere."

"Wait, I have one more question," Ruby hurried to say, though in truth, she had dozens. "Why are you telling *me* this? I mean, why didn't you ever tell Dahlia and Ginger?"

Her mother's soft mouth crooked up at the corner. "Ruby, Dahlia was my apprentice when she was a little older than you. You don't remember? Those nights when Ginger babysat you? Well, you were young."

But all of a sudden, she did remember: rare evenings when her mother sent her and Ginger upstairs, keeping Dahlia by her side. She and her middle sister would watch old movies with the volume turned up, and Ginger would braid her hair into a dark crown to match her bright one, and feed her blini from a stack she'd snuck away for them. This was before Ginger turned into a know-it-all in a black beanie who brought stacks of classic novels to the dentist's office, just to be seen reading them.

Ruby had forgotten those nights until now.

"I—I thought they were just . . . helping people."

"Hmm," her mother murmurs beside her. "Ruby, you know

I love your sisters. I love them for exactly who they are, and who they aren't. Ginger is so sure of everything. Two plus two equals four, and you can't tell her otherwise. She's very smart, but that stubbornness makes her incurious. And Dahlia . . . she's always been sweet, but flighty, since she was a little girl. Distracted by every passing thought or whim, like a little butterfly on the breeze, with no real purpose. I taught her the ritual the way teachers used to make us memorize a passage out of Shakespeare and recite it for the class. Do they still make you do that?" Evelina asked, but continued without an answer. "They accept the sacrifices and they say the words, but Dahlia doesn't speak the language, in more ways than one. She only knows the smallest part of what we can do, and it's enough for her. For so many of the women in this family. Polina could've helped you, if she'd dared, but not your sisters. Not even if they'd been honest with you, or if you'd told them about your Time. All they could've done was nudge it backward a bit. They aren't equipped for real power. They aren't hungry enough to learn to wield it.

"But you, Ruby! You have that hunger. You've had it since you were born. The second you figured out how to crawl, you wanted to walk. I taught you to count to ten, and you wouldn't stop asking till you could count to one hundred. I put a clock in your room when you were learning to tell time, and you climbed up your dresser, grabbed it off the wall, and took it apart to see how it worked. You always wanted to learn. If knowing your Time changed any of that . . . You might be young, but you're strong enough to carry this knowledge. I see it in you, the way Polina saw it in me. You're stronger than your sisters."

"Polina said you left us because you were scared," Ruby protested. "She said you were running away from your fate. Or . . . that's what Ginger said. That you were weak."

"They were wrong, Ruby. I left to figure out how to be strong. And I did it. I made myself strong for you, zerkal'tse. You don't have to believe me now. But I promise you," she said fiercely, reaching over to clutch Ruby's winter-numb hand in hers, "you will."

· TWENTY-THREE ·

The house on Stone Road had a tiny backyard, just a square
plot bordered by a tall wooden fence, weather-grayed,
half-consumed by a thick blackberry hedge that hardly
ever gave fruit. When it did, the Japanese beetles and june bugs
got there first. There was also a small concrete porch under
an awning just deep enough to protect their shabby swing, so
although Ruby sat swaddled in her hat and coat and an armful
of blankets, watching the waxy light of dawn peel away the
dark, at least she wasn't sitting in snow.

She'd been out here long enough that her nose and fingertips were strangers, numb and damp-feeling, but she'd been
awake much longer than that. In fact, she'd never fallen asleep.

Ruby had made it home just before midnight—though a

curfew never *had* been established, midnight seemed the magical hour, and to stay with her mother beyond that was to press her luck—and she'd expected her sisters to pounce the moment her key touched the lock, demanding the details of her date. But they'd been curled up on the couch watching an old season of *America's Next Top Model*, and though she knew they'd been waiting up for her, they barely stirred when she walked in. In fact, they hadn't asked a single question, except that Ginger wondered aloud whether she was ever planning to run the salt-encrusted Malibu through a car wash, or was waiting for it to molt in the spring.

Taking the reprieve, Ruby had collapsed onto her bed. Brain still buzzing, she'd tried listening to the latest episode of *Solving for X-traordinary*, in which Kerrigan Black attempted to help Katherine Harrison of Wethersfield, Connecticut, a woman accused of witchcraft, but after denying the advances of the powerful owner of the town sawmill over the course of her investigation, was (predictably) accused of witchcraft herself. Instead of the voice of Jessica Keating, the host, Ruby heard her mother's.

What are you willing to lose?

She'd ripped out her headphones and tried to sleep. But every time she lay back, she imagined herself falling. Every time she shut her eyes, she saw Mrs. Mahalel's, two blue icicles that made her cold to her core. She knew she should have told her mother about the Mahalels. It was just that everything had happened so quickly. There was so much information to process. And even alone with her thoughts in her own bedroom, she still couldn't figure out what there actually was to tell. That Mrs. Mahalel had come to town looking for them seemed certain, especially now that Ruby understood there was truth to the old stories, after all—more than she'd ever guessed. They still had secrets worth coveting. Ruby, of anybody, knew how far people would go for more time, more *life*. But how had Mrs. Mahalel found out about them, and what did she plan to do about it?

Somehow, Ruby didn't picture Dov's mother as a paying client, come to beg her sisters for their services.

And there was Dov. How much did he know? Where did he fit into the story? Against her will, she felt the lightning strike of whatever "Spark" Mrs. Mahalel had been talking about as she lay in the dark, and the fire in Dov's hands licking up her twisted leg, and remembered his lips, the way they'd parted to let her in.

She gave up on sleep completely when the sky lightened at last, settling on the creaking porch swing under her blanket pile. And that was where her sisters discovered her. Letting the back door bang shut behind them, they wedged themselves onto the swing on either side of her. Ruby found it difficult to look at them, so she stared into the all-but-dead blackberry hedge.

"We want the truth and the whole truth," Ginger commanded.

Her stomach tightened, but eased when Dahlia clapped her hands eagerly and chimed, "Yes, come on, tell us how it went with your *boyfriend*."

"He's not my boyfriend," Ruby said.

"Your *inamorato*, then," said Ginger.

"My what?"

"Your lover. Jeez, haven't you taken three years of Italian?"

"Oh gross. They didn't teach us *that*." She assumed they hadn't, anyway—Italian was a final-period class, and Ruby's attendance, therefore, erratic.

"Anyway," Dahlia said, "we feel, as your big sisters, that there's certain . . . wisdom we should be sharing with you."

"Uh-huh," she muttered, apprehensive.

"Wisdom about, you know, what takes place in a boy's bedroom, boyfriend or no—"

"Nooooo," Ruby moaned, dropping her face into her gloves. "Can you just . . . not do that?"

Beside her, she felt Dahlia stiffen, though she spoke gently. "If you'd rather talk about this stuff with Mom, it would be okay. We'd get it."

Ruby jerked herself upright. "Why would I do that?"

"Because she's your mother, Ruby. What she did to us . . . to the family . . . it's hard to forgive. Maybe impossible. But if you want her in your life—"

"How could you be okay with that, when she ruined *your* life?"

"Did she?" Dahlia tilted her head to the side and stared dreamily into the backyard, as if considering this. "It doesn't feel ruined."

"If she hadn't left, you could have graduated instead of raising us," Ruby insisted, unsure whether she was arguing with Dahlia, or herself.

"Ruby, I made my own choice," she said calmly.

And Ruby realized, for perhaps the first time, that it was true. Yes, their mother had relinquished custody of Ruby and Ginger before fleeing, but that didn't mean Dahlia had to take it up. Evelina hadn't even asked it of Dahlia in her letter. She could have let them live with Polina, where they'd have their own bathrooms, and a big-if-overgrown backyard, reliable electricity, and no wasp infestations. Dahlia could be somebody else, somewhere else, doing whatever twenty-seven-year-olds did. Having coffee with her coworkers in their fancy break room, or raising a daughter of her own, or getting sloppy drunk and stoned and having wild sex every night, just because she could; because there was no Ruby there needing help with homework she hadn't intended to do anyway.

Dahlia would be free, and the three of them would be a very different family right now.

She turned to Ginger, who didn't look so Zen as Dahlia. "Do you want Mom back?"

Her middle sister set her jaw so tightly, Ruby could almost hear molars grinding, small bones grating. "I'm too old to want a Mom again. I think she missed her window. But you could still have one, if you wanted. You're still young." For once, she didn't sound condescending about Ruby's age.

She sounded jealous.

"We're only saying it's up to you," Dahlia took over. "That we wouldn't judge you. But if you did want to talk to us about last night—"

"OH MY GOD, we didn't do anything." Nothing approaching sex, anyhow, though if Dov hadn't pulled away when he did . . .

"Well, what happened, then?"

"I don't know. It was . . . nice. He made us a fire pit. We held gloves."

Dahlia swooned, tilting sideways on the bench to toss her arms around Ruby. She let the hug happen.

She should tell her sisters everything—that in defiance of their elders and the most basic Chernyavsky laws, she and Cece had been on a mission to alter their Times (of course, Dahlia and Ginger would put a stop to it, once they knew) and that she had gone to their mother (though Ruby didn't quite know how to explain how she could trust the woman who'd abandoned them, if, in fact, she truly did) and absolutely, about the Mahalels.

But her sisters had lied to her, first, pretending that they were simple, humble women helping other women, hiding from Ruby the scraps of power they possessed.

They aren't equipped for real power, her mother had said.

That, Ruby believed. Certainly not her sisters, committed to their lives in Nowhere, Maine, with their terrible jobs and terrible boyfriends, because they believed they were safe as long as they were small, as if submission had ever really protected women. Not Vera or the aunts, who'd fled after the Reading, scared even to consider what Polina's outliving her Time had meant. None of them trusted Ruby with what was hers by birth, by right: the whole truth of who they were, and who they might be again.

Only the mother who barely knew her believed she was strong enough.

When Dahlia pulled back, her eyes glittered. "Let's spend the day together, just us three. We even got you a present." She looked to Ginger.

Ginger hoisted a plastic shopping bag Ruby hadn't noticed, and three small boxes tumbled out into her lap. Ruby leaned in to examine them: boxes of semipermanent hair color in three shades. One a bright penny copper, one a vivid candy-apple red, and one a velvety deep hue called Midnight Ruby.

"See?" Dahlia smiled, pleased with herself. "It's fate."

Guilt and anger still clawed for purchase inside of her, but in the end, she was too exhausted to sustain either. Instead, she let herself be led to the bathroom.

By the time they were done, the sink and tub were splashed with what looked like blood—human this time—in varying stages, from freshly spilled and bright to old-crime-scene dark. Because Ruby's box was made for brunettes, bleach hadn't been necessary, so they were examining their dyed and blow-dried hair in the steamed mirror before most of Saltville had finished its Sunday brunch.

Dahlia squeezed her hand and kissed her red-streaked cheek, lips smacking sloppily. "It's perfect. You're one of us, now."

If only Dahlia really meant that. If only she and Ginger would trust Ruby with what she was trying to accomplish . . . but they wouldn't. It was Ruby's future at stake—Ruby's and Cece's both—and since she couldn't wrest the truth from her own family . . .

Well, there was always her enemies.

· TWENTY-FOUR ·

She stood outside of Dov's bedroom door at noon on Monday, but didn't knock, afraid of what she'd find inside; though she'd forbidden herself from doing so, she pictured him on his deathbed. Piles of quilts, handkerchiefs spotted with lung's blood, black-veiled women sitting vigil.

Maybe not the last. She knew he was home alone.

Dov hadn't been at school, but Talia was. While Cece had gasped over her hair, Talia had ignored Ruby altogether. And that was fine, because it gave Ruby the chance to study Talia, striving to notice what she never had before. Like that she spoke with her hands, the silver charm bracelet on her slim olive wrist flashing in the cafeteria lights, as did a tiny diamond nose stud. And she talked a lot. About a show both she and Cece watched, and a book they were both reading outside of class, and all of the clubs she was trying to persuade Cece to join. She had a louder laugh than Ruby remembered. Not the worst, just high and echoing, like a cymbal beat.

Ruby found herself strangely relieved—if his sister could laugh so easily, Dov must not be too sick or hurt—then fought to pay closer attention. She tried to determine whether Talia was acting differently, more guarded, whether her smile was forced, her movements performative.

But it was impossible to guess what Talia knew.

That is, until Ruby left the caf at the end of the period, and an arm hooked roughly through hers from behind, marching her backward through the crowd and shoving her, stumbling, into the girls' locker room. The air inside was thick with shower steam and the smell of makeup and sweat, but it was empty between classes.

For the first time, she was alone with Talia Mahalel.

Talia's eyes narrowed to sharp amber points. "I want to know what you told Cece."

Ruby wasn't planning to have this conversation today, but that was all right. She needed information, something to take back to her mother, and had her strategy prepared. And it was ironic, because just when she was starting to feel strong, she had to pretend to be weak. Small already, she shrank down into her spine as if to protect her vulnerable parts. She made herself wild-eyed, as if searching for exits, and spoke with a tremble in her voice. "Nothing! I didn't tell her. I wouldn't."

That much was true, and it twisted her heart. She'd wanted to tell Cece everything, text her their Super-Actual-Emergency Code, conference with her over fries and ice waters. *Did you know that your girlfriend's mother is in Saltville because of us, probably with nefarious intentions? Do you think Talia . . . and Dov . . . might be in on it? Might be using you . . . or us? Has Talia ever asked you strange questions—whether our people are allergic to garlic or iron, if we have any special talents, where we store our family secrets?*

That was a terrible thought, but she couldn't pretend it wasn't a possibility, no matter how badly she wanted to. Had Talia known who she and Cece were from the beginning? Had Dov? Because that would be some coincidence, both siblings falling for the only of-age Chernyavsky progeny in Saltville.

Ruby told herself she wasn't keeping a secret, because she absolutely intended to tell Cece everything. She was only holding on to the truth, for a little while, to protect her. She'd always looked out for Cece—in second grade, when Austin Griggs called her fat, and Ruby beaned him from across the classroom with a hardcover copy of *From the Mixed-Up Files of Mrs. Basil E. Frankweiler* when their teacher had stepped out. On a school field trip to Funtown Splashdown, when Aunt Annie packed Cece a bikini, but all the other girls had coordinated their one-pieces the night before, so Ruby went down Liquid Lightning with Cece in her training bra and underwear, daring the park staff to call her out with murder in her eleven-year-old eyes. And the summer when Mikki and Lili developed their own secret language and spoke it constantly just to annoy the rest of them, but Cece was crushed, close to tears at the exclusion. Until Ruby got them in trouble with their mother by daring them to smoke the cigarette they found in Aunt Irina's purse when she knew Aunt Nelly would smell it on them. Then their sputtered protests were strictly in English.

So she was really protecting her cousin, possibly from the Mahalels, and definitely from herself. Cece wasn't a liar like Ruby. She couldn't keep a secret this big, and would try to stop Ruby for her own good by running to Aunt Annie to admit everything. She was loyal and sweet and good, but she wasn't . . . *brave*, Ruby had almost thought, and felt sick for echoing Cece's worst beliefs about herself.

Steeling herself on the inside, Ruby made herself weak and fluttery on the outside. "I promise, I just . . . I don't want anybody to get hurt."

Talia's cheeks blazed. "You think I'd hurt her? What, like you hurt my brother?"

"I wouldn't—"

"You already *did*. Dov is so dumb and noble, he couldn't just let you be in the tiniest bit of pain. He had to ruin everything and make himself sick and spill our secret, when he's barely known you a minute. Now he's home in bed, and you're perfectly fucking fine." She cast a disdaining glance at Ruby's leg. "And my mom wouldn't even let me stay home with him in case he needs something."

"She left him alone?"

"Well, she *works*, Ruby," she sneered, as if it were Ruby living the high life on Oak Lane, while Talia's family was saving pennies and wearing hand-me-downs on Stone Road. "And if we have to move again and I have to leave my—leave Cece because of you, I swear . . . Just stay away from us, so nobody *else* gets hurt." With that, she whirled and stormed from the locker room, as if Ruby had dragged her in and not the other way around.

Had that been a threat? It was hard to tell. The conversation—if it could be called that—hadn't been terribly illuminating. She would never get the truth from Talia, but that wasn't the plan anyway. Luckily, there was a Mahalel who thought better of Ruby.

Talia *had* been helpful in one way. Thanks to her, Ruby knew she had the opportunity to talk to Dov without the risk of running into his mother, if she left school for the Mahalels' right now. And when she took a chance and tried to let herself in through their garage door, she was grateful Dov had told her the truth: it was always unlocked.

Ruby raised her fist and pressed her hand against his bedroom door, gathering the courage to knock. But it was unlatched, and eased open at her touch. Through the gap she could see Dov in his bed, seemingly asleep despite the music playing at fairly high volume:

> *You are a raisin in the sun*
> *Your skin is warm and wrinkled*
> *I'm just a grape*
> *Cool in the shade*
> *The only difference is passion and age*
> *Oooh, what's thirty years*
> *Between two fruits from the same vine?*

Her heart staggered as she recognized the pluck of the ukulele, the singer's reedy voice. She must have made some strangle sound loud enough to hear above the song, because Dov turned his head to blink up at her.

"You're here." There was awe in his voice, as if it was a magic trick.

Ruby edged into his room, which in some ways looked exactly as she'd expected. The basic "manly" red-and-black-plaid bedspread and drapes, the jumbles of clothing on the floor, the scent—his spicy deodorant, laundry in varying states of fresh, and something uniquely Dov that didn't smell like fire and whiskey and snow, but reminded Ruby of it anyway.

There were little surprises, too. An aquarium in one corner, clear water with bright yellow fish weaving between the plastic ferns. Colored pencil drawings tacked to the bold blue walls: a band poster he'd copied, anime characters she didn't recognize. It was good work, if not stunning; it was . . . observant? There was a drawing of the aquarium, the ferns beautifully feathered, the fish delicately scaled.

Dov was a surprise up close, too, but not a happy one. He lay on top of his blankets in only pajama pants and a loose black V-neck tee, and she could see the sweat on him, the light sheen of a fever. One bare foot was propped up on pillows at the end of the bed, the leg of his sweatpants rucked up just enough to show his ankle, brown skin mottled purple and painful looking.

"It's not as bad as it looks," he said quickly, almost sounding embarrassed. "It just hurts. A little."

"Jesus . . . Dov, it was just a stupid bone. I would've been fine."

"You looked like you couldn't breathe. I thought it was worse. I thought maybe . . . I panicked, sue me. But I'm okay. What about you?" From the way his brown eyes wouldn't meet hers, she doubted he was asking about her ankle.

Ruby did a little tap dance to demonstrate its health, and he laughed. As she started to sit on the bed opposite his bad ankle, she realized she was still in her winter wear. She dragged her hat off, but remembered the last time they'd shed their clothing, and thought better of taking off her coat or gloves. As she perched stiffly, she saw that Dov was staring up at her. "What?"

"Your hair," he said. "It's pretty."

She tugged on the strands, painfully aware that while he'd been lying in bed with a busted ankle on her behalf, she'd been coloring her hair. "How's your hand?"

Dov spread his bandaged right hand palm up on the blanket, gazing down as if considering it for the first time.

"Does it hurt?"

"That was . . . kind of the point."

Unsure what he meant, she reached her gloved hand out and tucked it into his undamaged one. There was no electric thrill this time, but her stomach was bubbling lava. He looked so harmless in his bed, soft and sleep-rumpled, but he could have been lying to her the whole time, using her. All of his talk about wishing they'd known each other sooner might be sugared bullshit. Or he might be as oblivious as Cece. She didn't know, and so she didn't know how to feel about him. Ruby had never had an enemy before . . . but then, she'd never had anything to lose, and she has a suspicion the two went together. "Can you talk about it?" she asked, forcing her voice to patience.

He sort of laughed. "Mom says you already had a talk."

"Kind of." Ruby stepped carefully. "Did, um, did she say anything about me?"

His forehead puckered beneath his bangs. "She said . . . I should leave you alone. Let you go. She said it was wrong to make you a part of all this."

But she hadn't told him who she really was. Or was he lying? Ruby frowned, undecided. "Your mother is an intense lady."

"All the Volkovs are."

"The who?"

"That's my mom's side." He shrugged. "They're the ones with the *gifts*."

"So your dad doesn't have it," she guessed. "Does he know who you are?"

Dov flinched. "Yeah, of course."

"But he's not *like* you?"

At that, he raised an eyebrow. "He's short, dark, and allergic to eggplant. So we have that in common. But no, he doesn't go around recklessly healing people and fainting, if that's what you mean."

"Sorry. That was a bad question. But both you and Talia, you can fix people. Except, um, your mom says you shouldn't be practicing?"

"Talia's really good at it, like everything else." His smile was only a touch bitter. "I'm . . . complicated."

He levered himself upright in bed, wincing as his leg shifted. When Ruby scooted backward to give him space, he reached out and wrapped a hand around her wrist where the glove met her coat sleeve. If he moved his thumb just a little, they'd truly be touching.

Every blood cell in her body rushed to fill a square inch of skin.

She held very, very still until he let her go, and her held breath slipped away. "I want to know what that means, *complicated*."

Dov's bright-dark eyes searched hers. "Right. Okay."

And then Dov Mahalel told her his story.

When Dov was ten years old, he'd had a different name.

That name no longer mattered, and was never spoken except by those who mourned the loss of it, none of whom mattered to Dov anymore. If he ever thought of it now, it was as a bold red X. He pictured it struck through the pieces of his past that no longer fit.

An **X** *across the photo of him and Talia dressed to match on the first day of kindergarten, in skirt sets patterned with tropical fruit, hands linked, big brown eyes luminous with nerves.*

An **X** *through the second-grade sleepover where Kacie Lowell dared him to put on her big sister's bra to see what he'd look like when he grew up, and his body in her closet mirror made him nauseated and afraid.*

An **X** *over the board game corner in his fourth-grade homeroom, where he'd wanted to play the boy token, only to have the plastic silhouette of a girl pressed into his palm.*

An **X** *through the person he thought he had to be.*

Dov Mahalel had been born a boy but was mistaken for a girl by the world, until magic, of all things, set him free.

It wasn't the magic of fairy tales, though their bedtime stories about the Volkov ancestors could've been mistaken for such. But their mother was always careful to tell them otherwise. "This is a story," she'd say every night in their childhood bedroom, "but it is also true."

Once upon a time, every Volkov had been gifted. They could sense what was broken in others—a miner whose lungs were stoppered by coal dust, or a child wasting away without the will to nurse. They could take away illness and sadness and pain, for a cost. Not much of one, of course. A small pile of kopecks, or a few stringy chickens, or a pouch of salt for preserving food while they traveled the cold countryside, healing the sick and the heartsick. Dov's great-great-grandfather had saved a farm full of workers who had been drinking from a contaminated stream. His great-great-aunt had brought a child back from the brink of death by tuberculosis. A woman who'd gone dumb with grief at the death of her husband, wasting away in her bed, was seen in town the day after a visit from Dov's grandfather's older cousin. She was shopping at the fish markets, a spray of flowers pinned in her hair, humming "Yablochko." The Volkov name was spoken with awe on back roads and in taverns, their reputation spreading among the desperate. They were beloved by the people whose paths they crossed. Blessings were always whispered at their backs.

One day, the mayor of a town stricken by cholera heard

the rumors and summoned Dov's great-grandfather, who brought his wife and many children with him. This was not unusual, for the Volkov families had often gone their separate ways, traveling the roads to practice. Like moons with elliptical orbits, their journeys would occasionally bring them close before spinning them away again.

To perform such a large healing, the family went into the field. The girls stripped naked and covered their heads with white cloths. The man and his sons armed themselves with scythes and rocks and animal skulls and lit torches. They called out to the sickness, gathering it to themselves.

But the people were not healed.

"This is not a natural plague," Dov's great-grandfather told the mayor. "It is not in our nature to heal it."

"Then I fear we must turn to the woman in the woods," the mayor said, suddenly pale. "Those who seek her and return say she has the gift to grant life where it has run its course, though their cost is much higher than yours, and may not be known until the deed is done."

Dov's ancestor considered this. "There is always a price. Let me seek her out. I would learn of her gifts, and judge the cost for myself."

And so, leaving his wife and daughters behind to keep them safe, he and his sons did just that. And what happened within those woods, nobody knows, except that the youngest son—Dov's grandfather, a boy of seven—stumbled from the trees days later, weak with thirst and hunger, white skin flecked with blood. Wild-eyed and tight-lipped, he could not tell the story, only this: that they had seen a woman and her daughters in the forest, beyond the river. Of their meeting, he could recall nothing. But afterward, as they set up camp for the night, a strange fever had come over his father and brothers and himself. They had turned on each other disastrously, for their gift was a two-sided coin, and not only could they fix what was broken, they could, should they will it, break what was whole.

Thereafter, the men of their line were cursed—those still in Russia, and those who had gone abroad, from young to old, fathers and grandfathers and sons—that they should never attempt one without causing the other, and be left with blood on their hands and ash on their tongues. The Volkov name, once spoken with reverence, was now mumbled while spitting upon the path. Dov's ancestors no longer traveled with blessings at their backs, but were chased away with scythes and rifle barrels.

And so they ran. Family by family, they crossed the glittering ocean for a place that had never heard of them, joining the few relations who'd immigrated ahead of the war. They settled together on the outskirts of a small town, amid miles upon miles of wavering cornstalks in the center of America, hoping for peace. What had been done to them by the woman in the woods could not be undone—not by their hand—and *all that remained was to begin new lives in this new country. The men would no longer practice. It was the women who kept the old ways, sacred but secret. They traveled by night to heal for coin, their passings unnoticed as the mice that scurried through the cornfields. For if their name had not been so renowned in Russia, their pride so great, would their fall have been so terrible?*

It was here that Dov's mother was born, and these were the stories she was raised on. Even when she met a boy, a college student crossing through town who kissed her on the tire swing of the playground at dusk and took her with him when he left, she promised that she would return with children, and raise them the same. Dov's mother, the most talented healer of her generation, was beloved by her family. And, true to her word, when she visited with two seemingly perfect little girls on her hips, they, too, were beloved. Dark-haired and dark-eyed and tan-skinned like their father, Mahalels by name, they were declared Volkovs all the same. Beautiful and gifted and blessed.

But blessings can be revoked.

And love, like fortune, can turn sour in a moment.

If anybody knew that, it was the Volkovs. Just as they had lost the love of the people of Russia, there were things they themselves could neither understand, nor forgive. Not even of Mila and her children.

From a young age, the curse set upon them by the woman in

the woods was the black thread embroidering their mother's fantastical bedtime stories. While boys could pass along the gift in their blood, they were never to use it. Should they try, the pain and sickness they sought to cure in others would not be diminished, but multiply. It would be like a campfire that leapt the rocks to the woods around it and, once wild, could not be contained. The Volkov sons were no longer taught to practice, lest they burn themselves down, and innocents along with them.

But, believing that she had two daughters, Mila Volkov taught her children. "When you're women, you'll do the same for your daughters," she assured them, and Dov felt the terrible weight of When *baring down on his still-small, unchanged body.*

Then, at ten years of age, Dov used his gifts for the first time.

His mother was out in the backyard, in the little garden past the lawn, beyond the trees. She'd left water boiling on the stove for her work, and while Talia was old enough to know better, she'd reached for it. Advanced for her age in everything from math to gymnastics, she thought she could help. But she tripped and pulled the pot down on herself, a mistake any kid could make. Dov had been in the living room watching Max Steel *and eating broken, bottom-of-the-bag Doritos out of a cereal bowl with a spoon. He heard the scream and sprinted for the kitchen, where his sister was dripping wet, on the floor, writhing.*

Dov had never practiced before, but he'd heard the stories, had the lessons, knew the principles. And however much it hurt, he believed that as a Volkov daughter, the gift was his to use. Rather than leave his sister in pain, and with a ten-year-old's thoughtlessness, he dodged her flailing limbs and wrapped his hands around hers, willed what was broken to wholeness. He knew there would be consequences—his mother, after she'd practiced, was always a bit down for a day or two, as if with a light cold—but he could handle that.

He was not prepared for the pain when it set in.

It started in his hands and crept up his arms, covered his body as if he himself had been soaked with boiling water. Pain was a starburst behind his eyes, replacing the blood in his veins. He was an electrical wire, live and severed and whipping.

He was a bomb.

Seizing, he leapt away from Talia and stumbled backward, bracing himself against the stove, hand coming to rest on the still-hot burner. And then the pain was running down his body, back to that hand, and it was pulsing there, almost beyond managing . . . but at least he was a bomb no longer.

Dov collapsed, and woke up in the hospital days later with a crazed heartbeat and a burned arm thickly bandaged from fingertips to elbow. His mother sat beside his bed, studying his face as if she'd never truly seen it.

"I thought . . ." She swallowed. "Is there something you need to tell me, X? I'm ready to listen."

His mother had always suspected, she later told Dov. She had paid attention. Listened as, when he was just a toddler, he begged her to call him boys' names. Read the elementary school essays where he talked about being a fireman when he grew up, or a policeman, or an army man—anything with man in the title. Humored him when he dragged her to the boys' section of the department store to try on loose jeans and shapeless dark T-shirts, once she'd proclaimed him old enough to pick out his own clothes. And she'd wondered, but had never really accepted. Neither did their relatives back home, aging among the cornfields—they scolded her for helping Dov "pretend," allowing him to cut his hair and register as male when they moved schools, for letting a precious female heir to their gifts slip away. They shunned Mila, and her children as well; though Talia had been a family jewel, the most promising among the next generation, she, too, was cast out.

But the Volkov gifts knew, their mother told Dov. The magic had always known she had a son; it knew that it was not meant for Dov to practice. It accepted the truth of who he was before he did.

And as she said so, Dov felt the power of certainty, and the perfect lightness of freedom.

• • •

Ruby's heart was a bird, and it forced its way up, up her throat, trying to fly away. She pressed a hand against her chest to keep it caged.

Though she hadn't known for certain, she'd feared that Mrs. Mahalel was a bad guy, one of the grasping, desperate people in this world who the woman in the woods had predicted would come for her family, would *always* come for them. That a woman and not a man had shown up at long last was unexpected, but whatever. You couldn't take every single word of a story literally.

Ruby had never guessed that Dov's mother was *the* bad guy.

Or at least, that her ancestors were. Her people. Her family. And wasn't that the same thing?

"You're weirded out," Dov said. He didn't sound upset, only matter-of-fact, as if there could never have been another outcome.

And she was, though not by the part that he'd expected; it was impossibly strange to recognize herself—her family—in Dov's story. *The woman in the woods.* But she rushed to say, "I'm not."

"I wouldn't blame you."

"I'm *not*. I'm . . . glad you told me."

"I meant to sooner, before—"

Before the lightning, the kiss, pulled clothing and heated skin and crushed lips. The Spark. Ruby's ears flamed at the memory, and she fought the urge to hide behind the red curtain of her hair. "I remember."

"I know this probably sounds insane. Like . . . magic? Sometimes I can't believe it's real, and I've seen it. I've been around it my whole life. It's what my family does, but . . . I . . . I just don't want you to think that's who I am. I guess it's a part, but I want you to know *me*. Does that make sense?"

She understood now how he could separate the two; that family could be nothing but blood, just a jagged piece that no longer fit into the puzzle of him. Ruby couldn't, but she tried to push away the Chernyavsky part of herself and be a person. She focused on the gorgeous boy in his bed, waiting for her to react, ask questions, walk out or stay. She threaded her safely encased fingers more tightly between his. "That's why your family won't talk to your mom?"

He nodded, his hand pulsing inside hers. "Not since I was ten. They warned her they'd cut her off, but Mom didn't back down. She let me pick out new clothes, and cut my hair, and we moved school districts so I could start again as a boy. And we just kept moving—she says it's safer that way, without the family. When I started high school, I started hormones. And here I am. And . . . you're staring at me," Dov said, eyebrows knitting together.

Was she? Yes, she'd been studying his face, his rumpled black hair, the small, solid muscles in his shoulders, wondering what it meant that she wanted him. Because against her will and despite her scheming, she wanted Dov Mahalel, in a way she'd never wanted anybody before. She wasn't altogether sure she ever *had* wanted anybody, but in this, she was sure.

And he wanted her.

The realization was a pocket of warm, bright air inside of her. Dov didn't know who she was. If he did, he wouldn't have told her his story, offered up the details of his legacy, helplessly tangled with hers. He wasn't using her—which shouldn't matter, because she was, in fact, using him, but it did. He didn't know her, but he wanted to. And it felt like tea on a cold day, like a nightlight in the dark, like happiness.

Ruby shook herself. "Sorry. It's just . . . if I'm being honest, I'm really not comfortable with the fact that . . . you're allergic to eggplant."

"Tomatoes, too, if that does anything for you."

"Stop, it's *too* sexy."

He laughed, winced, pressed his bandaged hand to his ribs and winced again.

Bottling her guilt inside of her, she forced her voice to coolness and nodded at the hand. "What did you mean, that it was supposed to hurt?"

She watched him search for the words. "It's . . . You know flood control channels? They're these empty cement basins you build along roads for water to overflow into, like big gutters. So it stops the streets from flooding in heavy rain. It's kind of like that." He examined his palm, brushed his bent fingers against the dressing. "I didn't know what I was doing when I fixed Talia. Everything I took from her could've broken me, or burst out. But Mom said when I burned my hand that day, it created a channel. The pain made a space for more pain to flow into, to stop *me* from flooding." Dov let his hand fall back to the bed sheet. "But I almost never practice, so I don't know how much it would hold, or what would happen if it didn't."

"And you don't miss it? The gifts?"

He shrugged. "Like I said, they were never mine. But no, not really. Talia's the heir, and that's great for her, but I think it's heavy, too. You can see it weighing her down, sometimes. I just feel . . . like I used to be a character in a story somebody else wrote for me, you know? But not anymore. I walked off the page, and now I can do anything."

It sounded wonderful, when he put it like that, and it broke her heart a little.

Dov looked up at Ruby, his fever-bright eyes two search-lights. "You're taking this, like, suspiciously well, for somebody who worships Carl Sagan."

"You think so?"

"Maybe you're in shock," he suggested.

She couldn't rule it out. But he had given her his truth. And though for one hundred reasons she shouldn't, she wanted to give him the same—at least, however much of it she could—so she swallowed the rawness in her throat. "Carl Sagan didn't believe in superstition or the supernatural. But . . . he also said,

'Somewhere, something incredible is waiting to be known.' So I just always figured, if I ever discovered something new—if I ever had information he didn't—he'd want me to learn everything I could, and understand it."

"Am I something new?" Dov's lips twitched.

"Maybe you're something incredible," Ruby answered, wishing at once that she could take it back.

But when his still-pale cheeks dimpled, she knew it was too late.

• TWENTY-FIVE •

Ruby did not tell her mother about Dov.

At least, she didn't tell her who he had been before he became the boy she . . . had feelings for. What did it matter? He was who he was now, and the past was irrelevant.

The rest, she recounted in her mother's motel room as she sat on one of the beds, eating mini cookies out of a foil package from the vending machine. Ruby had driven straight from Dov's house, and since she'd been too busy studying Talia at lunch to eat lunch, she'd been starving by the time she arrived. Wiping cookie crumbs on an already-greasy-feeling quilt, she told her mother everything she could think of, starting with that beautiful disaster of a date, the lightning and the voices and the fall. How Dov had hurt himself to heal her, and what his mother had said about the Chernyavskys being good at survival. How she'd threatened Ruby even as she'd dismissed her. How Ruby had snuck back to hear the whole story of the Volkovs, and how the woman in the woods had been their downfall.

"That's definitely us, right? Vladlena, I mean."

It was almost dark in the room, the bedside lamp the only light on, and its glow cast Evelina as a stone, pale and unmoving. She wasn't looking at Ruby, but out the motel room window at the cold, dry sky. At last, she pressed her fingers to the dip in her collarbone, where Polina's necklace rested. "Yes," she said simply. "That's her."

"I thought so," Ruby said. Her head swam with strange knowledge, question upon question like breaking waves. "Except . . . they don't seem to think it happened the same way we do."

Her mother twisted Polina's locket around her neck, dragging it back and forth across its thin gold chain with a *zip, zip, zip*. "Stories are living things, Ruby, not just ink on a page. Stories are power. They're born, and they grow with time, and they die off if they're not cared for or fed. They exist to fulfill a purpose. They can be dangerous. And sometimes, they lie."

That made sense. Of course, Mrs. Mahalel—and everyone who'd come before her—would lie about what had happened to the Volkov men when they'd gone looking for Vladlena Chernyavsky. No, when they'd *hunted* her and her daughters, because that was the real story, not the soft version Dov had been told as a child. She shouldn't be surprised that the Volkovs were the heroes in their own tales, instead of the villains they truly were. Why else would they have chased the Chernyavskys out of Russia and all the way to America? Why else would Dov's mother threaten Ruby?

And Dov? If he truly wasn't a player in all of this, stripped of the role when he was ten years old, then what *was* he to her?

That last was a question her mother couldn't answer, so instead, Ruby asked, "What did Polina tell you about the Volkovs?"

Evelina's eyes snapped back to Ruby. "Not much more than I've always told you. That men came into the woods, wanting to pry Vladlena's gifts from her. Vladlena managed to chase them off, but knew more would follow, so she packed her daughters' trunks, loaded them onto their horse cart, and sent them far away, where they'd be weak but safe without their secrets."

"Except we're not safe."

"No." Evelina clasped a white-knuckled fist around the locket, then let it drop. "But we're not weak, either."

"How did Vladlena get rid of the first Volkovs when they came for her?"

"That she didn't tell me." Evelina said, something like a flame of anger in her voice, but it had cooled completely when she spoke again. "Have you told your sisters about this yet?"

Ruby shook her head.

"That's good. They're safer if they don't know, for now. Ruby . . . I'm leaving town tomorrow morning."

Creeping tendrils of panic climbed her heart, until Evelina reached across the bed and laced Ruby's fingers through hers. Her hand looked like Ginger's, small and hard-knuckled and practical, but it was warm. It was as a mother's hand should be.

"Only for a little while. There are some supplies I can't find in Hop River, shockingly, but we'll need them if we're going to get started."

Ruby clutched at her mother, fingertips pressing down. "To change my Time?"

"If you're ready."

"Yes," she breathed with relief, then held her breath again as she asked, "Can I come with you?"

She smiled kindly. "It will take me a week or two, and I think your sisters might notice. Besides, isn't your cousin's party this weekend?"

Her mother was right; Cece's party had finally been rescheduled, a date found at the end of March, past the respectable mourning period for Polina. And Ruby should be there. Whether Cece wanted it or not, the party was her rite of passage, even if they were always the same. Piles of traditional food, the family in their fanciest dresses, the ritual of the Recordings.

Her mother's hand pulsed in hers. "But there's something you can do while I'm gone. Something we need in order to help you." She watched Ruby closely in the feeble light. "This Volkov woman. Do you think her son would want to see you again?"

Ruby nodded, hoping it was dark enough that her blush didn't show.

"Good. Because we need something from their house—a glove, a comb, anything, but the more personal the better."

"Why?"

"You remember the story of Vasilisa? The price?"

"She risked her life to find the cure for death," Ruby recounted dutifully.

"This ritual, when we do it, will buy you more time than Nell could ever pay for. We're talking about years, Ruby. Decades without repeating the ritual, if we do it right. But we'll need a powerful token for that. Something from another who has abilities. Our enemies."

"So . . . you want me to take it from Dov?" She winced without meaning to.

Her mother shook her head. "That won't do it. He doesn't have the power, and neither do his possessions. We need something belonging to a Volkov woman, anything she touches regularly. Just promise me you won't let her catch you. It could be dangerous—"

"I can do it," Ruby promised, oddly relieved. She didn't *want* to steal anything from Dov. She only wanted from him . . . whatever he was willing to give her. Though it was true that stealing from Mrs. Mahalel would be harder.

"I know you can, brave girl. You're a Chernyavsky. That means you're a survivor. And we're going to make sure of that, me and you."

Ruby clutched Evelina's hand, feeling the fullness of her own heart. There was so much more to talk about, but it could wait until her mother returned. Right now, she couldn't think of a single question worth tossing away this feeling, this tentative hope she wanted to cup her palms around and protect. Hope for a chance at a longer life, a *real* life. For the years ahead spent with her mother, with her whole family, and—why not?—with Dov. Anything seemed possible in this moment, a perfect jewel glittering among sands that stretched on and on forever.

· TWENTY-SIX ·

Cece's party was held at Great-Aunt Vera's house, an hour's drive north in Abbot, some of which Ruby spent staring at the monochrome landscape as it blurred by, searching for that anonymous spot along the highway where Galina might have died. The place where her grandmother's choices supposedly led. But the piled snow and guardrails and tall, dead-gold weeds looked exactly the same, mile after mile.

They parked on a street of refurbished Victorian homes painted every shade of lilac and spring green and bright berry red. Except for Vera's; hers was buttercup yellow once, but had faded to bone over the years, and she'd never repainted. "The house and I, we're both old," she'd said whenever her daughters, Ruby's aunts, offered. "Let us age beautifully together."

And so it had aged, from its scalloped siding to the wine-colored shutters to the round porch, like a carousel stripped of horses. In late spring, the front garden would burst with lilac bushes, but in March it was an icy, dead-looking hovel of sticks studded with ceramic lawn gnomes. What's more, these were imported gnomes from Russia, not just bearded but with their faces and hands thatched with hair, bursting from their bright tunics. Vera called them her "domovoi" and joked that they guarded her house.

She claimed it was a joke, at least. But Mikki said her grandmother left bowls of milk or oatmeal or salt in the flowerbed for them, rolls of bread and pinches of tobacco from her cigarettes.

The place hadn't been a part of Ruby's childhood quite the way Polina's had been. She had never sat silently in a kitchen chair, short legs dangling, watching Vera cook solyanka, a soup made from every kind of meat and every sour thing you could possibly keep in your pantry. Nor had she ever vomited on the lace tablecloth after her very first bowl of solyanka. But she knew the house, full of polished wood and tchotchkes from Vera's travels. She knew the smell of her great-aunt's cigarettes, steeped into the thick woven drapes and rugs, which Ruby found welcoming when Vera ushered Ruby, Dahlia, and Ginger inside. Their great-aunt was always the first to greet them at the door, despite her age and position in the family; Polina had never once met them on the front steps, not even when they came for visits, but expected the sisters to let themselves in and wander toward the kitchen, just as she had barged into their houses.

Gone was the mourning veil. This time, Vera greeted them in a peacock-green satin pantsuit and orange lipstick. "Come, girls, the guest of honor has just arrived."

They found Cece in the living room, surrounded by family. Ruby almost didn't recognize her at first; her cousin wore a moss-green dress with long sleeves that buttoned at the wrists, and her white-blond hair, typically uncontained, was wound into a perfect ballerina bun. She looked so unlike herself in general, Ruby felt a twinge of loneliness, as if her cousin had aged overnight. They hadn't seen much of each other in the week since her catastrophic date with Dov. While Ruby was driving back and forth between school, the Mahalels', and the Molehill Motel, Cece had been pulled into her mother's preparations for today; Ruby hadn't even had the chance to share all she'd learned with her cousin. But when Ruby finally managed to lure Cece from her party into the cramped downstairs bathroom, she told her everything—everything except for the Mahalels. Talia was still an unknown threat, after all, and her mother was right. Her cousin was safer in ignorance.

It would be worth the secret, Ruby decided, when she'd saved Cece from her Time.

The rest, she spilled willingly, starting with Evelina. She shared the translation of Vasilisa the Beautiful, and the story of the Volkovs (also relayed by Evelina, Ruby claimed). The ritual from the other night, and the cost of time, and Ruby's resolution to pay it. That part was tricky, without mentioning the Mahalels, but she managed through careful editing.

Cece stood pressed against the sink basin, pulling at the buttons on her dress. Her green eyes glowed—Aunt Annie must've done her eye shadow in classic beiges and browns—and they were wide with disbelief. "Why didn't you tell me you were going to your mom?"

With everything she'd just been told, that was her first question?

Ruby shifted against the towel rack that dug into her back through her own plum dress, a thrift-store find of Dahlia's with the tacky white collar carefully exorcized. "Was I supposed to? I thought it was my choice."

"Right, of course it was." Cece frowned. "I just thought we were working together."

"We are!" Ruby rushed to say. "It's still our thing."

"Our thing?"

"Our *mission*, or whatever. Evelina is . . . she's helping. She wants to help us. First we fix me, and then we'll know how to fix you. Or, your Time. You know what I mean."

"Just be careful, okay?"

Be careful must be the most useless two words in the English language. Whoever told you to *be careful* was obviously convinced of your recklessness, yet had no actual advice or instructions to offer. Ruby clenched her fists around her slightly overlong sleeves, but swallowed her sharp reply. It wasn't Cece's fault, and she shouldn't be annoyed with her. Cece wasn't . . .

She was different from Ruby, was all.

"Nothing has changed, I promise. It's still you and me, working together."

Cece's eyes slivered. "I don't know. You should have told me. Because I sort of had this whole plan for today, but now—"

"No, let's do your plan!"

"Don't patronize."

"I'm not, Cece, I want to hear it!"

So she listened as Cece told her, green eyes aglow once more.

After they'd rejoined the crowd, there were appetizers and mayonnaise-based salads to make it through, and so much family chatter—baby cousins shrieking as their mothers plucked them away from sharp corners and delicate collectibles, Oksana gushing about her date to the upcoming spring dance at Oakleaf Prep, aunts *ooh*ing over each other's beaded dresses, their pearl necklaces and pinned hairstyles. It seemed hours before Vera finally summoned them all into the living room, where she followed the script for parties as set by Polina. Ruby stood on her toes, trying to see over the crowd—there wasn't as much space or seating here as the house on Ivory Road, only a few mismatched chairs and a patchy velveteen chaise lounge—while Vera presented Cece the Recordings.

"Write down your Time, Cece. Write your truth."

Aunt Annie gave her daughter a thick-tipped pen.

"It . . . um, it might take me a while," Cece said, her voice like a rung bell, clear but trembling.

"You'll have as long as you need. Choose a private place, and we'll wait for you here."

This was always how it happened, so Cece hadn't really needed to ask, but this was her plan, so she was in charge of it. And if she sounded nervous, who in the family would blame her? She was about to set her death down in writing . . . or close enough. Aunts and cousins split to leave a path for Cece, and as she passed by, she cut her eyes toward Ruby for only a second, then set her teeth and walked on, shoulders pulled low by the weight of the book.

Ruby waited a few minutes while the room resettled and the chatter picked up, then tapped Lili on the shoulder. Her cousin was dressed like the sugarplum fairy in a pale pink cor-set dress that glowed against her dark skin, its tulle skirt full and beaded. Her dark hair was scooped into an updo topped by her natural Afro puff, and she smelled like coconut oil and lip gloss.

Ruby tugged again on her sleeves. A party was a time to glory in Chernyavsky pride, and she supposed she could've shown a bit more by putting a little effort in. Ginger and Dahlia looked like the prettiest witches at the prom despite their thrift-store style.

Oh well, it was too late now.

"I have to go," she mumbled. "Like, *go*. Cover for me?"

Lili frowned. "We're not supposed to leave. Can't you hold it for a few minutes?"

"I don't know," Ruby snapped, clutching her stomach dramatically. "Want to place bets?"

"Oh, fine." Her cousin walked with her to the very back of the living room, then shifted to block her from view as she slipped into the hall.

As she made her way toward Vera's room, which Cece had promised to pick for her private spot, Ruby stopped to look at a framed black-and-white photo perched on a little antique side table. It was of Galina, maybe in her early thirties, and Vera, a few years younger. They stood on the banks of a lake in their high-waisted bikinis, stomachs sucked in. Maybe Polina had taken the picture, though Ruby couldn't picture her on that shore, the toes of her sensible shoes in the pebbled sand, a summer breeze stirring wisps out of her tight, steely bun. Maybe a man had taken it, one of her aunts' fathers, or even Evelina's, tan-skinned and sunscreen-slick, handsome in a mustachioed, old-fashioned way. She couldn't imagine that either—a grandfather or a great-uncle—even though she knew that powers or no, Chernyavskys did not get pregnant by wind pollination. Men were there, and then they weren't.

Boys, too.

Shoving aside unwelcome thoughts of one boy in particular, Ruby went on, knocking softly at Vera's bedroom door. It opened a crack and Cece peeked out warily, then stepped back to let her in. "Did anyone stop you?"

"I wouldn't be here if they did, Cece."

Vera's room was much like the rest of the house, with its rich wood furniture, heavy curtains, tobacco smell and strange collections. On one pale pink wall, a display rack of delicate plates. On top of a bureau, a row of colored glass bottles, empty, their fading labels in every language. And on a little table in the corner between two mismatched, high-backed chairs, the Recordings.

Ruby had held the book, thick with uneven yellowed pages, its brown leather binding water-spotted, one time only. She'd written down her Time at her own party three years ago. And yet it hadn't occurred to her that the book she and Cece had been after months before would be present at Cece's own party.

All they'd had to do was wait.

Ruby wasn't sure what the book could tell her that Evelina could not, but this was Cece's moment, her plan, and—wracked with guilt as Ruby was—she would let her have this.

She moved forward, but Cece stepped in her path. "Wait, Bebe."

Despite their nearness, her cousin wasn't looking at her, but down at their shoes.

"*What*, Cece?"

"It just feels wrong. It's everyone's *Times*. Ours and Oksana's and Lili's and my mom's, these are their futures—"

"Their *maybe* futures," Ruby corrected, because what else had it all been for?

"I know, but still. We can't just read them, Bebe. It wouldn't be right." Though her voice was high and anxious, it was firm; she'd decided.

Ruby threw her arms up. "This was your plan! I mean, do you want to change your Time, or not?" Her cousin's chin crumpled. Ruby took a deep breath. "I'm sorry, okay?"

Cece pressed her lips together and breathed through her nose. "Fine, how about this: we won't read anybody's entry that's still alive. It would be *wrong*, and it wouldn't actually help us anyway. Like, how would we know whether it was gonna come true? It's the older ones that matter, right? Besides, they've already been read when those women died, so . . . technically . . . they're not secrets anymore."

She had a point. And Ruby wasn't at all sure she'd want to read about the deaths of her sisters and aunts, even their maybe deaths, so she agreed and swept a hand for Cece to lead the way.

Hovering over the little table, Cece reached out to touch the book. She pulled her hand back, then tapped the cover lightly with her fingertips, as if testing a fence for electricity. When nothing happened—no shocks or sprung booby traps—she sat in one of the chairs, pulled the heavy Recordings into her lap, and opened it. Ruby stood over her shoulder, watching.

There was no table of contents, just page after page filled in as their ancestors saw their Times; aunts and great-aunts and grandmothers, and great-grandmother Vladlena, and the women who had come before. Because of course, Vladlena hadn't sprung from nowhere. Ruby had no idea whether she'd been born in the woods—Polina had never said—but resolved to ask Evelina that night, if she had the chance.

The earliest entries were scrawled in ink-speckled Russian, and therefore useless to the quest at hand. But even without touching them, Ruby felt the pulse of time, and power, and blood. The weight of history. The doomed flutter of the lives of women she'd never met, but stored inside of her anyhow. She'd heard them all calling out to her at the Mahalels'.

Take everything . . .

Ruby clamped her muscles around a shiver, wondering what kind of answer they'd expected.

Flipping carefully through, Cece found Polina's entry, penned in clumsy English. "Why didn't she write in Russian?" she wondered aloud. "If she was sixteen, she'd have just gotten here."

"Maybe so her daughters could read it when she died," Ruby guessed.

It was exactly as Vera had read it. And though Ruby hadn't been alive for Galina's Reading, it, too, was as she'd expected when they'd turned a few pages, having heard the stories.

Entry in the Chernyavsky Recordings

September the 4th, 1942

I watch my children through the window. Two little girls, walking hand in hand down the street, so like Vera and myself at their age. When they're gone, I let the curtain fall in place and return to my shop. I sell tea to Americans, promising them better health, calmer sleep, peaceful hearts. It is a good business, and I am old enough and wise enough to have made a life for us at it, even if it isn't a fancy life. I sip my own cup, and think of my little sister—it's been a few days since we've spoken. Maybe I will call her. But I think of my girls, and I think I want to be near her instead. I will visit, and we will speak of our childhoods, and drink a tea to help us remember the best and oldest of times. As soon as I finish my cup, I decide, that is just what I'll do.

—Galina Chernyavsky, age 15

It was sweet and sad at once, especially when she pictured Vera listening at her sister's Reading, but as she'd expected, it didn't tell them anything new.

Why, then, was there a strange look on Cece's face?

"What?" she asked.

"This isn't Galina's handwriting." Her cousin flipped back and forth between Polina's entry and Galina's. "I think . . . I think they're the same."

Ruby squinted, inspecting Polina's entry once more, the bold pen strokes, narrow o's and spiked m's and n's. She recognized them from the writing on the key ring, and from notes she'd seen stuffed inside books in Polina's library, and the recipes her great-aunt had always pinned to the kitchen walls.

They matched Galina's entry, too.

"So Galina didn't write her own Time?"

"Or she did," Cece said, shifting uncomfortably on the chair, "and this isn't it." Her cousin lay the book as flat as she could on the tabletop, pressing the pages down on either side, and ran a finger in the seam between them.

Draping herself over Cece's shoulder, Ruby did the same. The sheet of paper with Galina's entry looked like any other page, but right at the binding, nearly too close to see, there was the slightest of ripples. Like a tear that had been meticulously mended until it was barely detectible. Nobody would ever notice, unless they were searching for it. And who would be? The only one who'd held the Recordings in Galina's lifetime, the same Chernyavsky who'd recited their grandmother's Time at her Reading, would be—

Cece drew the same conclusion. "Polina had the book when Galina died. It had to be her."

Why would Polina have tampered with her sister's entry?

"There's something really wrong about this," her cousin muttered, letting the book fall closed.

"I know. Come on." But as Ruby stood to leave, Cece didn't.

"Bebe . . . I'm not done yet."

"Oh." Ruby lingered, then took a step back. "*Oh.*"

She wished that she could wrap her arms around Cece, or better yet, throw the once-lush, now-sun-faded embroidered quilt on Vera's bed over their heads and forget about the Recordings, the family, the party. But tradition was tradition, and with a sympathetic smile, she slipped out the door, leaving Cece alone to set her fate down in permanent ink.

Still, that didn't mean her fate was permanent. Not anymore. Evelina might be unreachable for the moment—back in America for nearly two months, she still had yet to buy a phone—but she'd return with whatever ingredients she needed, and the answers to this new question as well.

Whether Ruby had realized it or not, she'd been waiting for Evelina since she was ten years old; a week or two more wouldn't hurt her.

Besides, she had her own task to complete in the meantime.

• TWENTY-SEVEN •

Dov returned to school on Monday, and with him, opportunity.

She'd known he was coming back. They'd been texting nightly (and daily) though not about anything important. In fact, at times when Ruby might've texted Cece—to report on a particularly stupid episode of *Finding Bigfoot*, for instance, or to recommend a song that *wasn't* by Creatures Such As We—she'd found herself telling Dov instead. To maintain her cover, she told herself. To make sure he had no cause to doubt Ruby after telling her the truth. And when he sent her updates from his convalescence ("Day 6: Gatorade ran dry this morning, and Talia bought jalapeño Cheez-Its instead of hot & spicy. Send help"), she answered right away, and with passionate combinations of emojis and exclamation points. So that he wouldn't forget about her while he was healing, wouldn't suddenly stop liking her, wanting her . . .

She wished that she could tell herself it was all for the plan. She was using Dov, and that was inescapable. It was scientific fact.

But she also wanted Dov, wanted to be around him, wanted him in her present, and in her uncertain future. That was fact, too.

She did not know how two such truths could coexist, and so she tried very hard not to think about it.

Ruby heard his signature, surprised-sounding laugh before she saw him—not seated with the slacker bros but across from Cece and Talia. Flustered, Ruby rushed through the lunch line, piling random and uncomplimentary food up on her tray—a cold bagel, a ketchup packet, a little cup of fruit cobbler she didn't take a spoon for—and hurried to her table.

He looked much healthier than she'd last seen him, without the gray-tinged skin or fever sweat, his sweats exchanged for a cream-colored knit sweater and dark jeans. His brown eyes were no longer sunken, but lit up as she slid onto the bench beside him.

"See, Ruby, Dov's back," Cece said, as subtly as if through a bullhorn.

"It's true, I've finally been liberated. The flu was a bitch. Anything good happen while I was barfing?"

Talia wrinkled her nose. "My charming brother."

She hadn't glanced Ruby's way yet, which was no surprise—in the week since their showdown in the locker room, Talia hadn't had a word to say to her. If Cece noticed, it wasn't in her nature to bring it up, but to speak more sweetly, to smile more widely, to pretend that everybody was happy and everything was fine.

Dov lurched across the table to tug one of Talia's braids before she swatted him off. Then he turned to Ruby. "So hey, there's a thing at Petey's tonight." He gestured vaguely toward his usual table, where no bro in particular stood out. "He says it's to celebrate my triumphant return. But it's really because his dad is staying with his girlfriend tonight, and Petey has the house."

"Your parents don't want you home after, you know, being sick?"

"Dad wants me home by nine, but he goes to bed at like eight, so he won't notice if we're a little late."

"What about your mom?"

"She's working late, but she doesn't care. She doesn't worry about me like that."

On the bench opposite them, Talia shifted, looking as though she wanted to speak. But when she met Ruby's eyes at last, she clamped her mouth shut and turned away, her face a mask of indifference.

"I'll go. Meet at your house first?" With his mother gone,

this was the perfect chance to take what she and Evelina needed.

"Deal." Dov scooped up her hand, squeezed, then dropped it to heft his cheeseburger.

Ruby cooled her cheeks after his public display of affection by plotting, doing her best to ignore Cece's delighted grin.

The Mahalels' house smelled green when Dov let her into the mudroom, like fresh-cut flowers. She sniffed to see if it was him—if he was wearing cologne for what would be their first public date—but Dov was his usual mixture of Old Spice and cleanish, comforting laundry, and something extra that reminded Ruby of their first kiss: a sharp, bright smell like the tinge of ozone after lightning.

"My dad wants to meet you before we go," he said shyly, pushing fingers through his disorderly sweep of black hair. "Is that okay?"

She nodded; anything to get inside. "Does he know about me? I mean, about us?"

"Yeah, and he wants to know your intentions," Dov said, expression serious.

"I'll tell him your virtue is safe with me," she answered.

His frown cleared as he laughed, brief and loose and honey warm.

Mr. Mahalel was a small but sturdy middle-aged man in shiny loafers, a white button-up, and a burgundy sweater vest;

Dov had told her in a text that his father owned this exact make and model of vest in one dozen colors, and rotated them daily. Black hair clung to the crown of his head, though not by much, and wire-framed glasses perched on the brown wedge of his nose, which he scrunched in greeting when they entered the kitchen—a Talia-like gesture. "Hello, young lady," he said with a very light accent. He was stirring a pot on the stove, but tapped the sauce off his wooden spoon and set it deliberately on a spoon rest before reaching out to shake her hand.

"Ruby," she clarified, in case he didn't know.

"Of course you are." Though Mr. Mahalel didn't smile, his eyes crinkled. They were the darkest brown and round like Dov's, only half the size. "I've heard a lot about you, Ruby."

Again, she wondered what his wife had told him, whether she'd explained everything. If this were a normal date, if she and Dov were normal, she might be nervous to meet her maybe-but-unconfirmed-boyfriend's father, and would ask about his job, tell him she'd always loved science, ask where he went to school and what he'd studied. But with the knowledge of her true purpose heavy in her chest, she simply nodded at the stove and said, "That smells good."

"It's Talia's and my signature dish. She's supposed to be helping, but she's wandered off. Find her before you go, Dov?" A timer beeped and he drew open the oven door, the perfume of baking fish billowing out.

"Sure," Dov said, taking her hand to lead her away.

"Nice to meet you," she called behind them.

His father looked up, glasses clouded with steam. "And you. You're welcome here anytime, Ruby. Anytime."

At that, she decided he didn't *truly* know who she was.

"Let me find Talia really quick, then we can go," Dov said in the hallway, leaving her at the bottom of the stairs.

The second he was gone, she hurried back toward the mudroom, meaning to sift through the coats that hung on the pegs. Surely there'd be something in one of his mother's pockets. She'd take a heel if she had to, though where she would keep it at the party, she wasn't sure—

The door to the downstairs bathroom swung open, narrowly missing her as she rushed by. She pressed herself against the wall, and Talia Mahalel blinked back at her in the hallway.

"Oh, right. I forgot *you* were coming."

This wasn't the time to start a fight with Dov's sister, especially when she was supposed to be feigning weakness and fear.

But this wasn't just about Ruby.

For all that she was—for the moment—keeping the Mahalels' secret from Cece, Talia had lied to her cousin for months. She was constantly lying to her, pretending to love her back while her mother was plotting against Cece and her family. And she must be plotting—whether the Volkovs were in Saltville because of the Chernyavskys or the opposite, as Mrs. Mahalel claimed, their families were clearly as tangled as snakes wrestling in the forest underbrush. The mysterious "business" that had brought the Mahalel's to town could only be about them. And as the only Mahalel girl and her mother's true heir, why would Talia have been kept in the dark?

Rage boiled in Ruby's small body until it escaped with an almost audible *hiss*. "You don't like me."

Talia smirked. "That's insightful."

"No, I mean you never did. You didn't like me before I found out about you. Why?" She wanted to rattle this truth out of Talia, force her to finally admit that she knew who Ruby was, and had all along. What did her pretense matter now, if the fight was about to begin?

"Ruby, I honestly never cared about you either way," she said coolly, crossing her arms. "The only one I care about is my brother."

"Like I care about Cece—"

"Who doesn't need *you* to protect her from *me*," Talia snapped, composure slipping. "She's a big girl."

"Then why haven't you told her who you are?"

Her amber eyes burned candle bright. "You think that was my idea? You think I'm not pissed that *you* know about us, and Cece doesn't? Between you and Cece, if I was gonna trust one of you with our secret? Yeah, you're not the one I'd pick." Talia shoved Ruby aside, her anger a living force crackling the air around them. "Dov doesn't think, but he's a good guy. The best. You . . . I don't even know what you are." Like a hurricane, she swept off to the kitchen, leaving Ruby stunned in her wake. She hadn't even turned off the bathroom light behind her.

And she'd left her purse right on the sink counter.

Quickly, Ruby ducked into the bathroom. She reached for the little black purse and pulled back the flap, sifting through hairpins and thick elastics and tubes of ChapStick inside. Any of it might work, but she stopped when she found the thin silver bracelet tinkling with charms—a butterfly, a rose, a hamsa, a heart-shaped lock. Thinly beaten metal, nothing expensive, but she'd seen Talia wearing it before.

The more personal, the better.

Ruby slid it inside her coat pocket, then slipped back into the hall.

Her mother had said they needed a token from their enemies for the ritual, something belonging to a Volkov woman.

She hadn't specified which.

• TWENTY-EIGHT •

The elusive Petey lived on a wooded, narrow back road, the kind that was rarely plowed, so they drove over inches of tire-packed snow to get to it. Apparently, it hadn't stopped her classmates from forging on toward the "thing" like moths to a porch lamp, nor had the fact of it being a Monday.

Petey's house was cozy, cabin-like, with lots of throw blankets and dark couches and wood-beamed ceilings, the stone fireplace lit. It was also crowded and loud, music and slightly wild voices competing with one another. The girl who'd come in before Ruby was snared by a group around the sofa, shrieking as they tugged her into their midst. She and Dov plunged forward. Except for a pause to drop their coats in a pile at the foot of the overburdened coatrack, he hadn't let go of her hand.

In the kitchen, they found his people. A clump of flannel shirts and uncombed hair, the boys bellowed indistinctly when they saw Dov, arms tossed up, Solo cups sloshing. A boy with uneven beard stubble slapped his knuckles against Dov's chest, and did a sort of double take when he saw who was with him. "Hey . . ."

"Ruby," she shouted over the music, impossibly louder in here.

"Oh right. Let me get you guys something!" He turned and fought his way across the room toward the fridge.

"That's Petey!" Dov leaned in so she could hear him, lips brushing her earlobe. The song that thumped through the kitchen was a whispery woman's voice over insistent bass, cranked until it rattled the cups on the counters, the furniture, the floorboards. She imagined she felt it in Dov's hand, pulsing through his body into hers, as if she held a beating heart.

Petey came back with a red cup for each of them. "Rum and Coke," he yelled, handing them off. "Have fun!" Then, in a great gust of body spray and beer breath, he was absorbed back into the flannel hydra.

Dov drank and grimaced. "Careful, I don't think that's rum."

Ruby took a sip that spiraled hotly down her throat. "I don't think it's Coke, either."

He led them out of the kitchen to a staircase that descended into the basement. It was packed as well, and coolers of all kinds were set up beside a pool table, on top of which sat sticky-looking bottles. She scanned the selection of whatever strange drinks that wouldn't be missed from parents' cabinets—Grand Marnier, peppermint schnapps, the largest bottle of Fireball she'd ever seen.

Ruby set her half-full cup delicately into a paper bag bulging with empties. Dov set his on the pool table (Ruby doubted the felt would survive the night) and dipped his free hand into a cooler. He fished out two dripping Sea Dogs, one of which Ruby took. It was better than their mystery mixes.

They wound through kids she half knew in search of a quieter spot. In the corner by a set of steps leading up to the hatch, there was another door. Dov opened it tentatively. She saw his lips shape around a "whoa," and then after raising an eyebrow—she shrugged—he went inside.

The room was empty. Of people, anyhow. There was a workbench along one wall, but the small room's most prominent feature was one whole golf cart, parked right in the middle of the concrete floor.

"Why?" she asked, bewildered.

"I don't know."

"How did they even get this in here?"

"I don't know!" He laughed. He dropped her hand to circle the cart, examining its tires, the yellow-and-black-striped upholstery, the driver's seat and a back-facing bench mounted to the rear. They climbed up onto it; Dov had to duck under the rippled awning, and his hair nearly brushed the roof once they were aboard. He slid his hand back into Ruby's, and they sat side by side, taking in the view of the workbench, its scattered tools.

"It could be like a project," she suggested. "Like a DIY golf cart he's building with his dad. Or his mom."

"Yeah, those DIY father-son golf cart kits you see everywhere."

"*Or* mother-son." She drank her beer, letting it wash away the pucker of the mystery mix and warm her stomach. "Does, um, your mother know we're together? Tonight, I mean, not—" Another frantic sip for courage. "Wouldn't she be mad?"

"I don't know. She'd probably be disappointed. Maybe she'd say I'm being selfish." He shifted subtly so his arm was against Ruby's arm, his hip against hers, hands still clasped. "I probably am. But I never expected to find someone who was okay with . . ." He gestured broadly to himself with his beer can. "Everything. All of this. I mean, like, I hoped, but I wasn't holding my breath. And now I have, and it's kind of hard to believe you could be this cool. And pretty, and smart, and fuck, I have to stop talking." He knocked the beer can against his forehead, eyes pinched, an embarrassed flush beneath his brown skin.

"*No*, it's sweet. It just proves you don't really know me," she reminded them both, but with a grin. Now she pressed closer to Dov, breathing in the same square inch of air as him.

"Do you want—"

She kissed him. This time, she was definitively the kisser, he the kissee, and if it wasn't as electrical as their first touch, it was heat and breath and heartbeat, and the identical taste of beer on their tongues, though neither of them minded that.

His hands were on her hips, but she steered herself, shifting to straddle his lap.

"Are you sure you want to?" he asked.

She nodded. "But I should probably say I haven't done . . . anything like this."

Dov paused with his fingertips at the hem of her sweater, an old one of Dahlia's, soft gold, big enough so it slouched off her shoulder. "With someone like me?"

"No, with anybody." She plucked at the top button of his flannel, in the hollow of his throat. "Have you?"

"Yeah."

"In Saltville?"

He jerked his head to knock his hair back—her eager fingers had dragged it out of place. "In St. Pete's. And, uh, Virginia, before that. But just twice."

She considered this. "Did *they* know you were a Volkov?"

His hands bunched in her sweater, and he pecked his lips against her bare shoulder. "I'm not. I'm a Mahalel. Plus I figured being trans was, like, the more pressing issue."

Nobody had known Dov the way she did, and that thought sweetened the moment again. She shivered under his mouth.

"You have to tell me what to do, okay?"

Dov pulled back. "So do you."

Was this really happening? She resettled herself in his lap. "Deal. Should—can we take our shirts off?"

He laughed. "Yes please. But so you know, I'm wearing a half binder. It's . . . kind of like a long sports bra, but it has this thick panel that flattens you in front. It's gonna be rough, if you feel it, because I'm wearing it inside out. Otherwise it's not that comfortable."

She remembered the panic that had cleared Dov's eyes when she went to lift his shirt that first night. "Is that why you wanted me to stop?"

"Yeah. I should've told you before that," he said. His leg jumped anxiously beneath her.

"I think you tried."

He frowned. "I don't even know what got into me."

But Ruby did. They still hadn't spoken of the Spark. *The Annihilation Event,* she tried not to call it. *Nothing without a price.*

She'd have to talk to Cece, ask her how it had felt the first time she'd touched Talia. The first time they'd kissed. That was safe territory without explaining everything—they were cousins, best friends, and could talk about things like that, even if they'd never had occasion to before.

Then Ruby didn't want to think of Cece, or of Talia's simmering amber eyes, because Dov was tentatively lifting her sweater while she unbuttoned his shirt. Only he was working up at the same time she worked down, so her sweater got tangled around her elbows, but they were laughing as she stopped to tug it over her head. She wore a black camisole beneath, but it was rucked up over her hips, and her skin rippled with goose bumps as he ran his hands across them. Everything she'd normally be self-conscious of—the natural swell of flesh above the waistband of her skinny jeans, or the flatness of her breasts, or the knobbiness of her collarbone, or the permanently dry patches of pink skin on her elbows—she shoved aside as the pads of his fingers drifted up her spine to her bra, touching, but not unclasping.

She tugged off his flannel and, waiting for his help, the white T-shirt underneath. The gray binder wasn't quite snug against him—the bottom ridged out about a half inch—but when they pressed urgently together, they were still so much skin and warmth, hands in each other's hair one second, tracing his stomach and her waistline the next. His beer can tipped off the seat and clanked as it spun away across the cement floor, but Ruby only heard it distantly. Mostly, there was the vague bass pounding through the walls and the ceiling, matched beat for beat by the blood in her ears.

It was like the swell of a wave building behind a seawall.

How far they would've gone—how far he wanted to go, or who would've stopped first (probably not Ruby), if the door hadn't opened, she didn't know.

But it did, letting in the music and the sounds of the crowd behind her.

"Oh shit . . . sorry guys . . ."

Ruby craned around to watch a flash of army-green jacket and the heel of a boot disappear as the hapless intruder pulled the door closed behind them.

When she turned back, Dov was breathing as if he'd just finished a long run. He wiped the heel of his hand across his forehead.

"Are you okay?" she asked, remembering he'd only been on his feet for a day or two.

"Yeah." He let out a puff of laughter. "Maybe I need some electrolytes or something." He leaned in to kiss her again, sweetly and once, not like the start of something, but like the ending.

For the moment, anyway.

Hopping down from the cart, she pulled on her camisole and sweater, smoothing down the static halo of her hair, massaging her lips with one finger; they felt red and sore, but in a good sort of way. Dov rebuttoned his shirt, a little pale all of a sudden, and seemed to limp slightly as he dismounted. But he smiled as he watched her.

Ruby realized she was smiling, too.

As they melted back into the party, pausing to grab her another Sea Dog out of a cooler, and Dov a Sprite, their togetherness was acknowledged by the people around them in surprised glances and sly nods. She didn't mind the attention. It was nice to have something all to herself that she didn't have to take, because a beautiful boy was giving it to her already.

Because by some kind of luck or magic, he wanted her to have it.

· TWENTY-NINE ·

As March turned over into April, the weather finally began to change. Nothing was green and wouldn't be for a while yet. But the snow melt kicked off mud season, the stretch of early spring where lawns became shoe-swallowing bogs, and cars floundered on dirt roads as if caught in quicksand. Dov persuaded Ruby to go mud-running with his friends that first Saturday, but the wind was cold and he wasn't a true devotee, so they spent the trip parked in his truck instead. After briefly explaining the plot and making him promise not to laugh, she let him listen to the latest episode of *Solving for X-traordinary* through shared head-phones—Kerrigan Black was currently in prison, awaiting her own trial for witchcraft.

My cell is predictably bleak, very small and dark. Though there are no windows, I can tell time a bit by the sweltering temperatures as it grows closer to noon, and then the slow break in the heat some while after. It always stinks of dung and tobacco, and I know there must be lice in the straw bedding scattered across the stones. I hear rats in the night. It goes without saying that I won't have access to anything I might use to make an explosion while I'm wasting away in jail, which could be for months.

Though I try to remain hopeful, I know my history, and I know how these trials went. I will be examined for witch marks, humiliatingly, I'm sure. If they find anything, I'll be whipped or worse until I confess, and with no friend to testify for me, I'll likely be hanged, all on the word of a corrupt and horny businessman, delivered from atop his petty throne of lumber.

After all of this, after everywhere I've been and everybody I've left behind, to never make it back home . . . this can't be how my story ends.

"She's right, though," Dov said thoughtfully.

"About what?"

"Come on, you know she's going to be okay because it's a

story, and stories don't work like that. Main characters don't just die in jail cells in the middle of a random episode."

Ruby reached over to pinch his cheek. "Oh, you sweet summer child. You've never seen *Game of Thrones*."

That same night, she and her sisters celebrated Dahlia's twenty-eighth birthday. The three of them lounged in a pile on the sofa watching *Practical Magic*, eating chocolate cake for dinner and blueberry pie for dessert. Ruby swooned along with them at the retro sundresses and broom skirts and rippling hairstyles, but half-heartedly. It had been almost two weeks since Evelina had left town, and with no way to contact her mother, she was trapped in limbo: making excuses to avoid Talia and Mrs. Mahalel while sneaking out to meet Dov—and making excuses to herself to avoid all thoughts of what might happen between them once her mother returned—and scheming with Cece while the secret she still kept from her cousin clawed at her. She'd slipped Talia's bracelet in between the pages of the fairy-tale book in her backpack, but when she and her cousin were together, she imagined she could hear its cold tinkling with every step.

When the end credits played and they set their scraped-clean plates on the floor, Ginger draped her leg over Dahlia's and nudged Ruby's shoulder with her slipper. "Okay, present time! Mine's in my room. Can you go get it?"

Ruby thrust her socked foot in Ginger's face, jostling Dahlia between them. "I thought I was banned."

"Congratulations, I'm lifting it temporarily. Go get my present."

"Sure." She smiled sweetly. "Be right back, Dahlia, going to get your exciting new desk planner."

From the way Ginger's eyes pinched, Ruby supposed she wasn't far off. She had made Dahlia an unstable jewelry stand in wood shop, wrapped in magazine paper and masking tape. Their big sister would pretend to be thrilled by both gifts.

Dropping her plate off in the kitchen sink instead of the dishwasher—a passive-aggressive present for Ginger—she trudged to her sister's bedroom. It was as she remembered: her bed perfectly made with edges sharp enough to cut a throat, her books organized alphabetically and by subgenre on dustless shelves, and the faint, fake scent of orange blossoms from a fabric spray bottle. Ginger's was the only room in the house where multicolored strands of hair didn't collect in the corners. Even Dahlia's pristinely wrapped present sat dead center of her little office desk. The only hint of a mess was a thick stack of papers beside the gift, the page on top brittle and wrinkled. Ruby glanced down at it: a certificate of title for a 2005 Volvo V70, Maroon.

Polina's car.

Curious, she sifted through the pile, careful to keep everything in order. Insurance policies, bank statements, a copy of Polina's social security card. It all must've come from the fire safe in her library—she remembered that Dahlia and

Ginger were taking care of the house for the time being, until the estate was settled. Her heart quickened, but none of it seemed very interesting or important, except to finalize affairs for the dead. Polina had saved a list of the medications she'd been taking—not many for a woman of ninety-five—and paper-clipped documents with the note "for renovations" attached . . . though not in Polina's now-familiar handwriting. Among them was a City of Saltville electrical permit, dated 1946. After the Chernyavsky sisters arrived in Maine, but before they'd inherited the house.

Sure enough, the name under "Owner" read "Pyotr Volkov" in faded ink.

"Hey!" she barked aloud to nobody. Setting down the stack, she pulled out her phone, searching "Pyotr Volkov Saltville Maine."

The first result was a public records site that announced a death record had been found. Ruby tapped the link and scanned the limited information given for free. His last location—Saltville—a short list of relatives, no Mila among them, and his age at the time of death: thirty-eight.

"Ruby!" Ginger bellowed from the living room. "Are you lost?"

Grabbing Dahlia's present (roughly the size and shape of a desk planner), she texted Cece as she made her slow way back to her sisters.

Ruby: Is your mom going to MoM tomorrow?

Cece: Yeah why?

Because none of this made sense. First Galina's tampered entry in the Recordings, and now this knowledge: a Volkov had lived in Saltville before the Chernyavskys even got here.

That wasn't how the stories went. The Chernyavskys had fled Russia to escape their enemies, not to meet up with them again in America. Her mom had never mentioned that Polina had inherited the house on Ivory Road from one of them. And while it was true that the story of how Polina came to settle in the house for good didn't specifically state that the widower had died of old age, it didn't say otherwise.

Lisichka, you're here because *of us.*

In another two weeks it would be her own birthday—seventeen seemed old and young at once—and she couldn't help feeling that when she woke on April 16, the countdown to her final birthday would truly begin. Yet here she was, waiting on her mother to come home once more, scrabbling at pieces of a puzzle she couldn't make fit.

Except Ruby wasn't ten years old anymore. She wasn't helpless, and Evelina wasn't the only one who'd grown up in Polina's house.

The Meeting of Moms was known to gather from 10:00 to 11:00 a.m. every Sunday at the long back table of the Busy Bean Café, Saltville's only coffee shop outside of the Dunkin' Donuts. Ruby arrived, as planned, when the group was just breaking up, stopping briefly at the counter to buy two small black coffees. She spotted Aunt Annie in the crowd by her hair, the same winter-blond as Cece's but ironed into a glossy sheet. Her aunt stood chatting with a fellow MoM mom while collecting her purse and coat, but when Ruby materialized in front of her, she dropped back onto the cushioned bench with a soft *whuff.*

"Ruby?" she asked, incredulous.

She had counted on this, catching Aunt Annie off guard. In their world and surrounded by family, she was composed, cagey about delicate subjects. Among *normal* people, exposed by daylight, she was vulnerable.

"Can I sit?" Ruby asked, sitting already.

"What . . . are you doing here?"

Ruby didn't have a perfect answer prepared, because she wasn't certain herself. She didn't know what the mysterious Pyotr had to do with any of it, let alone their quest to change her Time. But he seemed important, and Carl Sagan himself would've told her to collect all available facts before proceeding. Kerrigan Black, as well. And though she could have waited for Evelina to come back and make sense of him, it seemed more and more like every passing minute counted for so much.

"I bought us coffees." Ruby slid one peppermint-striped mug across the whimsically rough wooden tabletop.

Her aunt took it cautiously, but smiled, as if she suspected the cup was poisoned but was too polite to say so. "Is this a happy coincidence?" she asked brightly.

"Actually, I wanted to talk to you," she admitted, then charged in. "About Pyotr Volkov."

"Who?" Annie asked. Her tone was untroubled, in a way Ruby didn't think she could fake; she didn't recognize the name.

"The widower? The man who lived in Polina's house first."

At that, something slid closed in her aunt's eyes, like storm shutters over windows. She picked up her mug, staring into the steam, then set it back without drinking. "That was a very long time ago, and there's not much to say about it. You should try looking forward in life, Ruby. Some history isn't worth dredging up."

"That's not what Mom says."

Now Annie's lips parted in surprise. Her jam-colored lipstick had bled in one corner, Ruby noticed, and it might have been the most unkempt she'd ever seen her aunt. Either that, or she'd never looked too closely before.

She was looking now.

"It's so nice to hear you and my sister are rebuilding your relationship," Aunt Annie said, but the smudged corner of her mouth pulled slightly downward. "Even if she hasn't had the decency to speak to the rest of us. Perhaps she expects us to—" She stopped abruptly, took a sip of her coffee, restored her casual composure. "Have you seen much of her?"

"Not a lot." The last thing she needed was for Annie to

call Dahlia and Ginger, anxious to tell them what their little sister had been getting up to when they had no idea Ruby and her mother were meeting. "But Mom said our family and the widower's family might have known each other in Russia." Or she would've, Ruby reasoned, if Evelina were around to ask.

"Well, I don't know any more than your mother does."

"Did you know he died in his thirties?"

Aunt Annie's gaze darted between the moms still milling about, comparing soccer scores and schedules over the dregs of their lattes. "Why are we talking about this, Ruby?" She kept her voice low.

"The truth that wasn't in the stories." She let her own voice rise so that the nearest women paused in their conversation, glancing over with interest.

Aunt Annie clasped her mug, knuckles white around the handle, perhaps to stop herself from grabbing Ruby. She leaned in, smile souring to a grimace. "I don't know the truth," she gritted out. "Just what your mom and I used to talk about in bed when we were your and Cece's age. It's all rumors."

"Then I want to hear them."

Her aunt shrugged helplessly, eyes rolling. "I don't know, Ruby. People said a lot of things—they talk when they have nothing better to do. They said Polina and the widower were . . . that there was a romance between them. One of the old women who lived down the road claimed he got her *with child*, but she lost it after he died. It was mean gossip. When we were in middle school, one of the kids told us that *his* mother told him our aunt had poisoned the man she worked for to get his house—that's the sort of gossip I'm talking about. He died of an asthma attack; it was in the newspaper. Ev and I saw a copy, back when they kept old papers in the library basement."

"Why were you looking?"

Aunt Annie paused.

"If you knew it was all stupid rumors, why'd you have to check?"

To her surprise, a tiny laugh bubbled up from her aunt's berry lips. "Maybe we wondered, for a second. Polina was complicated, Ruby. She wasn't everything they said she was, but she wasn't . . . somebody you want to grow up to be like. Polina was right, though. We'll be safe so long as we keep our heads down. So long as we don't go looking for trouble." Then she stood abruptly, slinging her purse over her shoulder. "Your mother should know that better than anyone."

With a last long look at Ruby, she pasted on a polite smile, stopping here or there to say goodbye as she made her way out of the coffee shop.

• THIRTY •

"Tell me a story," Ruby said.

"What kind?" Dov asked, tipping his head back against the driver's seat of his truck to stare out the windshield.

Together, they watched people come and go through the doors of the Cone Zone. It was busy for a Thursday night, and a cold one, the black clouds over the roof heavy with what might be the last snow of the season. But the place had only just opened for spring, and there wasn't much else to do in Saltville. The marquee out front with its rotating border of pastel twinkle lights advertised:

THIS WEEK'S DANGER CONE IS . . . BUTTERED LOBSTER!

Ruby had been tempted out of habit. She'd fought the impulse and picked a simple strawberry cone. Dov's rocky road was wild by comparison. But it had been almost a week since she'd cornered Aunt Annie in the coffee shop, and with her mother yet to return, no new leads, and her seventeenth birthday just over a week away, Ruby felt anxious all the time, her muscles tight and her brain cranked up to eleven. So tonight, she'd chosen comfort over adventure.

"I don't care," she said, licking a thick pink rivulet from her thumb. "Just a story where the good guys always win and there aren't any bad guys."

"How can there even be good guys if there are no bad guys?"

Ruby considered this. "Okay, fine. A story where nice things happen to nice people, and everybody gets what they want. No conflict whatsoever."

"So, a fantasy." Dov laughed, but not bitterly, the way Ginger would have.

"Sure. But no magic, either . . . no offense."

"None taken." He set his plastic bowl of rocky road in the cup holder—Dov preferred bowls to cones so that he could savor the ice cream even after it melted—and took her free hand in his, lacing their fingers together. "Once upon a time, there was, um, a young scientist. A scientist who worked in a lab. And one day there was an explosion that sent her back in time through—"

"Uuuuugh," Ruby groaned.

"Through *science*," Dov plowed ahead. "At first she was pretty nervous, because time travel is, like, some serious shit. But then!" He held his finger in the air, jerking her hand upward where it was still linked with his. "She realized that she had actually been transported to a beautiful farm full of puppies. And butterflies. And dolphins."

"Oh yes, the famous dolphin fields of Pennsylvania."

"Exactly—maybe you've heard this story before." He paused to scoop a bite of rocky road, quickly transitioning to soup under the dashboard vents. "And basically, she had a great day playing with the puppies. She had some lunch— a nice sandwich—and took a nap in some wildflowers, and then she was sent back home. Through *science*. She went to bed early, which was also enjoyable, because she was kind of tired."

"That's a terrible story." Ruby rolled down the window to toss her half-eaten cone at the trash can by the curb, then slumped to the side so she could rest her head on Dov's shoulder.

He leaned over the stick shift to make it easier for her, even though it was an awkward position for him. "I thought you wanted a happy ending."

"I guess I did."

"Your turn. You tell me a story."

She sighed, scrubbing her cheek into his scratchy-soft wool

sweater. "What kind?"

"A true one. About you. Your life, before I knew you."

"Okay . . . Once upon a time when I was really little, I was in the car with my mom, and I was mad at her. Who knows over what. To make me feel better, she drove us out to this tiny, tin-roofed ice cream stand on Magnolia Street with plastic flamingos along the walkway. I don't remember the name of it, but it was our favorite place until the Cone Zone opened and put it out of business. Mom bought us each a Bomb Pop to eat at the picnic table out front. But I was still pissed about . . . whatever, so I refused to get out of the car even though it was, like, dead summer and sweltering. My mom sat at the table all by herself, a Popsicle in each hand, just sort of licking half-heartedly, but mostly letting them melt into the dirt. And neither of us got what we wanted."

Why that particular memory had surfaced, she wasn't sure, except that she'd been thinking a lot about her childhood lately. About the time before her Time, before her mother left, and before she knew what was coming for her. It wasn't the best feeling—she both pitied and missed and resented kid Ruby for her innocence, her softness—but it was still easier than thinking about the future.

Ruby hadn't given up hope. How could she, now that she and her mother were so close to fixing things? She had faith in their powers, in their birthright, and, though she never would've believed it, in her mother. Evelina was on her side, willing to do whatever it took to save her. And—unlike Cece, though she hated to think it—Evelina was just as hungry as Ruby.

Still . . . so much remained uncertain. And sometimes, usually when she was alone in the dark with her thoughts, the future whirled in the near distance like a black hole: terrifyingly inevitable in its gravitational pull, capable of wonders, sure, but also of utter destruction.

Better not to be alone, if she could help it.

Dov squeezed her fingers between his. "Wow. You are . . . really bad at happy endings, Ruby Chernyavsky. There were, like, zero dolphins in that story."

She shrugged her shoulder against his. "I'll work on it," she said, snuggling closer.

If the future was a black hole, then Dov was a sun.

And when a quick, acid flash of guilt over her and her mother's scheming threatened to curdle her momentary happiness, she replayed their conversation in Petey's basement:

Did they know you were a Volkov?

I'm not. I'm a Mahalel.

The Volkovs were their enemies, not Dov. He didn't belong to them anymore—they'd cast him out in the first place. He only wanted to be free.

So why couldn't they each have what they wanted? Who was to say that a happy ending wasn't possible for them both?

• • •

By two days before her birthday, hope and fear had swirled into a small storm inside of Ruby. So it was that she came home from school, heart thundering, to find her mother on their sofa, perched on the very edge of a couch cushion with a cup of tea between her hands.

"What—"

Evelina cut her eyes to the kitchen doorway, where Dahlia suddenly stood with her own steaming mug, a stack of papers under one arm. She stopped short when she saw Ruby.

Their mother was first to speak. "Dahlia left a message with the desk manager at my motel last week—I've been out of town visiting an old friend. She asked me here to go over some of the details of Polina's estate. And I wanted to give Dahlia her birthday present. Belated, alas."

Ruby noticed the package at her feet, wrapped in paper that might belong at a baby shower: a parade of elephants held pink balloons twined around their trunks, and a massive bow exploded out of crossed pink ribbons.

"I didn't think you'd be home till three," Dahlia said, casting anxious eyes back and forth between Ruby and Evelina.

"We got out early," Ruby said, slightly breathless. "Substitute teacher."

Untrue—she'd left class halfway through Italian, claiming cramps. She hadn't expected her sister to be home yet, either.

"Dahlia, can we . . . do you mind if I have a few minutes alone with your sister?" their mother asked—not as if she expected obedience, but with respect, like a guest in the house.

"Ruby?" her sister asked.

She nodded. "It's fine."

"Okay. If you're sure." Dahlia looked into her eyes until she felt her skin prickle, and glanced away. "Let me put this stuff back," Dahlia said, "and I'll just . . . I'll run down to the store really quick. We need . . . milk."

Ruby and her mother sat in silence while Dahlia got her coat. She squeezed Ruby's arm on her way out.

The second the door shut behind her, Evelina relaxed back into the couch, resting her cup between her knees. As she did, she scanned the tiny living room, and Ruby saw it all anew through her mother's eyes. The rugged coffee table they'd hauled home from a garage sale five years ago. Pizza menus and potato chip crumbs strewn beside Dahlia's salt lamp. The faded '90s wallpaper, green pinstripes with a row of dancing palm trees bordering the low popcorn ceiling. The little TV, silent for once. "How long have you all been here?"

"Almost six years."

Her mother's face was a careful mask. "We'll get you out of here. Polina left me her house in the will, did you know?"

Ruby shook her head.

"That's why Dahlia wanted to see me. She called the motel desk and left a message asking to come by, but I asked to come here. I was hoping to see you. Do you have something for me?"

Wildly, Ruby thought her mother was asking for a present of her own, until she remembered her mission. She shed her backpack and burrowed into the front pouch, finding Talia's bracelet. It was so thin between her fingers, the charms like little pieces of foil she could pinch and ruin if she wanted to.

She paused before pulling it out. "Mom . . . do you remember that ice cream shop? The little one on Magnolia Street? With the flamingoes? What was that place called?"

Her mother blinked. "I don't know, Ruby. I . . . maybe it was called Scoops N' Smiles? Or Smiles N' Sprinkles?" Evelina touched her fingers to Polina's locket, apparently ever-present these days. "I haven't thought of that place in a long time," she said softly.

"We went there once because I was mad at you, didn't we?" Ruby pressed. "I was just wondering . . . if maybe you knew why. What had happened."

"I can't say that I do. Why—"

"And remember that haunted hayride we went on when I was ten? At that farm with the corn maze? I know I was scared, but I don't actually remember the ride. Do you?"

"I don't." Her mother frowned. "Does that really matter right now?"

Ruby felt that it did. She felt that everything that had ever happened between her and Evelina mattered a great deal. Because they kept using big words like *family* and *blood*. But if they couldn't remember the moments that had made them—every stupid fight and sweet lullaby and nothing after-noon passed as mother and daughter so long ago—then who would they be to each other once the ritual was behind them, and they had time to just *be*? They would be Chernyavskys, of course. Always that. But . . . who else?

Mrs. Mahalel was not simply a Volkov, or some dude in a Cossack hat with a hunting rifle, but Dov's mother, as Talia was his sister. And they had six more years of accumulated memories than Ruby and her mother did. Weren't their lives made up of moments and lullabies and fights and ice cream shops and hayrides?

Shouldn't that matter too?

Evelina held out her hand, eager-eyed and impatient. "Let's prioritize here, zerkal'tse. Time is literally of the essence. Did you get what we need?"

Ruby shook her head to clear it. "I did . . . but it's not from Mrs. Mahalel," she said, keeping hold of the delicate metal. "It's her daughter's."

Something shifted in her mother's face so quickly—a shadow briefly cast by a cloud over the sun—that Ruby didn't recognize the expression before it had passed.

"Will that not work?" Ruby asked, not sure which answer she was hoping for.

"It'll serve," her mother said at last.

Ruby pulled the bracelet out of her backpack but held it to her chest, surprising herself.

Evelina let her hand drop into her lap. "What is it? Why are you acting like this? Did something happen while I was gone?"

She listened as Ruby recounted her discovery in Polina's paperwork, the ambush she'd set for Aunt Annie, and her aunt's warning. "She said I didn't want to be like Polina. And she said you should know better."

Her mother strummed her fingers across a small fray in the thigh of her jeans. "I told you our relationship with our aunt was complicated."

Ruby groaned. "People use that word whenever they don't want to explain."

"Then I'll explain, if you have a question." Her tone was patient, her soft smile inviting, but the words blew Ruby back like a billow of heat from an oven door.

She rooted her legs to keep from retreating, and didn't even bother slow-rolling her question—she was sure, by now, that her mother would know exactly what she meant when she asked, "Why didn't you tell me the widower was a Volkov?"

Evelina set her teacup down on the coffee table with a hard *click* so she could fold her hands in her lap. "Why didn't you tell me who Dov Mahalel really was?"

"I did."

But her mother shook her head. "Not the whole truth."

Then, Ruby understood. "Because it was none of your business," she snapped, face aflame, though she couldn't say why she was so angry. She wrapped her fist around the bracelet until its charms bit into her palm, fragile but sharp. "How did you even find out?"

"I didn't just leave to gather supplies. I needed information. So, like I told Dahlia, I visited an old friend while I was away. An old contact, anyway." Her green eyes shone. "A psychic."

"Right," Ruby snorted.

But an almost-wicked smile danced upon Evelina's lips.

"You're serious? An actual psychic? Those exist?"

"This is a big world, Ruby. A big country, even, with hundreds of millions of strangers, and some of them are stranger than most. Some of them are like us. If there can be Chernyavskys living in Saltville, Maine, why can't there be a psychic in Cape May, New Jersey? Honestly, at this point, I'm a little surprised that you're surprised."

Ruby shook her head as if to rattle the thought into place. "All right, there are legit psychics. Good to know. What did this one say?"

"'Your enemies are strong in number, but far away—the wolf at your door prowls alone,'" her mother closed her eyes and repeated. "'She's been chasing your scent for years. She hopes to return with blood on her muzzle, and win back her place in the pack.'"

"How . . . mystical."

"Very. When I asked about her weaknesses, he saw two children. Pups, he called them." Ruby couldn't help but roll her eyes, but her mother pressed on. "I got the gist—two children, seemingly both girls, but then not. He saw the she-wolf hugging her pups to her body all the same, and said for that, she was cast out, and her son and daughter with her."

This was no more than Dov had told Ruby, but it was no less painful to hear a second time. "So," she said, clearing something rough from her throat. "Mrs. Mahalel thinks if she gets vengeance on us, her family will take them back?"

Evelina tipped her head. "That seems to be the translation. But you didn't answer my question. Why didn't you tell me the truth?"

"I didn't think it mattered," Ruby said honestly, calmer now.

Her mother looked skeptical. "You weren't trying to protect the boy?"

"Maybe," she admitted, because this was also true. "So what?"

"You asked why I didn't tell you the whole truth about the widower. I suppose I was trying to protect Polina. At least, your memory of her."

"From what?" But Ruby didn't require an answer. At least, not one she didn't already have deep down. "Pyotr Volkov didn't die of an asthma attack."

"Not so. That's *what* killed him."

Ruby squinted down at her mother, trying to read between the lines; Evelina looked up at her expectantly, as if demanding she do so. "Okay, that's *what* killed him. *Who* killed him?"

Again, she didn't need her mother to answer.

"I . . . why?"

Evelina spread her hands. "He was our enemy, Ruby."

"But . . . That's why we were here. Why we didn't know of our powers. So they—whoever *they* are—couldn't find us."

"And Polina made sure of that."

"He didn't have any powers. Or he couldn't use them," she amended, thinking of Dov.

"As if a man needs powers to be a threat," her mother scoffed.

"Fine, but why would she live in his house for so long if he was dangerous? Why did it take her ten years?" Though they were discussing murder, Ruby felt strangely detached from the conversation, a little cloud floating above herself, watching tiny lives unfold below.

Her mother regarded her, then nodded slightly, as if deciding. "Because her Time was approaching, just like yours is."

All at once, she sunk back to earth and into her body, finding it heavier than she remembered.

"When she sensed it was near," Evelina continued, "she performed a ritual, like the one I did for Nell, but . . . more intense. She wasn't asking for days or weeks, she needed something more powerful—and she knew how to get it." Her mother saw that Ruby understood, but she pressed on. "We need something powerful as well, for you, zerkal'tse. More time than your sisters could ever buy you. That's what all of this is for—the supplies I left town for, and a personal belonging. A sacrifice."

The word triggered a memory—Nell pulling a towel from her bag, encrusted with something dark. Something *personal*, apparently.

"So the bracelet is our sacrifice?"

Her mother sighed, as if they were discussing a book Ruby had been assigned, but neglected to read. "It's a symbol, of the *true* sacrifice."

Ruby imagined Polina, preparing her own ritual to preserve herself. She'd have done it in the tower, back when it was just a bedroom for three immigrant girls. Before she took the house from Pyotr Volkov, and his life, and . . .

His time.

She drew in all the air her lungs would hold. It wasn't enough, and her voice was weak when she spoke. "Pyotr Volkov was Polina's sacrifice. That's how it works." The words stuck in her throat. "Some innocent person was Nell's."

Evelina picked up her teacup again. "Who says they were innocent? Not many people are, baby."

"I won't kill anybody." Of that, she was fairly certain. "I definitely won't kill Talia. She's—" Dov's sister. Cece's girlfriend. "She's sixteen years old."

"And you don't have to! Talia is powerful. I believe she can spare what we need. You've seen how these people spend themselves to practice, then bounce back the next day—you told me so."

It was true, Dov had said as much. And Ruby had seen his mother fully recovered. "But Dov wouldn't," Ruby pointed out. "Pyotr didn't."

"The men in that line aren't strong enough. You've heard their story. But it doesn't need to be like that. Nobody has to die. *You* don't have to die."

With a stumbling step forward, Ruby sank to the couch beside her mother, the wind going out of her. "I didn't think it would be like this."

Evelina wrapped her arms around Ruby, pulling her nearly into her small lap. "But this is the way it is. You have to fight for your life, and fighting doesn't always look like it does in movies, guns and wands and fists. Sometimes we do it in the dark. But everything will be okay, zerkal'tse. You'll see. By tomorrow night it'll all be over, and you'll be safe, and we'll have plenty of time to put things right between all of us."

"We do this once," Ruby said, "and then what? I die when I'm ninety-five?"

For just one moment, Evelina ceased to breathe.

"Was Pyotr Volkov Polina's only sacrifice?" she pressed.

"Ruby . . ."

She tried to squirm out of her mother's reach, but Evelina pulled her back, thin arms deceptively strong.

"You're my daughter," she said fiercely, "and if it's them or you, I choose you."

"Is *them* the Volkovs, or anybody who's not a Cherny-avsky?" Ruby muttered into her mother's sweater.

"Does it matter?"

"To me it does."

"Then I'm sorry. Maybe it's not what you want to hear, but I choose you over anybody. This is not the choice I want to make—it's the choice our family has been forced to make, for generations. Not all of the women in our families who have died young have done so in a car, Ruby. There have been dozens of Times where our ancestors have seen themselves killed by those in society who don't understand them, by men who fear them. They made a choice, to use the power they had to survive. We are only doing the same. Your life is all that matters to me. Yours and your sisters'. Don't you want a life?"

"Of course I do."

"Well, you can't get something for nothing, zerkal'tse."

As if Ruby hadn't figured that out already.

Evelina pulled back to look at her. "Let's just get through tomorrow, baby, and then focus on the future. We'll concentrate on becoming a family again."

It was everything Ruby wanted to hear, but it didn't feel like hope; instead of her heart rising through her chest, it sank, settling on the floor of its own dark forest.

This wasn't how it was supposed to be. Like Vasilisa, she was meant to march into the woods, winning her miracle through cleverness and bravery, walking out again with new power. Of course, Vasilisa hadn't known the full truth . . . or maybe she had. Maybe Vasilisa knew exactly what would happen to her wicked stepfamily when she knocked at their gate to be let in, bringing fiery death to their door. It didn't say so in the story.

But stories lied.

Then again, perhaps Ruby had willfully misunderstood from the start. The Chernyavskys were thieves and liars. They used people—hadn't she been using Dov?—and used them up. They kept secrets from the people who loved them most. Apparently, they murdered. What if the Chernyavskys weren't the heroines, but the witches?

And maybe witches didn't get to lead long or happy lives . . . not unless they took them.

• THIRTY-ONE •

Once Dahlia returned from the store, Ruby waited in her bedroom until her sister and mother had finished their business. Then, before Dahlia could come and check on her, she announced that she was going to Cece's, pausing only to lift Polina's keys from the ring. Though it was a school night, Dahlia didn't try to stop her from leaving. Ginger thought their big sister was too permissive, but Dahlia became reluctant when she bumped up against the border between Sister and Mother; so often, she retreated. Ruby had always sensed it, and used it, with some guilt. Now, though, her only goal was to be somewhere that nobody could find her. At least, nobody she didn't want to.

What she needed was to be around something good.

Something she didn't have to steal. Something that was already hers.

Ruby watched from the window as Dov's black truck churned through the slick snow and mud to climb the driveway. Before he'd even parked, she'd thrown open the door to meet him. He wasn't looking at her as he approached the front steps, but had his head tipped back to take in the whole house. When he stepped across the threshold, toed off his boots, and stood in his socks on the mat, his dark jeans were soaked to black above the ankles from the muddy trek across the lawn. He didn't seem bothered; in fact, he seemed in a trance as he padded by her and down the hall, pausing in the archway of the great room to take it in.

Would he recognize it? she wondered. Sense that this house had belonged to a relative, like a monarch butterfly that knows its home without ever having been there? She was curious, but felt detached, a scientist studying her subject from afar.

"This was your grandma's?" he asked, unsteady-sounding.

"Just my great-aunt's. Want the tour?" Without waiting for him to answer—or to blink—she folded their hands together. His was warm, and when he finally looked at her, brown eyes focusing, her whole body warmed, too.

She tugged Dov down the hallway and up the stairs, not bothering with any of the rooms they passed until they reached the foot of the staircase spiraling into the tower. He followed her up and through the door, unlocked since her and Cece's last visit. When her fingers found the familiar pull cord, they both winced in the sudden light.

This was what she'd wanted to show him, why she'd asked him to come in the first place, she now realized. She wanted him to stand among the Chernyavsky secrets, see Ruby, truly know her at last. "What do you think?" she prompted.

Dov turned a slow half circle, taking it in. "I think . . . it's cool?" He seemed to guess at the answer she wanted, then chuckled. "Kind of Goth."

He'd guessed wrong.

She dropped his hand, drifting toward the rough worktable and the little object that glinted on top. It was the clock Cece had knocked over. She picked it up, held it to her nose, and she could see how fragile it was—the delicate gold scrollwork around the face, the slim wooden finials like flattened clovers, its black metal hands as thin and sharp as toothpicks beneath the finely cracked glass—yet still it ticked away, even after the fall. As if nothing could stop it.

Ruby pressed her thumb into the glass and watched it splinter. Harder, until it caved, until glass shards tinkled around her feet. Her finger seared with a small, sharp fire.

"Stop, stop!" Dov took the clock and dropped it carelessly back on the tabletop. He took her hand in both of his, holding it up to examine. "What the hell, Ruby?"

An ugly slice ran down her thumb, oozing blood that

looked black in the attic light. She peered at it with mild interest. "Can you fix it?" she whispered hoarsely.

"What?"

"That's what you do, right? You fix broken things."

Dov froze in place, his face stricken. "*I* don't."

"But you *did*." There was a horrible desperate whine in her voice. "You fixed me. You could do it again if you tried."

His mouth set in a grim line, eyes huge and damp, before he reached back for the broken clock. His fingers drifted toward the sharp glass.

"Wait, stop!" She grabbed his wrist at the last moment, pulling him back. "Never mind. I shouldn't have asked. I'm sorry."

Dov looked at her uncertainly, so she plastered on a calm smile to show the danger had passed.

"Let's go down," she said. "There're Band-Aids in the bathroom."

But after they'd descended the tower staircase, she didn't stop to grab the first aid kit in the bathroom cabinet. She continued on, to her mother's old bedroom instead, towing Dov behind her.

It didn't happen the way she'd pictured her first time, not exactly. For one, it wasn't a solemn, dramatic affair. When Dov's watch clasp got tangled in her hair by the root, he worked it carefully free as they grinned into each other's faces. He was nervous, she could tell, though it wasn't his first time. But he was also patient, and sweet, and talked her through everything, stopping often to ask questions. He told her where he wanted to be touched and how, and Ruby did the same (everywhere, and every way, just to be sure). Afterward, he hopped out of bed in his binder and boxers to fish her clothes off the floor so she wouldn't be cold. Back under the covers, they coiled against each other until Dov dozed off, and then Ruby twisted carefully around to look at him.

He lay on his belly, lean muscles loose. One arm was outstretched, fingers curled against the blankets where she'd lain a moment before. Dark hair flopped over the angled plane of his cheek, and little puffs of breath from between his parted lips warmed her face.

She rolled away from him.

Regret sat jagged inside of her. Not for the sex; she didn't regret that. She'd liked it, and part of her wanted to kiss him awake and begin all over again. She was glad they'd done it.

And yet, she did not feel fixed.

That had been a stupid thought, of course. Dov couldn't fix what was really broken in Ruby, even if he'd been a true Volkov heir. That was just the little-kid story she'd started to tell herself at bedtime to stave off the fear that came in the dark: that she was nothing, and would never have the chance to be anything more, whether she deserved it or not, despite her mother's promises. It had gotten so the only way to fall asleep was to let herself believe that *love* might save her.

But it was time to grow up.

• THIRTY-TWO •

T hough she set her phone alarm when she got home so that she'd get up in time to get up for school the next day, when it went off on Wednesday morning, Ruby didn't get out of bed.

"I'm sick," she croaked at Ginger, who lay a skeptical hand across her forehead, examined her red cheeks and eyes bloodshot from rubbing, with bags beneath she didn't have to fake, as she hadn't slept at all. Dahlia dutifully stuck the thermometer beneath Ruby's tongue, but as she rushed off to get ready for work, Ruby held it briefly against her bare light bulb until the temperature was just high enough that her sisters wouldn't bother to argue.

She'd be in trouble when they came home from work to find

her gone, with some unsatisfying excuse on a Post-it stuck to the fridge. Grounded from electronics, maybe, until Dahlia forgot that she was being punished and invited her to watch a *Bachelorette* marathon. It didn't matter, and would pass quickly.

None of this was strictly necessary. Skipping school wasn't part of the plan. She could've gone to class as if everything were normal. Her mother probably would've preferred it, though it's not like she'd ever shown much interest in her education. But Ruby couldn't stomach the thought of seeing Talia in the halls, of holding still while Dov pressed a quick kiss into her cheek by her locker, of looking Cece in the eye at lunch as she forced down rubbery chicken nuggets and sweating french fries. She couldn't imagine making it to seventh period, collecting her books at the end of the day, and waiting patiently in the parking lot line while student's cars squeezed out onto the main road one by one.

Instead, she texted Cece a few face-with-thermometer emojis to explain her absence and her silence, waited until seventh period would've started, then dressed in jeans and Ginger's old cheeseburger baseball tee, grabbed her backpack, and got in her car.

As she drove, she blocked out stray dark thoughts by pretending this was an ordinary day: that she had cut school just because and was headed to the mini mall in Hop River, where she would sniff every soap bar in the body store for show as she palmed a bath bomb into her pocket. She turned on the end of the latest episode of *Solving for X-traordinary* and half listened, fingers jumping on the steering wheel.

I stand on the platform before the people of Wethersfield, the hangman's rope rough around my neck, my wrists aching in their bonds. The heat of the day beats upon me, and though I've got far bigger problems, I pray for the soft breath of a breeze. Anything else seems too much to ask for, even in my final moments.

But then I hear it. My name, my real name, bellowed from the back of the gathered crowd. I search for the voice and smile—it's handsome Josiah, sandy hair undone from its leather binding, billowing around his flushed face as he claws his way through the masses to get to me, his hunting musket clutched in one hand. It ignites a spark of hope in me, however faint, though I don't know if he'll reach me in time; between him and me are so many people, their faces twisted by rage, and suspicion, and fear.

They are an ugly sight, and if these are my last moments, then I am determined that this view will not be my last before I die.

Instead, I picture the places I have been, the whole wide world with its plains and rivers and forests, its bridges and roads and skyscrapers. I've stood in the shadow of the Great Sphinx of Giza, ridden a horse through a gunfight in the Wild West, attended the crowning of King Louis XVI. I've known people everywhere, and some of them have been monstrous, and some have been heroes, but most have been every natural and heartbreaking and breathtaking shade in between.

Josiah calls out to me, nearer now, caught up behind the first row of townsfolk, but I close my eyes, and smile. I think of the poster that hangs in my lab back home: the image of Earth from Apollo 17 called "the Blue Marble." The planet with its white swirls of weather, its continents pressed flat with distance, and its oceans, vast and deep and interconnected, one big body of water beyond time, without end.

This is the view I choose.

The end-of-episode song played as always, familiar bars of Cyndi Lauper's "Time After Time." But instead of the teaser for next week's episode, the voice of Kerrigan Black returned:

Hello, listeners. I have some sad news for you—
this week's episode of Solving for X-traordinary *will*
be the last.

Wait . . . what?

You all might know that I, your friendly host, Jes-
sica Keating, and Sabine Durand, my co-writer for
X-traordinary, started this podcast two years ago,
together, with borrowed recording equipment in the
corner of the little bedroom we shared. Unfortunately,
our relationship has come to an end, and it was just
too hard to think about either of us continuing Kerri-
gan's adventures alone. We have to move on, to other
podcasts, separate bedrooms, and separate lives.

When we thought about finishing Kerrigan's story,
there were a few possibilities. With a final explosion,
we could bring her home at last. Or we could have
her killed. Or she could continue her journey, finding
romance and solving equations across time and space.
We talked about all of these endings, even when it was
painful to talk to each other. All of them seemed pos-
sible, but none of them seemed perfect.

So listeners, after one last adventure in Connecti-
cut, this is where we leave you: with a choice, just like

Kerrigan. The story ends how you want it to, because
it isn't just mine and Sabine's. It's yours, too. You've
been here with us all along, and now, you're a part of
the story.

It belongs to you.

Ruby swerved into the nearest parking lot outside the pink
brick storefront of Vacuums Plus, hands trembling on the
steering wheel. It was over; *Solving for X-traordinary* was all
over, and it was ridiculous to be heartbroken by the passing of
a podcast, the end of a relationship she hadn't known existed.
But when she ground a palm into her stinging eyes, it came
away damp.

Kerrigan couldn't just be *gone.* . . .

Text after text chimed in the silence, loud enough that she
jumped in her seat. Ruby picked up her phone, trying to focus
her blurred vision on the screen.

**Cece: Oooooh, Dov just asked what kind of soup you like so he
can bring you some <3 <3 <3**

Cece: I said split pea

Cece: It's a surprise though, shhhh

Cece: P.S. hope you're feeling ok!

Ruby's cheeks felt hot and tight under the dried salt trails
of her pointless tears, but there was a cold flutter in her chest,
like the first snowflakes of the season that melt before you can
catch hold of them. It wasn't the stirrings of her Chernyavsky

senses, she knew. Cece was fine, and healthy, and happily unaware. This feeling wasn't mystical at all.

It was doubt.

The ritual wouldn't kill Talia. Maybe Polina had been a murderer, or maybe she'd been a survivor. Possibly both. But her mother was . . . well, she was *her mother.* She smelled like mint, and wore winter hats with pom-poms, and folded colorful paper squares into butterflies to tuck inside her daughter's lunchbox. She had, anyways, before she'd left. And perhaps she'd changed, grown stronger with age and absence, or perhaps she'd never been as scared or weak or warm as Ruby believed. But Evelina only wanted to help Ruby, not to kill anybody. Talia would be fine, because her mother had promised, even if Ruby wasn't sure how her mother could know for certain. She must know that Ruby would never forgive herself for hurting Cece's girlfriend, Dov's sister.

But again, the cold quiver of doubt in the hollow of her chest.

With enough time, Ruby might rewrite the whole story. She could see it. In her own tale, Ruby would be the innocent heroine Vasilisa once more, battered by circumstance, alone in the woods without a choice, without hope. Talia, the ugly, bitter daughter of the woman who wished her dead. And that evil, iron-toothed witch in the woods would be . . . complicated. A wise old goddess of death and regeneration, helping the pure of heart (Ruby) and devouring the wicked (anybody who wasn't Ruby). It seemed impossible, but with a few months or years—years Ruby would have, if all went according to plan— she might come to believe it all. And that a price which once seemed unpayable had been worth it.

But if that came to pass, what would stop her from paying it again and again, as Polina had done? Maybe her great-aunt had done it to keep the family safe, to protect them from anybody that might come for them. But what about the families she'd destroyed?

Maybe that was the true cost of time. What you lost, when you took life from others to keep yourself alive: the knowledge that those lives mattered, too, even if they belonged to your enemies. You lost what was *right* in you. What was *good* in you. What was *human*.

Ruby didn't want to die—she really, really, really didn't— but she couldn't let that happen, to herself or to her mother, who was prepared to risk anything to help her.

So she would go to Polina's and tell Evelina the ritual was off. The fight was canceled.

She shifted the car into gear, only to throw it back into park, rocking her head against the seat in disgust. She didn't want to hurt Talia, not truly, but as Talia herself would testify, Ruby wasn't Vasilisa. She wasn't pure of heart. She definitely wasn't a hero. And if she went into the woods alone, would she really stop her mother? When it came to it, would she want to?

She grabbed her phone out of the cup holder where she'd dropped it.

Ruby: Can you get out of school?

Ruby: I'll come pick you up

Ruby: It's an emergency

Ruby: I need you, please

A full five minutes later, the answer came.

Cece: OK

She almost sobbed with relief. Cece Baker was the only person on earth she trusted to walk into those woods and come out clean on the other side, even if it meant spilling every secret. Even if she would realize that she and Ruby were not the same, that she hadn't known Ruby at all, and now that she did, would hate her forever.

• THIRTY-THREE •

"Say something," Ruby begged. She had told Cece every-thing. The whole truth. Who the Volkovs were—who Dov and Talia were—and how she'd kept their secret from everybody but Evelina. How she'd been lying to Dov to learn about their family. That her mother had been gathering supplies and secrets from a psychic in Cape May, while Ruby had stolen Talia's bracelet for a ritual to save herself at Talia's expense, without stopping to fully understand the cost. Without caring—at least, not caring enough—until now. "I'm . . . I'm really sorry."

"For what?" Cece asked. She'd had her face turned to the passenger window since halfway through Ruby's story, listening without once looking at her.

"For—I mean, I should've told you."

"I know why you didn't," Cece said, still without looking, her voice oddly dull-sounding. "You were trying to save yourself. You wanted a life. I get that. I want it, too, and my Time is much better than yours."

"That's not true," Ruby hurried to correct her. "I never said that. I wanted this to work for both of us."

Cece swiveled to face her at last, and Ruby wished she hadn't. The look in her narrowed green eyes . . . like she was seeing Ruby for the first time, and was disappointed by the view. "Then how could you lie to me? I thought we were working together. But you didn't tell me about Talia, and she's . . . she's my *girlfriend*, Ruby. And she isn't just that, or your boyfriend's sister. I don't care if she's a Volkov or whatever. She's a *person*. Your mother could've killed a real person."

"But I didn't know—"

"You didn't want to. You trusted Evelina over those of us who've actually been here for you. Have you told Dahlia or Ginger anything about this? Or do they not matter either, now that your mother is back?"

She was right, of course she was. It was no less than Ruby had realized herself. So why, even as her ears burned with shame, did she want to scream?

"I know it was wrong, okay? I fucked up, I know I did! I thought—I thought I was keeping you safe by lying, but . . . I just really didn't want you to stop me. And you would have, because you're so much better than me. You're the good one, and I'm the bad one. That's always been true. That's why I need you to help me unfuck it all up."

After a long moment, Cece said gently, "You're *not* bad. That's why you know you can't do this, Bebe. Not this way. It's wrong."

"I *know*." Grinding away hot tears with her palm, she focused on the road in front of them. Though they were parked, she didn't dare glance over at Cece; if there was disgust, or hatred, or pity in her eyes, Ruby couldn't stand to see it. "I am sorry. Really, really sorry. You're my best . . . everything, and I wish I was better for you. But that's why I need your help. You can help me be better. We'll just go to Polina's, and I'll tell Mom I don't want this. And Talia will be safe. It'll be okay, like it never happened."

Cece turned back to face the window again. "Just drive. We need to hurry."

And, like the ivy that climbed the stones of 54 Ivory Road, Ruby felt a tendril of fear creep up her heart.

When they got to Polina's, they clawed their way up the gravel driveway, still a muddy Slip 'N Slide, until they stood on the doorstep, panting and shivering. Ruby jabbed her stolen keys toward the lock, but her mother must have been waiting, and she opened the door.

Ruby, she expected, but her cousin's presence took Evelina

by surprise. Her lips formed a perfect O. "Cece, look at you!"

"H-hi, Aunt Ev." Cece breathed raggedly as she straightened, cheeks pink and damp.

"Well . . . let's all get inside. I guess we've got some talking to do." She looked questioningly at Ruby as they passed, but by the time they'd kicked off their boots and peeled off their coats, her mother was warm and welcoming once more. Today, she wore the same buttercup-yellow cardigan she had to Polina's Reading, the locket cold-looking against her neck, exposed by her simple ponytail. Her khakis were rolled up to show tennis socks with pink heels—they looked like they belonged to a little girl.

Meanwhile, Ruby and Cece were wet messes. The galaxy tights her cousin had worn to school were soaked through by their climb, the stars blotted out. Her bright purple skirt was mud splattered, and her precariously contained bun unraveled in white-blond streamers down her back. Ruby's jeans were mud-blackened, and she was sweating through the armpits of her cheeseburger baseball tee.

That's when she realized it wasn't just their efforts outside, but the old house itself making her overwarm. For once, the temperature bordered on tropical, and when they went into the great room, she understood why.

Logs crackled in the fireplace, but that wasn't all. Set on the floor in the four corners of the room, there were bowls of beaten metal, propped on squat, four-legged stands. With a start, Ruby recognized them from the storage shelves in the tower. She edged into the room and peered into the closest, filled with smoldering coals, aglow but not aflame. Settled among them, a small kitchen pot, water simmering inside. The smell wafting on the steam was bitter and sharp, and strangely pointed leaves churned in the waters.

The furniture had all been pushed back to the walls, so all that remained was the coffee table, now in the dead center between the four bowls. The spread on top was familiar enough from the ritual in her mother's motel room: a black cloth set with burning candles, a bowl of speckled brown eggs, a plate of blini, and a teapot on a mat. There was also a pile of white pebbles instead of corn kernels, which she recognized from the apothecary cabinet, and another mason jar of cloudy water, bits of twig and root inside.

And, twinkling against the black cloth between the candles, Talia's bracelet.

Her cousin stood frozen in the doorway.

"I wasn't expecting you, Cece," Evelina said behind her.

Cece jumped, stumbling nervously down the step into the great room.

"I asked her to come," Ruby hurried to say. "For, um, moral support."

"I know you're nervous, zerkal'tse—"

"She's not nervous." Cece found her voice, stronger than Ruby's. "She doesn't want to do this."

· 319 ·

Her mother looked to her. "Is this true?"

Ruby swallowed, nodding. "We—I just came here to tell you."

"I can see we have a lot to talk about." Evelina frowned. "Can I make you girls some tea?"

Ruby glanced in the direction of the pot on the table.

Her mother laughed. "Not that kind, I promise. Honestly, I don't have a taste for Russian tea anymore. Too bitter. Celestial Seasonings, only." Then she laid a gentle hand on Cece's flushed cheek, running it down her unspooled hair. "It truly is good to see you, plemyannitsa."

Once she'd left them for the kitchen, Cece skirted the edge of the room anxiously, staying as far from the loaded table as possible. She perched on the very edge of a sofa shoved up against the wall by the fireplace, and Ruby joined her. Though her cousin hadn't said a thing to her since the car, hadn't forgiven her or anything like that, she slid her hand over Ruby's on the couch cushion. Her gentle squeeze announced: *Keep going. You can do this.*

Ruby turned her hand palm up, lacing her fingers through Cece's.

They sat that way until her mother came back with two steaming cups in the familiar podstakannik, one of which was still buried in Ruby's underwear drawer. "Black Cherry Berry all right?" She handed them their cups and settled into Polina's old armchair, pushed up against the couch. "When I left, Cece, you were a quiet, round little thing. And now you're a woman, like my Ruby. You've had your own Time, I guess?"

Cece looked sideways to Ruby, then back. "Yeah. Yes I did."

"And do you know about Ruby's Time?"

"I do."

"Then you know what I'm trying to do. All I want is to protect my daughter, the way Annie would want to protect you. Do you understand?"

"We know, Mom," Ruby cut in. "You love me, and you're just trying to help, and that . . . it means everything to me, seriously."

"But Ruby doesn't want this kind of help," Cece spoke up. "You can't hurt Talia."

"The Volkov girl?" Evelina studied Cece. "She means something to you, doesn't she?"

Her cousin flushed, cheeks hot as the coals in the braziers.

"It's not just about Talia," Ruby protested. "I know they're our enemies. And I know you think it's worth it, if they die and I live . . . but, Mom, I think we got the price wrong. I don't think it's about risking our lives. I think it's . . . fuck." Ruby fisted her free hand in her hair. "I don't know if there's such a thing as a soul. I mean, scientifically, there isn't, and maybe Carl Sagan wouldn't approve," Ruby rambled. "Except that he thought all life was precious, from the cosmic perspective, just because it was life . . . I'm saying that if there is *something*, whatever it is in us that thinks life is precious no matter who it belongs to, I don't want either of us to lose that."

"I see." Her mother pressed a hand to her lips, sphinx-like.

"You said there's always a choice," Ruby continued, when it seemed like her mother wasn't going to say anything more. "That's the way it works, even for Chernyavskys. And this is mine." Ruby set her chin, willing it not to wobble as this last hope extinguished, treacherous though it was.

Her mother glanced back and forth between them. "You girls." She looked down and laughed to herself, soft and rumbling and familiar. "You're both so beautiful. And so young. It's hard to believe I was like that, but I was, once. I thought I knew exactly how the world worked, and where I fit into it." She gazed into the fireplace, then stood and strode to the firewood rack beside it. Stooping gracefully, she fed another log into the fire, though the flames had yet to burn low, and it was still so warm in the room, Ruby's head swam.

She set her teacup down on the floor—it was too much, with the steam dampening her face, and the fire, and the heat from the simmering pots. Cece put her cup down, too, looking dizzy.

"But I left everything I loved and everyone who loved me," her mother said. "And I learned how big and strange the world really is. You'd be amazed. You girls can't possibly know, because you've spent your whole short lives here in Saltville, without any idea where you really come from, or what you're really capable of. Polina made sure of that. *She's the one who betrayed this family.* But when you're older, when you leave, as you surely will"—here, she gave them both a penetrating look, as if she knew more of their fates than they did—"you'll see."

"That's not . . ." Ruby's swallowed, her mouth so dry in the strange heat that her tongue felt swollen, and tried again. "Polina loved the family. She *was* the family. She never betrayed us."

Her mother didn't answer. She reached for a photo on the mantel—one of the pictures the aunts had set out for the Reading, of Polina standing in her backyard beside a teenaged Evelina and Anfisa. Instead of picking it up, she plucked out a small bundle from behind the frame. Like a white cloth napkin, tied up with red yarn. Balancing it in her open palm, she wrapped something Ruby couldn't see around the neck of the bundle. A piece of string so thin, it was invisible from where they sat. "You learn a lot about yourself when you're alone," her mother said, as if Ruby hadn't spoken. "You figure out exactly how strong you are, and what really matters to you, and what you'll do to protect it."

Evelina looked at them through the shimmering heat of the fire, and very deliberately, she closed her fingers around the cloth, slowly crushing its contents.

Beside Ruby, Cece doubled over.

She coughed violently, and Ruby reached out to pat her

back, but her cousin pitched forward off the edge of the couch, landing on all fours.

"Cece!" She scrambled down to help her. . . .

And saw the blood just as it spattered the floorboards. Still coughing, she looked up at Ruby, panic in her streaming green eyes, her teeth and the spit clinging to them stained red.

Stupidly, Ruby turned to Evelina for help, and in her mother's eyes, she saw something colder even than Polina at her very coldest staring back.

• THIRTY-FOUR •

B efore she could speak, her mother's fingers relaxed around the bundle, and Cece's cough eased.

"What's happening?" Ruby asked, her voice as insubstantial as the steam and smoke wafting through the room.

"She's—" Her cousin choked, then spit a mouthful of thin blood onto the boards between her splayed, shaking fingers. "It's *her*, Bebe," she mumbled wetly.

Ruby didn't want to believe. She searched her mother's face, and thought she saw the shade of uncertainty. But when she spoke, she sounded sure. "One day, you'll understand. I did."

"What does that mean?"

Evelina stared down at her, considering Ruby in the shifting firelight.

Then she told one last story.

Polina set her tea glass in its podstakannik down with a clink, watching her little sister from across the kitchen table. Though she was in her midforties, Galina looked considerably younger, with her round, gem-like green eyes, the pale blond hair twined into a crown of braids, and the sweetness of her heart-shaped face. Polina, on the other hand, looked her age and felt older.

It was why she'd called Galina over this afternoon, why she'd sent the girls outside when they arrived. Little Anfisa, with her mother's light coloring but without her beauty, angular and scrawny, always complaining. And then there was Evelina. Nine and quiet, but clearly the leader, even among her older cousins, her small heart-shaped face ever serious under coils of dark blond hair. Polina could see the two of them through the window over her kitchen sink, which looked out on the backyard. It was a sunny September day, and the girls sifted through the erratically tended grass for acorns dropped by the bordering oaks, picked spiny purple flowers from the creeping thistle to stick in their own braids. As Polina watched, Evelina plucked a flower and straightened, examining it. Then she crushed it between her palms, slowly and deliberately, rolling the bud back and forth. She buried her face in her hands to breathe it in, then opened them, letting the tiny petals flutter away on the breeze.

"She's like Vera at that age, don't you think?"

Polina turned back to her sister, who was watching her

watch Evelina. She shook her head briskly. "Your memory of home is poor. Vera was not so quiet. She could never be."

Galina laughed at the memory, but asked, "You still think of that old log shack as home? That was all so long ago."

"It's where we are born. It's in our blood. How long is too long? How soon did you forget who we are, sestrichka?"

Now Galina set her own cup down. "Please tell me we're not talking about this again."

Polina reached for her sister's hand and found it stiff in her grip, like holding on to a store mannequin. "We are, again and again until you see the truth. You must send her to me. I will teach her. You don't see she is made for it? She can carry the knowledge. It is meant for her. And you, you will not be alone. You have Anfisa still."

"No!" Her sister yanked her hand away, then glanced back out the window, wincing as if her daughters might have heard her outburst. She lowered her voice to a hiss. "I've told you, I don't want her learning all of that. We're in America now, and we're not going back. We have jobs. We have lives here. We don't have to do that anymore."

"It is not what we do, Galina. It is who—"

"Who we are," her sister finished wearily. "But it's not who I want Evelina to be."

"You think you have a choice?"

"We always do. That's what I believe."

Polina leaned back in her chair, steeling her gaze until her sister squirmed beneath it. "Enough. I am patient for too long. I wait for too long, but it is time. Evelina is ready. She is sharp. She is hungry. Of all the children, she will keep our traditions. The family needs her. We forget our past, we forget our power, and we die. We must survive, Galina. Even a kuritsa like you can see this."

The women sat motionless, staring each other down with matching eyes. Then Galina stood, so quickly the motion sent her chair skittering away from her across the floorboards. "Perhaps if you wanted a child to train so badly," she said coolly, "you should've had one of your own. If you'll excuse me, I'm going to take mine home."

Gathering her purse and coat, she crossed the kitchen and rapped on the window above the sink. When the girls looked up, shirt fronts sagging under piles of acorns, Galina beckoned them sharply, and the girls headed for the house.

"You say you have a choice?" Polina spoke from her seat at the table, watching her sister's shoulders stiffen. "Choose carefully, sestrichka. I don't wait forever."

As it turned out, Polina had only to wait three more days. When her telephone rang, she knew before answering that it was Galina, whether through some Chernyavsky gift, or because only her sisters had ever called her.

Galina's answer, too, she'd anticipated, though not the venom in her voice.

"You can't have her," Galina said through gritted teeth;

Polina could picture her in that tea shop of hers, fist clenched around the phone cord, pale hair frazzled with sleepless worry. "You'd ruin her to make her like you. Like Mama. I'm going to Vera, and we'll make sure you won't have any of the children. I mean it. These so-called gifts end with us, Polina. But if they mean so much to you, then you can live alone with them for the rest of your too-long life. And that's my final word."

That was all she said before the call ended with a click, and then the maddening dial tone. Calmly, Polina set her phone down on its cradle.

She had prepared for this.

All her life, really, she had been prepared to do what it took to keep them going, to ensure their continued existence. Vladlena had taught her, as her own mother had taught her, just as Polina would teach Evelina. Because there was nothing more important than family: strong, towering and ancient, with roots sunk deep into the dirt, whether it be the dark and sometimes bitter soil of Russia, or the cool earth of Maine. Perhaps the family needed Evelina, an acorn to be tended and replanted, grown under just the right circumstances to achieve her potential. But the tree did not depend upon a single, shivering leaf on a single branch to survive.

Without Polina's sestrichka, the Chernyavskys would go on.

"She killed her," Ruby said faintly, head spinning with smoke and stories. "Polina killed your mother because she wouldn't give you to her. And then she changed Galina's entry in the Recordings to hide it. And you *knew*?"

"Not then." Evelina sighed. "Decades later, when she admitted it."

Cece's arm started to tremble, and Ruby pressed her pathetically small body against hers. "But . . . why would she tell you?"

Her mother actually laughed, though it was a flat, joyless note. "Because she was scared. She claimed she wanted the family to survive, to be strong, but when push came to shove, she was weak."

That sounded nothing like the Polina Ruby remembered. "But she taught you everything you know!"

"She told me stories," Evelina sneered. "Taught me a little Russian. She'd taken me from my mother to train me to be like her, but in the end, she gave me crumbs. She only showed me what she showed your sisters—to nudge fate back a bit— but not to fend it off. She never gave me the knowledge she used to save herself for so long, or what we'll need to save you. After everything she'd done, after she'd killed her own sister to keep the family secrets alive, she couldn't go through with it. I wanted her to make me like her, strong enough so that we would never have to fear anybody, ever again. 'When you're older,' she kept saying. 'When you're ready.' But I grew up, and she never let me in all the way.

"So I went to Polina when you were ten. I knew you were strong. I saw that you had the potential to be powerful. I asked Polina to work with me to train you. All I wanted was for her to keep her promise."

"She said no?" Ruby guessed.

Evelina's fingertips drifting to the locket at her throat, winking in the firelight. "Time had made her soft, and sad. She said the power wasn't worth what it had cost the family, or would continue to cost us. And she told me what she'd done to my mother, and why." She took the locket into her fist then, and squeezed until her knuckles went white. She finished softly, "That's when I . . . did what I did."

"You left us," Ruby clarified. "Across town from a murderer."

"She would never have hurt you. And I always planned to come back. But it took a lot longer than I thought." Her lips twisting as if the words were bitter. "Suddenly I was alone, without my family for the first time, and my daughters back home hating me, and me hating Polina. She'd killed my mother for nothing. I wanted revenge. I wanted to . . . to topple her from her throne. I wanted to take everything from her and protect this family in the way she never could. But I never would've beaten her, with what little she'd taught me. I wasn't strong enough.

"So I went searching. I followed rumors and fairy tales across the world. Along the way, I found a lot of other folks with their own gifts. I told you they're all over, when you start to look." She glanced toward the windows on the far wall, as if one of them might be peeking over the sill. "Some of them came to America to survive, just like us. Some of them are in hiding, too. But I found them out there."

"That's what you were doing for six years?" Ruby burst out, angrier than she was afraid. "What, were you traveling around Europe by fucking donkey cart?"

A muscle in her mother's delicate jaw twitched. "I suppose I got lost in the woods, for a while."

"And when you came out, you were *evil*?"

Her mother's lips parted in protest, but Cece interrupted. "You could've told the family what Polina did. My mom—"

"You think I didn't try? I went to Annie the same night I learned the truth. I begged her to stand up to Polina with me. I told her we were strong together. I gave her the story to remind her where we'd come from, and what we were capable of. But my little sister . . . she was scared. *She* was weak, too. Ask her about it. She'll probably cry—she cried then—but she kept quiet. She protected the tiny life she'd made for herself with that Baker."

Evelina clenched the fist around the bundle. Only long enough that Cece began to choke, spittle and blood dribbling from between her teeth. Ruby threw her body over her cousin's to hold her up and screamed, "Stop!"

Her mother's hand unfurled. "It didn't matter, because I didn't need her. I tracked down our people, after all."

"All of *our people* are here," Ruby challenged, and then, thinking of Vladlena, "or dead."

A light smile danced over her mother's soft lips, so much like Dahlia's. "Who says they are?"

Ruby looked to Cece, who stared up at her with wide, red-rimmed eyes.

"Anyways, I found the knowledge I went looking for. And I would've come back to face my aunt. I was about to come back." She said this defensively, small shoulders thrust back, as if desperate for both of them to believe. "But I was a little too late, and the Volkov bitch got her first."

"How do you know that?" Ruby demanded, even as she thought back to that bright, clean kitchen with its expensive appliances and its gleaming countertops, Mrs. Mahalel's eyes as sharp as the knives in the block.

"Polina. After the Reading, when I ran into you in my old bedroom, I was looking for, well, *something* from her—my aunt was too powerful to be caught unaware, even if she'd slipped with age. We parted badly, obviously, but I know she always hoped I'd come back to her. I didn't think she'd leave me totally unprepared. And she didn't. There was a letter under my mattress, where I used to hide my diary from Annie. And other contraband, until Polina found it all." Her mother smirked, fondly remembering her teenage exploits, perhaps a squashed joint or R-rated love notes stashed beneath her bed.

Meanwhile, Ruby's lungs contracted. She'd thought her mother was searching for her that afternoon, desperate to explain herself. Apparently, it was the first lie Ruby had made herself believe.

She shook the memory free—she'd feel sorry for herself later. "Polina told you in a letter that she'd be murdered?"

"She said she sensed trouble coming. Old enemies and a fight she didn't think she was strong enough to win. She was right."

Abandoning her post by the fire, Evelina crossed the room to kneel on the floor beside them. They shrunk backward, but her mother ignored Cece, looking only at Ruby. Her eyes were as green as the shadows at the bottom of a lake. "Polina was right about this, once, even if she lost her nerve. Strength matters. Power matters. It's what kept the Chernyavsky women alive in this hard world. Your family needs you, and it needs me, if it's going to survive. There are so many of us . . . but they're leaves on a branch. We're the root. Do you understand?"

"I . . . I thought you loved me." Ruby's voice was hoarse, her throat pricked by glass when she tried to swallow. "I thought that's what all of this was for."

"Ruby, I do love you." Evelina dropped back onto her heels. "It doesn't have to be like this. None of us needs to get hurt.

We can do the ritual tonight and buy you years. We can be together, you and me and your sisters. I learned so much while I was away, and I can teach you everything."

"What if I don't want that?" she dared to ask.

The cloth bundle still rested in her mother's open palm, and she plucked idly at the red yarn wrapped around its neck. She didn't need to speak.

Evelina truly was Polina's heir. She was the monster Polina's choices had made her, and more. While Polina's hunger had dulled with time and regret, Evelina's had only sharpened. She was willing to do terrible things, to hurt anybody—to hurt her own niece—to get what she wanted.

And though Ruby wouldn't have thought it in the last six years, what Evelina wanted most was Ruby.

"If I do this," Ruby began, sucking in a breath of potent air, "will the family be safe? From—" From *you*, she could've said. "From the Volkovs?"

Cece grabbed at her ankle. "Bebe, *don't*."

Evelina ignored her. "As long as they exist, our family will be in danger. But with you by my side? I know whose survival I'll be betting on."

Ruby recognized the new fire in her mother's voice—not bitterness toward the past, but hope for the future. Hadn't she had that, once? Wouldn't she have done anything to hold on to it?

Well, almost anything.

"Okay," she gave in.

Her mother smiled, proud of Ruby's choice. "Good. That's good, baby. Let's get started." She stood and strode toward the fireplace, stoking the flames again with an iron poker from beside the rack.

With one eye on her mother, Ruby reached back to pry her cousin off. But then she slipped a hand into her back pocket and, in the brief moment they weren't watched, pulled out what was inside and slid it beneath Cece's hand. Because she had a bad idea, desperate and uncertain, and she whispered it to her cousin before her mother came back to claim her.

Preparations for the ritual were more intense than they had been before Nell's, which Ruby might have expected.

She and Evelina sat beside the spread on the coffee table while her mother did her best to braid the dried stalks of a plant stacked with withered violet-blue blossoms into Ruby's hair, which had grown out and faded, though it still gleamed red. Evelina managed to weave them through the strands, and the smell of the flowers and their crisped gray leaves was a strange mix of lilac and turpentine.

Ruby shook her head to listen to the rattle of dead plants.

Otherwise, she kept still and tried not to look at Cece, or at the clock on the wall above the fireplace.

As her mother worked, Ruby shut her eyes tight and thought of her Time.

I'm in Ginger's car, the Malibu, except I'm driving.

Evelina knotted a length of red string around Ruby's left wrist.

I'm young, maybe seventeen or eighteen? I can feel it. Plus there's a Physics 2 textbook on the floor of the passenger seat with a badger sticker on the cover, and that's the Saltville High mascot. So unless it's seriously overdue, I'm still in high school.

A length around her right wrist.

It's morning, and the sun is coming up through the windshield, but I know I'm not driving to school. I'm on a street I don't recognize, and I'm drinking gross coffee out of a foam to-go cup from a diner I've never heard of, so I don't think it's in Saltville. There are empty ones just like it stuffed into every cup holder and side pocket, and crumpled up turnpike tickets, too. Like the kind we got that summer Mom took us to Pennsylvania on vacation, when it was my job to hold onto them for her between the tollbooths.

Around each of her ankles, now. The string against her limbs felt . . . heavy. Like the ties were made of iron links instead of cotton fiber.

This okay band, Creatures Such As We, comes on the radio, and I turn it up. Somebody's waiting for me. I'm singing along to this song, even though it's not my favorite, but I'm really excited to get where I'm going and see them.

Then I don't see anything else.

Ruby opened her eyes as her mother slid Talia's brace-let onto Ruby's wrist, cold fingers brushing the flushed skin above her pulse. She shivered as Evelina touched her cheek and announced, "You're ready, zerkal'tse."

The candles on the black cloth had burned low, but they flickered as her mother took up position on one side of the coffee table. Ruby risked a glance at Cece, pale and huddled on the couch, arms wrapped around her knees, her stained lips pressed painfully tight.

It wasn't long enough, but what could she do?

Evelina poured a cup of tea from the pot into one of Polina's cups, drank, handed it over. Ruby stared into the thin amber liquid before she sipped, gagging. It had gone cold while it sat, and worse, it tasted the way rotting things smelled—damp black earth and berries ground into mulch.

Next, she passed Ruby a blini from a dull silver platter, also cold, spongelike, without any of the sweetness Ruby remem-bered from family parties.

She opened her mouth, and Ruby knew what was coming.

"Mom, wait."

There was so much she wanted to say. Her mother had left her, and had lied to her and convinced her to lie, to her sisters and her best friend and to herself . . . though it hadn't taken much persuasion, if she were being honest now.

If time is a prize you want to win, you must prepare to lose.

She had told herself stories because she wanted to live, really live, and didn't care to know the true price. And it had cost her, just as it had cost the women before her.

None of this was easy, or simple. Part of her would always hate her mother, and would always love her, and would always wonder who they might have been.

But even with all the time in the world, she couldn't begin to say so. In the end, she settled on, "I'm sorry."

Evelina frowned. "For what?"

Ruby touched the charms at her wrist, preparing to rip the bracelet free, whatever the consequences. "Just . . . that this is who Polina made you. And who you thought you had to become."

For a single moment, the firelit angles of her mother's face softened. Not toward Ruby, she didn't think, but toward some younger version of herself, far away and long ago. It blurred her wrinkles, and with the flames burnishing her hair gold, she looked like the Evelina Ruby remembered.

Then her eyes darted past Ruby and crystalized, hard and cold once more. "This house isn't yours," she said, her voice a distant thunderclap, promising destruction.

Ruby knew without turning to whom she spoke, but spun around anyway. There stood Mrs. Mahalel in the doorway of the great room: her great-aunt's murderer, and her desperate hope. "It should've been. But why would I want it now?" She glanced around the room, taking in the gathered dust, the cobwebs in the high corners, the misplaced furniture casting bold shadows. "The place is rotting, and it's starting to show."

"Then why are you here?" Evelina snarled, so unlike the quiet woman Ruby remembered that even after everything, it shocked her.

"Didn't you know? I was invited."

Both women turned as one to look at Ruby.

This wasn't technically true. What Ruby had done was whisper instructions to Cece as she passed her cousin her phone. "Tell Dov he needs to tell his mom to come to Polina's, now. Say Polina's heir is back, and Talia's in trouble." She'd left it to Cece to decide how best to fit that into the few texts she could send while Ruby distracted Evelina, allowing herself to be prepared for the ritual. Then she'd prayed to nothing—or to the laws of nature she'd yet to break, or to the four unseen suns in a faraway sky—that Mrs. Mahalel, the only person who might be strong enough to stand up to her mother, would make it in time.

Mila Mahalel eyed the tablecloth, eyes flickering across the spread with disgust. "You people will never stop trying to take what isn't yours."

As Evelina rose and rounded the table to face her, Ruby snatched up the cloth bundle she'd left on the floor at her feet, forgotten for the moment. Holding it between pinched fingers, she grabbed Talia's bracelet off the cloth as well, then scuttled backward toward Cece, away from the women.

"It's all ours," her mother answered. "You people should've learned that by now. You shouldn't have come back to Salt-ville."

From the pocket of crisp tan trousers, Mrs. Mahalel pulled a knife, its handle smooth and pale and knobbed at the end, spotted already with blood, like a bone filleted from a fresh kill. Its blade flashed in the fire's glow. "We'll be leaving soon," she said calmly.

Every muscle in Ruby seized, but instead of pointing the knife at her mother, Mrs. Mahalel dragged the blade's edge across her own palm, unspooling a thin ribbon of blood. She murmured through barely parted lips, her words lost beneath a sound like radio static that stuffed up the air.

No, that wasn't it exactly—the static wasn't around them, but in Ruby's ears. In her head. And it was deeper, darker than white noise, the buzzing of flies, or a rattlesnake's tail.

Evelina wavered on her feet, a small red stream dripping from her freckled nose to spatter the floorboards. Between her mother and Mrs. Mahalel and Cece, Ruby imagined she could taste the blood in the room, the taint of iron, like water from a rusted spout. But there was no moisture in the air—impos-sibly, it grew hotter still.

Her mother sagged against the fireplace, catching herself on the mantel.

This was how the Volkov women broke what was whole.

Ruby made herself crawl the rest of the way to the couch,

where Cece sat transfixed. She reached for her cousin and grabbed her wrist—she wasn't gentle—pulling until Cece tumbled to the floor. "We have to go," she wheezed through a parched throat. She managed to get them both to their feet. They couldn't stand fully—the air high up was too hot, as if the flames had leapt the fireplace, as if the braziers had toppled and caught the room on fire.

Mrs. Mahalel closed her eyes and her smile stretched wide, the shadows of unseen things flitting from her lips.

Between great gasps of scorched air, her mother was speaking now, too, words Ruby did and did not know. Russian chanting she'd heard outside of Dov's bedroom, his hands on her and hers on him, their skin alight with the Spark. She recognized her mother's voice, at once coarse and velvet, but Polina's, too, and there was Galina's voice, too, though she'd never heard it, and her great-grandmother, and whoever had come before her, though she'd never wondered much about Vladlena's genesis; she was where all their stories began.

"Prinyat' vse," the voices ungoverned by time called from her mother's slim throat, and she straightened, snatching up the fireplace poker from its stand.

Mrs. Mahalel's eyes snapped open.

Ruby took Cece's hand and ran.

Out of the great room. Down the hall. To the front door, where she made them stop just long enough to scoop up their shoes and coats—whatever the outcome, Ruby wouldn't leave anything behind for either woman to use. Cece flung open the door just as the wild buzzing in the room behind them became a roar.

Nearly blind in the darkness, the moon and stars blotted out by trees once they reached the driveway, she and Cece skidded halfway down, ankle-deep mud sucking at their feet. Cece fell hard with a heavy grunt, and Ruby tugged her up, not letting go until they reached the bottom of the hill, her beautiful old Malibu gleaming under a streetlight. Soaked and shaking, they threw themselves into the car. As she started the engine and swerved them into the road, Ruby passed her cousin the little white bundle, which she'd been holding so carefully since she'd stolen it, as if cradling a cactus. She clawed the flowers and leaves from her hair, then tore at the clasp of Talia's bracelet with her teeth. It broke away, and she handed that to Cece, too. The red string still around her wrists would have to wait; she couldn't free herself while driving.

Cece lifted the bundle in one filthy hand to inspect. "It's got my hair around it," she said, still panting.

Ruby hoped it was exertion, rather than pain.

She chanced a look, and her cousin was right. A strand of long, glistening blond hair was wrapped tightly around the yarn.

Cece bared her teeth, still red-tinged, remembering, as Ruby was, the way Evelina had stroked her hair and cheek, as if because she'd missed her. As if she cared for her niece.

· 343 ·

Fumbling with the cloth and knotted yarn, she lay it open in her lap. Ruby kept her eyes mostly on the road, but caught snatches of its contents. Burned bits of some root, charred beyond naming, and dried leaves, and a heap of the tiniest bones, smaller than matchsticks. Before she could examine it all, Cece wound down her window, letting in the night and the fresh smell of pine. She held up the open cloth, and the cold April wind took it all, whipped away and lost along the road, never to be found. Finally, she let go of the white cloth, and it fluttered out the window like a freed dove.

Talia's bracelet, she clutched with muddy fingers to her chest. "What now?" she asked numbly.

As with one million other questions, Ruby didn't have the answer.

• THIRTY-FIVE •

There was no way to know what had happened between Evelina and Mrs. Mahalel, but Ruby didn't think her mother was dead. She didn't feel that familiar, icicle cold. All she felt inside of her was . . . quiet. Like the ringing silence after a door slams shut on the outside world. Already, the words of her ancestors seemed to be fading from memory. Even her own mother's voice was a slippery thing; had it been gruff, at the end, or sugar-sweet, or knife sharp? What was the last thing she'd said, not to her enemy, but to her daughter? Ruby couldn't remember. It might mean that her mother was weakened. It might mean everything, or nothing.

As for Dov's mother, Ruby supposed she wanted her to be all right. Mrs. Mahalel had killed Polina, had probably meant to kill Ruby's mother from the start. But Polina had killed, too. Murdered. Did that make Mrs. Mahalel right? Did it make her good?

She didn't know. Maybe there weren't any villains or heroes in the world.

Maybe there were just people.

Exhausted but afraid to go home—if Evelina made it out and came after them, she might head straight for Stone Road—Ruby pulled into the parking lot of the first place that felt safe.

The crowd at the Cone Zone had calmed some in the weeks since its opening. This week's Danger Cone: Foie Gras.

Cece was toying with Talia's bracelet, running the little silver charms through her fingers one at a time, the way Ruby had seen religious people do with rosary beads in movies. Now she dropped the bracelet into her lap. "We need to tell Talia. And Dov. They should know about . . . about everything."

Ruby slumped back in the driver's seat, watching a cluster of kids she recognized but couldn't name spill out the brightly lit doors. "They'll hate me."

Cece sighed through her nose, then coughed at the effort. "I don't think they will," she said once she'd recovered. "You lied to me, and you did a really shitty thing to Talia, even if she is a Volkov. But you're not, like, evil. You were scared."

"My mom was scared, too," Ruby pointed out.

"That just proves you're stronger than her, because you couldn't go through with it. You couldn't hurt someone to save yourself. You're not like your mom."

Not yet, Ruby thought but didn't say.

Cece pulled the phone out of her boot where she'd tucked it. She set it in Ruby's lap, and Ruby obeyed her wordless command, answering Dov's increasingly frantic texts over the past few hours with instructions to meet at the Cone Zone.

Before she could toss her phone aside, Dahlia's name flashed on the screen. She didn't want to talk to her sisters yet, but she didn't want them calling around, either, comparing notes with Aunt Annie.

"Hey, Dahlia," she said in a breathless rush. "I'm sleeping over Cece's tonight if that's—"

"What? Hold on . . ." Silence, then a muffled argument in the background before Dahlia returned. "Ginger wants to—"

"You'll be disappointed to know our trash can remains inanimate," Ginger said dryly, having snatched Dahlia's phone away from her.

"Huh?"

"You mean you weren't expecting our trash can to gain sentience and walk itself out to the curb this morning?"

"I—"

"Because once you recovered so miraculously from your terrible illness, you'd think you would've been able to complete one of your two weekly chores."

"Ginger . . ." Her voice cracked down the middle, and she had to stop to clear her throat. "Hey, I have to go now. I'm with Cece. But . . . I'm sorry, okay? I . . . I'll remember next time," she finished, because she couldn't say 'I love you' without casting suspicion on the whole conversation.

It was almost six years to the day since her sisters had brought her here for their speech. At the memory, Ruby felt such a wave of love for them, it was almost like drowning, and she undid her seat belt to fill her lungs with all the fresh air she could. Her mother didn't think very much of them. Not Ginger, with her piles of Russian classics topped by *Anna Kar-e-nin-a*, and her unfathomable blind spot for flannel-wearing mailmen, and all of the nights she'd spent with Ruby at the dinner table, going over history essays and creative writing assignments she'd never got the point of. Or Dahlia, with her piles of costume jewelry, and the patient way she'd taught Ruby to shave her legs, to make mac and cheese, to ignore whatever insults kids tossed her way because none of it mattered; she knew who she truly was, a Chernyavsky, and it was somebody to be proud of.

Evelina had called them flighty and stubborn, and Ruby had listened, so desperate to be special. But Evelina didn't know the sisters who'd raised her, not anymore. If she did, she'd know they weren't expendable, weren't just leaves shivering on a branch.

"We have to tell them, too," Cece said, though it wasn't necessary.

"I know." Ruby owed them the whole truth, and she would give it to them. "But I don't think they can protect us," she admitted, to her cousin and to herself. Evelina had been right about one thing: Her sisters weren't hungry the way their mother was. They were better women by far, and for this reason rather than in spite of it, they didn't have anything approaching her power. "If Mom wants me for her heir, if that's the only way she thinks she can win, she won't stop. And they can't stop her. I don't think anyone in the family can."

"Maybe Vera can help?"

Ruby considered this. Galina had wanted to go to Vera. She'd believed that her little sister would help her, and they could stand against Polina together. Maybe they could have. But that was over forty years ago, and Vera was an eighty-five-year-old woman without Polina's secrets to aid them. Slowly, Ruby shook her head.

She was only telling Cece what her cousin already knew; Ruby saw it in her decisive nod, and heard her steadiness when she said, "So we'll leave Saltville. We can go tonight."

"Go where?"

"I don't know, but there has to be another way to save you. Polina was a bad guy, sure, but she proved that we can change our Time. There has to be someone who can help us. Someone . . . not evil. We'll find the kind of people your mom talked about, people like us and the Volkovs. We can do it, Bebe, I know we can!" Her cousin looked awful, blond hair mud-clumped and wild, round chin still smeared red, and the white of one eye dark with burst blood vessels from coughing so violently.

Still, she burned so brightly, ablaze with hope, that Ruby badly wanted to believe her.

"Cece . . ."

Her answer withered on her lips as the sharp rap of knuckles on glass startled them both. Talia was stooped over, staring in through Cece's window. Behind her stood Dov, and their dark eyes were as round as moons in the black-and-neon night.

The Mahalels sat in the back of the Malibu while Ruby and Cece, twisted in their seats, told them everything in turns.

It wasn't as hard for them to accept as Ruby would have guessed. But then, they already knew the part that had happened before they were born, the birth of the feud between their ancestors and the woman in the woods. Ruby wasn't even sure the Volkov version of events was the skewed one, anymore.

They'd also gleaned some of the truth from Cece's desperate texts to Dov, and from Mrs. Mahalel before she left for Polina's. But of course, they hadn't put all of the pieces together.

By the time Ruby and Cece finished the story, the Mahalels sat in stunned silence. Talia had her hands braced against the back of Cece's seat, as if to ward off attack, while Dov was folded in on himself. Arms wrapped around his body, elbows in a bear grip, he kept his gaze determinedly on the car ceiling. When he finally spoke, his voice rattled brokenly. "I told you everything. Like . . . every single secret I have. And you didn't say a word."

"Of course she didn't." Talia sighed in exasperation—not with Ruby, it soon became clear, but with her brother. "We're enemies. And she's not a complete blockhead. It's not her fault you spilled the fucking beans."

Ruby hadn't expected Talia to come to her defense—she deserved Dov's disgust and more—and the shock of it rocked her back like a sudden wind.

"We're not enemies," Cece jumped in. "Okay, maybe our families were. Or are. But that's not us. It doesn't have to be. Right?" She glanced between the three of them, eyes pleading.

Dov wouldn't look away from the dome light that cast them all in its thin glow, but Talia appraised Ruby coolly. Ruby tried not to twitch, examining her right back. If they weren't enemies, they'd done a good job pretending to be. Talia had every reason to hate her, and only one reason not to: although they lived on opposite sides of a cold world, the same two suns lit their skies.

This time, Talia blinked first. She put a hand on Dov's shoulder, then reached the other around Cece's headrest to gently work a clump of mud from one wild, white-blond curl. "No," she said. "I guess we're not."

Cece relaxed against her touch. "Good. That's good. So the question is . . . what do we do about it?"

Dov exchanged a complicated glance with his sister.

"Mom told us to leave town if she wasn't back by midnight," Talia explained. "She made us promise. Dad's at a professional development conference or whatever, but we're not supposed to wait for him. We're supposed to call him from the road. She said we wouldn't be safe here, and she'd come and find us when she could."

Dov snorted his dissent.

"Mom knows what she's talking about!" Talia snapped back. "Anyway, we were . . . kind of fighting about it, when you guys texted."

Just by the look of them, Ruby could have guessed which side each fell on. Talia was fully dressed in black skinny jeans, boots and a high-collared wool coat, her hair braided back into a tight ponytail, as if for battle. Even her diamond nose stud winked fiercely. Dov, meanwhile, did not look ready to run for his life. He wore sweatpants tucked sloppily into unlaced sneakers, and the green Creatures Such As We hoodie that no longer annoyed her. His hair stuck up in black tufts, and she wanted nothing more than to reach out and smooth it down.

Ruby resisted the urge. Instead, she said, "Your mom's right," she said, surprised to agree with Talia for the second time tonight. "As long as my mother's around, it's not safe for you. Or for Cece." She sucked in a deep breath in preparation. "Which is why you guys have to go, and take Cece with you."

"What? Without you? Um, no," Cece spluttered. "We're going together. We're going to save you."

"Mom's convinced herself she needs me as her heir, and she'll hurt you to get to me. She would've killed you tonight. You and Talia."

"Yeah, that's why we're all going together. We're gonna save you."

Dov met Ruby's eyes at last, and the look in his as he remembered her Time lit a fire behind her cheeks.

She made herself turn away from him, toward her cousin. "Cece, I can't do that."

"But—"

"Wait, just listen," she begged, then fell silent as she sifted through her thoughts. "Chernyavsky magic, Volkov magic . . . it all has a cost. And somebody else always has to pay it. Polina figured that out too late, after she'd already killed one of the people she loved most. She tried to warn Mom. I think . . . I think she tried to warn me, once."

Family is everything. The most important power we Chernyavskys have.

Ruby hadn't fully understood at the time. How could she have, when she hadn't known what her great-aunt had—that Evelina had left them in search of a darker power? And Ruby had been so young; too young to sense the regret in Polina's words. Neither had she known what price Polina had paid for her long years, over and over again. Though even for her wicked great-aunt, spilling Chernyavsky blood had turned out to be too high a cost.

Judging by the dried blood caked in the corners of Cece's lips, the rust-brown streaks down her chin, her mother didn't intend to learn from Polina's mistakes.

But Ruby did.

"The closer I get to—to my next birthday, the more desperate I might get. And as long as I'm looking for a way out, any way, I might make a choice I don't want to make. I . . . could become somebody I don't want to be. Someone like Polina, or my mother. That's why this has to stop here, with me."

"So you're really giving up?" Cece whispered, horror written on her face. "You're quitting on us?"

Ruby wiped her nose with the back of her wrist, and dried mud crumbled away. "No," she said gently. "I'm not quitting, I'm just . . . I'm going to stop playing."

"That's the same thing!"

"It's not," she insisted. And suddenly, she was very sure that it wasn't.

Ruby had already made the wrong choices, done terrible things she couldn't take back. She'd lied and spied and stolen, so sure, once upon a time, that she would sacrifice anything and anybody for more time, more power. That she would do whatever it took to win, just as her mother had, and their ancestors before her.

But she didn't want the kind of victory that tasted of blood. So maybe . . . maybe the only way to win this fight was to leave it.

Ruby couldn't figure out how to say all of this to Cece, not around the rock lodged in her throat, so she simply said, "I'm trying to be good."

And perhaps that was enough for Cece, who whimpered, but didn't argue.

"Besides," Ruby said, swallowing hard, "someone has to warn the rest of the family. You said so."

"And you said they can't help us."

"Well, there's always hope?" It felt like the right thing to say, the thing Cece needed to hear.

Her cousin threw her hands up, face pink and shining. With tears, Ruby realized. "Fine, that's very noble and all, but you don't have to like, punish yourself. If—if your Time really is your Time . . . you don't have to be alone, Ruby."

"I agree." Dov spoke in a low voice that carried throughout the car and stopped their argument, all the same.

Talia turned sharply. "You better not mean what I think you mean. Because you're coming with me. Mom said—"

"Mom isn't in this car. And one of us should stay. For her." He looked at Ruby when he spoke, and as he did, it felt like a sunrise after the longest night of the year.

"You can't help her if that Chernyavsky bitch"—Talia paused to wince at Cece—"if she kills you."

"Why would she?" He shrugged. "I'm not a Volkov woman, so I'm useless to her. I don't matter. It's you she wants." And then, gently, "I'll be careful, Tal. You're a badass, everybody knows that, but you can't protect me forever."

Talia sniffed, turning to look at Ruby. "Fine. Then you better."

Ruby nodded, her chest too full for speech.

"You guys should get going. Take the truck," Dov said. "I think it'll get you a little further. No offense to the Malibu." He patted the vinyl seat beside him apologetically.

Talia flung herself through space to crush Dov against her in a drawn-out hug. "You call me," she commanded. "Like, all the time. Not just text. And come as soon as you can."

"I will," he promised, patting the back of his sister's head and pressing a kiss into her hair.

Then, quick and businesslike, Talia detatched herself, slipped out of the car, and came around the front to open Cece's door.

Cece stayed for a long moment, fingers white against the dashboard, until Ruby thought Talia would have to pry her out. But at last, she managed a tiny, bloodstained smile. "I'm not going to give up, you know? Maybe you're done with magic, but I'm not. I'm going to save you. In fact, I'm going to save all of us."

Then her cousin was gone, too, pulled along after Talia toward the black truck. Because Ruby didn't want to cry, she didn't watch Cece tuck herself inside, didn't watch their taillights in her rearview mirror as they drove away. Instead, she stared intently out the windshield, where a little girl up past her bedtime sat at a picnic table, lamenting her fallen ice cream cone. She watched the girl as Dov came out and climbed into the passenger seat beside her. Ruby reached for his hand and clung to it, so hard his knucklebones shifted beneath her fingertips. Dov held on just as tightly.

Ruby didn't trust fairy tales anymore. She still didn't believe that love could save a person.

But what could it hurt?

"Talia won't let anything happen to Cece. She'll be okay," Dov said.

"I know." In fact, her cousin might be better than okay. All that awaited Cece in Saltville were long and lonely years, the tight bonds of their family turned to shackles that would keep her from living and loving how she wanted. Without her mother and aunts and cousins to tell Cece who she was, Cece could find out for herself. Wasn't it possible that fate could be nudged, just a little, just this once?

"And maybe they will find a way to help you. I mean, what if they can? Like, some kind of magic that really won't hurt anybody else?"

Ruby chose her words carefully. "I guess that'll be a whole other story."

"Good." Then he asked softly, "So, um . . . do you want to tell me more about your Time?"

Ruby had skimmed over the exact details. Now she opened her mouth to describe them, to describe the memory that hadn't yet come to pass, but would one year from now: the

Malibu, a terrible band on the radio, and the sun glaring pink ahead of her. All of the meaningless particulars of her death, her final moment. For the last three years, it had seemed like the only one that mattered. But there were so many moments in a life, even a little one. Surely they couldn't all be erased so easily.

Surely a story still meant something, even after it had ended.

"I will," she promised. "But let's just . . . be here, for a minute, okay?"

When Dov nodded and squeezed her hand again, she reached for the radio and scanned through until she found the familiar intertwined chords of electric guitars and ukuleles—Creatures Such As We was always on some station or other. Ruby leaned into Dov's warmth and his weight, and let the song play.

She didn't know if she was any of the things the people who loved her believed her to be—if she was strong, or brave, or worth saving. She didn't know if she deserved a happy ending, or stood any chance of finding one, whether it happened a year from now, or not.

But at least the story belonged to her.

ACKNOWLEDGMENTS

Thanks, first and foremost, to my husband, Tom, and to my in-laws, Dick and Jeanne Wiley, and my parents, Brandon and Linda Podos, for all of the childcare required to complete this book. I appreciate every Saturday afternoon spent bean-wrangling while I hid in the office with a laptop and a coffee for two hours. I literally couldn't have done it without you!

Thanks to Lana Popovic, my beloved first agent, for all you've done for me over the years. I apologize for the panicked late-night "omg no wait read this version instead" emails, but I regret nothing. And thanks to my incredible second agent, Eric Smith, for taking a chance on me. I can't wait to see what happens next.

Thank you to my editor, Jordan Brown, for all of the work you put into helping me write and shape a damn fantasy novel (and it was sooo much work). Thank you for being a partner, champion, and cheerleader in one. I couldn't ask for better.

Thanks to the amazing team at HarperCollins! To Sarah Kaufman, the best designer in the biz, and Gina Triplett, who created the astonishing cover art. To Alessandra Balzer and Donna Bray, Tiara Kittrell, Alison Donalty, Laura Harshberger, Shannon Cox and Bess Braswell, and Mitch Thorpe—thank you all for everything.

To my earliest readers, Ashley Herring Blake and Rachael Inciarte, for your enthusiasm and invaluable feedback. And thanks to Gabe for your help in making this book as strong and respectful as possible. And thanks to Claire Legrand, one of my literary heroes, for reading and blurbing. I'm still verklempt.

And thank you to the beans, Anya and Asher. You are a constant source of love, delight, and inspiration . . . though perhaps your naps could last a little bit longer while I'm writing Book 4?